A TEMPTING F

There was a knock on the door, and after Denby's call to enter, his valet came into the room followed by servants with the bathtub, steaming jugs of water, and several big towels which were placed on the other side of the hearth.

"Can I persuade you to join me?" Denby whispered in Melanie's ear. "There's room enough in that big bathtub for two."

Her cheeks turned a fiery red, and she shook her head, though she suddenly wondered what his warm, soapy hands might feel like as they caressed her bare skin.

"Very well," he said softly, "some other time, when we know each other a little better, I'll show you just how delightful the sharing of a bathtub can be."

Melanie rose quickly, more than a little embarrassed.

"When that time comes, and you have learned to relax and trust me not to hurt you, we can see how you will enjoy a number of things you've probably never heard of, my dear . . ."

IRENE SAUNDERS, a native of Yorkshire, England, worked a number of years for the U.S. Air Force in London. A love of travel brought her to New York City, where she met her husband, Ray. She now lives in Port St. Lucie, Florida, dividing her time between writing, bookkeeping, gardening, needlepoint, and travel.

The Contentious Countess

IRENE SAUNDERS

A SIGNET BOOK

SIGNET
Published by the Penguin Group
Penguin Books USA Inc., 375 Hudson Street,
New York, New York 10014, U.S.A.
Penguin Books, Ltd, 27 Wrights Lane,
London W8 5TZ, England
Penguin Books Australia Ltd, Ringwood,
Victoria, Australia
Penguin Books Canada Ltd, 10 Alcorn Avenue,
Toronto, Ontario, Canada M4V 3B2
Penguin Books (N.Z.) Ltd, 182-190 Wairau Road,
Auckland 10, New Zealand

Penguin Books Ltd, Registered Offices:
Harmondsworth, Middlesex, England

First published by Signet, an imprint of New American Library,
a division of Penguin Books USA Inc.

First Printing, April, 1992
10 9 8 7 6 5 4 3 2 1

Copyright © Irene Saunders, 1992

REGISTERED TRADEMARK—MARCA REGISTRADA

PRINTED IN THE UNITED STATES OF AMERICA

1

The traveling carriage, which brought the Somerfields' eldest daughter, the Honorable Melanie Grenville, to town was not quite of the first stare, but there were few about to notice, for it was late August, and the Little Season would not yet commence for several weeks. By that time Lady Somerfield and her other children would have arrived in a more up-to-date equipage and the old one would have been sent back to the country.

Accompanying the twenty-two-year-old young lady were her abigail, Bridget, and a number of servants, whose duty it was to set the London town house to rights before the rest of the family arrived. Lady Somerfield had been in poor health for a couple of years, and did not feel quite up to the task.

As they pulled up in front of the house on Upper Grosvenor Street, Melanie frowned, for a glance out of the window told her that the steps and pavement had not been swept for some time, and there was a general appearance of neglect about the place.

"Do you think something is wrong, Miss Melanie?" Bridget asked, "for you did send word to the Baldwins that we were coming, didn't you?"

Her mistress nodded. "Several days ago," she said, "but I have a key to the front door, if one of the Baldwins doesn't come through to open it soon."

She gave the key to the footman who handed her down, and a moment later entered what at first seemed to be a dusty, abandoned home. It was only a moment, however, before she heard someone coming through from the back of the house, and Mr. Baldwin came shuffling toward her.

She had not seen him for more than three years, and he appeared to her to have aged considerably in that time.

"Miss Melanie, isn't it?" he asked. "I thought it was her ladyship that was coming, and right sorry I am for the state of things. You see, Mrs. Baldwin's gone a bit queer in her head, and I've had all I could do, these last months, just seeing to her."

It was a shock to Melanie, for she had liked the old couple who had, for as long as she could remember, taken care of the house while they were out of town.

"Don't worry about it for now, Mr. Baldwin," she said quietly. "I'm very sorry to hear about Mrs. Baldwin, but I've brought staff with me, and they can make a start on things right away. I'll come back to see you both as soon as I set everyone to work."

The next few hours were busy ones, but by the time darkness fell, the kitchens, breakfast room, and Melanie's own bedchamber were at least habitable.

It was Bridget who, at her mistress's insistence, brought a light supper for them both into the breakfast room and then sat down herself, with some relief, to eat it while giving her mistress a lengthy report.

"I never did see such a mess in all my life," the abigail told her. "And we need a lot more hands helping if we're to have the place the way your mama wants it before she gets here."

"I know," Melanie said briskly. "First thing in the morning, I want you to go to a register office and hire extra hands. I'd go myself, but—"

"You'd do no such thing, Miss Melanie," Bridget sternly interrupted. "What would your mama say if she heard about it? You couldn't go alone, for it's not done, and I'll find you some good strong Irish lasses and lads who'll have this place clean as a new pin in no time at all."

Melanie smiled gratefully. "I'm sure you will," she said; then her soft gray eyes saddened. "I went through to see Mrs. Baldwin and she is in quite a bad way, it seems. She didn't recognize me, of course, and most of the time she doesn't know her husband either. I feel so very sorry for him, for she needs constant watching.

"I don't know who is doing the cooking here, but do you think they could put in another two portions for the Baldwins? I caught a glimpse of their larder, and it was almost bare."

Bridget chuckled. "You didn't know that I've studied under every cook your mama has had, did you?" she said proudly. "I cooked for all of us tonight, and for once the help ate exactly the same food as their betters."

Melanie had to laugh despite herself. "Oh, Bridget, you're a treasure beyond price. I don't know what I'd have done today without you," she said, shaking her head.

"You've have done what you've been doing ever since we got here," Bridget said quietly. "Working with us and encouraging us, and you just a little bit of a thing. It's such a pity that your grandma and grandpa died one year after the other, for if you'd have had just one more come-out, you'd have been all right, and found a good man to love you. It was just that you were so shy at eighteen that nobody noticed you."

Melanie sighed. "I was certainly a lot different from Martha, in looks and everything else," she agreed, "for she just can't wait to get here and take London by storm."

That night she tried to send Bridget directly to her bed, but the abigail would not hear of it.

"I've brushed your hair and seen you into bed every night for as long as I can remember, Miss Melanie," she said, "and I'll not have you get up in the morning with that lovely brown hair all tangled. You just sit down and let me see to it, and I warrant you'll sleep better for it."

With a heavy sigh Melanie gave in, and the next morning she did not even protest when the abigail came up with a cup of tea and began to lay out her clothes, for she knew it would be just a waste of breath.

Once Bridget had left, Melanie went through to the rooms the Baldwins shared, to see how the old lady was feeling this morning, and to consult with Mr. Baldwin on where she might find a piano tuner, a clock repairer, and a chimney sweep, for in previous years the couple had been used to taking care of all these chores in advance of the family coming to town.

Six days later, when the family arrived a day earlier than planned, it was to find the house in such a spotless condition that even Lady Somerfield could find nothing to complain about—at least not at first.

"I hope you've been to the modiste already, Melanie, and ordered some new gowns, for the rags you're wearing are scarcely fit to give to a maid," she remarked. "Madame LeBlanc will have enough to keep her occupied for the next few weeks with just mine and Martha's things."

Melanie concealed the twinge of irritation she felt, and managed a soft chuckle instead. "If you believe there was time to think of gowns these last few days, then you can have no idea what condition this house was in when we arrived, Mama," she told her. "But in any case, my gowns are of little importance. If Madame LeBlanc is too busy, I think I'll try a quite genuine Frenchwoman that Bridget told me about the other day. Her work is excellent, I hear, and her prices a great deal lower than usual."

Lady Somerfield's eyebrows rose. "Just be sure the quality of her fabrics is high, for she might be cutting corners by buying inferior materials," she warned, adding, "but if she's any good, I'll try her myself. Only last week your papa was complaining bitterly about how much the Little Season is going to cost him."

"Well, it really is an added expense when Martha is not going to come out officially until next spring," Melanie said thoughtfully. "And it's not as though she is a bundle of nerves, with knees that knock, as I was when I had my come-out. Nor is she an ugly duckling, like me. Wouldn't it be lovely if she should get a wonderful offer before the end of this year, and then she wouldn't need to bother having a Season at all."

"No it would not," Martha declared emphatically. "I'm not going to miss my Season for anything. If I get the kind of offer you mean, I'll just tell him he must wait until next year, that's all."

"But just think, Martha," Melanie went on. "What if he was everything you've ever hoped for in a husband? Young, handsome, wealthy, a marquess or a duke, perhaps. Would you dare to tell someone like that to wait?"

"I wouldn't need to do so if he was so rich," Martha said airily. "We'd get married right away and then go off on a trip to Paris and Vienna instead of bothering with a Season at all. Then, when we finally returned, the patronesses would fall over each other trying to get me to accept a voucher for Almack's."

"I couldn't wish anything better for you myself," Lady Somerfield said, wondering a little how she and her husband had managed to produce such a beautiful daughter. Martha was so very much like she herself had been at the same age, she decided, but no one could call Lord Somerfield handsome, particularly as he grew older.

There was the sound of footsteps in the hall and Michael Grenville came bursting in. He had the same coloring as Melanie, though he was considerably taller, and at twenty he thought himself very much the young man-about-town. He had set out immediately they arrived, to look up some of his friends who he knew had already come up to London, for he felt that he had more than done his duty by escorting his mama and Martha to town, and, while here, he did not intend to spend all of his time with his two sisters.

"Is there any tea left, Melanie?" he asked hopefully.

"I'm afraid it's a little cold by now," she told him, grinning as she noticed the eager way in which he was eyeing the cakes and pastries, "but if you can wait a moment, I'll ring for a fresh pot. In the meantime, why don't you help yourself to some of the sandwiches?"

He needed no encouragement, for he was still growing and at an age when his appetite was rarely completely satisfied.

"Were you able to find your friends?" Lady Somerfield asked her son.

"Oh, yes," he mumbled, pushing a dainty cucumber sandwich into his mouth in one piece. "Old Rushworth is here, and George Caster."

"Is Lady Caster here also?" his mama asked, anxious to get in touch with one of her bosom bows.

Michael shook his head. "Not for a couple of weeks, according to George, but Lady Rushworth and Barbara will be here in a few days."

Lady Somerfield beamed. "That is good news, Michael, for Martha will have someone to keep her company right away. And it's no use frowning, Melanie, for there's too much difference in your ages for the two of you to have much in common. I clearly recall how it was just the same between me and my sister—until we got married, of course, and started to have babies."

"I didn't know that I was frowning, Mama," Melanie said with some amusement. "As a matter of fact, I'm only too glad that Martha will have a friend her own age to talk to right away, for I was hoping to see some of the sights of London that I missed last time, and I know how very much that would bore my sister."

"Just remember to take your maid with you if you do go out," Lady Somerfield warned. "You know that you can't just go wandering off alone in London the way you always do in the country."

"You forget that I've already been here a week, Mama, and I can assure you that Bridget is worse than you are for insisting I observe the proprieties," Melanie said, smiling. "And, I might add, she's been a wonderful help to me in getting everything in order before you arrived. Did you have a chance to look in on the Baldwins yet?"

"Good gracious, Melanie, when have I had the time, may I ask?" Lady Somerfield snapped. "And in any case, I feel that his wife's illness was insufficient reason for him to shirk his duties, causing us all so much inconvenience. I mean to ask Lord Somerfield to speak most severely to him when he comes to town."

Melanie was about to say something, then changed her mind, thinking there was little point in doing so. She could always explain the situation to her father before he said anything to poor Mr. Baldwin. To her relief there was a knock on the door. And with the arrival of fresh tea, the subject was quickly forgotten.

She suddenly remembered a message she had promised to convey to Lady Somerfield. "By the way, Mama, I ran into Lady Settle in Hookham's the other day. She introduced herself and asked me how soon you would be in town. She had just arrived, and her daughter, Josephine, will be joining her shortly. She is apparently about Martha's age, and is also making her come-out next Season. Lady Settle said she would be calling upon you once you were here and receiving visitors."

Lady Somerfield smiled. "How very interesting. I'll look forward to seeing her again. Did she say if they are staying at Settle House?"

Frowning, Melanie shook her head. "No, in fact she made a point of telling me that she is staying with her brother at Denby House. I'm afraid I really did not recall having met either her or her brother before, but then, it is a long time since I was in town."

"It's an even longer time since he was in England, for he was with Wellington all through the war, I believe, except for when he came home to recuperate from a wound." Lady Somerfield smiled at her younger daughter. "Lady Settle's brother is the Earl of Denby, my dear, still a bachelor, and one of the wealthiest men in England, for he owns at least half a dozen vast estates."

Martha's hazel eyes seemed to take on a greenish glint as she smiled thoughtfully and twisted one of her golden ringlets around a finger. "Perhaps we could pay a call on Lady Settle at Denby House and I could get to know Josephine, if she is in town yet," she murmured. "It's always nice to make new friends, isn't it? I'm sure we would have much in common."

"If they don't come to call in the next few days, then we will pay a call on Lady Settle," Lady Somerfield agreed. "In fact, I think we should take you to the modiste in the morning, and then we can find out from her just who is already in residence. After that we will leave my card at their homes, letting them know when I will be receiving.''

It all sounded so simple now, Melanie thought, but at the time of her own come-out, more than three years ago, her mama had not known quite so many ladies of the *ton*, and whenever they paid a visit or attended a function, her own tongue always seemed to become tied and she found little in common with the other young ladies. As for the gentlemen, she was dreadfully uncomfortable, for she had not the slightest idea how to giggle and flirt with them, as all the other girls did. But the past disappeared quickly when she heard her mama addressing her again.

''You will, of course, accompany your sister and me on these first visits, Melanie, for it would appear very strange if you were not to do so,'' Lady Somerfield said. As Melanie nodded, she could not help wondering why it would appear strange, but she did not like to refuse her mama's request.

The following morning, while Lady Somerfield and Martha called at Madame LeBlanc's establishment, Melanie went with Bridget to visit Marie Dubois, the Frenchwoman the abigail had told her about. To her surprise, she was able to order the first half-dozen gowns she would need at half the price Madame LeBlanc would have charged, and she made sure the fabrics she chose were of the very finest quality. As the modiste did much of the work herself, however, she could promise her only one gown in a couple of days' time, and the others two or three days after that.

The Earl of Denby, though a strikingly handsome man of some thirty summers, was fully aware that he was regarded as somewhat of a dull dog by many of the *ton*, including his widowed mama and his two older sisters. In fact, he quite deliberately did nothing to dispel such an idea, for it was entirely the conclusion he preferred them to reach.

One of those sisters was, at this moment, giving him a most profound look of disapproval as she sipped a cup of bohea tea and nibbled daintily on a feathery pastry. Denby had just professed his extreme reluctance to become personally involved in the activities of the *beau monde* during the Little Season, which was now almost upon them.

"I recall quite clearly, Broderick," Lady Settle told him, the plaintive note in her voice most pronounced, "that when our sister, Agatha, was bringing out her youngest girl, Barbara, you were only too willing, almost eager in fact, to allow her to use Denby House for the come-out ball. And you also went so far as to put in an appearance at several other entertainments they attended. What is more, you even went to Almack's on more than one occasion."

"Certainly I did," her brother agreed quietly, "but that was, if I remember, in the regular Season, and I just happened to be home on leave recuperating from a wound I had sustained. At the present moment, however, though Parliament is not in session, I have a great deal of work to do for Lord Liverpool, and cannot spend my time at balls and dinners. Frankly, I do not understand why you wish to have Josephine's come-out at this time of year when the weather is so frequently inclement. I'm sure the chit would have a far better opportunity of making a match in the spring, when more young people will be about."

"Oh, I mean her to attend next Season also," Lady Settle put in quickly, "but you know very well that she has always been a rather nervous child and is still somewhat lacking in polish. If she could but attend one or two parties in the Little Season, and make a few close friends at this time, I'm sure she would then take very well indeed next year. She's really a most attractive child when she smiles, though she's still rather leggy and needs to fill out a little more."

Though Denby was now a decidedly good-looking man, tall, with strong, rugged features and luxuriant fair hair, he could still clearly recall the time when he had been a spotty youngster, tall and lanky and with hands and feet that seemed far too big for the rest of his body. And from what he recalled of his niece Josephine, though he hadn't seen her for some time, he felt that she was probably experiencing that same discomfort. If such was the case, then his heart went out to her, for it was even worse for a girl than for a boy. Lydia was probably right to let her get used to the Season slowly, he decided, and it was up to him to do what he could to help.

He grunted, and a light came into his sister's eyes as she realized that she was going to get her way.

"If you're merely talking about a few parties this winter, why are you asking me about it, Lydia? She certainly doesn't need an old codger like me to escort her when she has her handsome papa. There's time enough for me to lend a hand when you have a ball for her next year."

Lady Settle sighed, for she'd hoped not to have to go into so much detail.

"Well, if you must know," she said, "Settle simply couldn't leave the estates at this time of year, and so Mama is coming to town to give me support. I didn't want to go to all the bother of opening up Settle House on my own, so we thought . . ."

"So you thought you'd come here for a few days first, and then have everyone join you later," Denby said dryly.

"Well, for goodness' sake, this place is big enough for fifty guests, let alone five," Lady Settle declared. "I clearly recall times when we've had thirty or forty people staying here."

"Did you say five guests? You, Mama, Josephine, and who else?" His voice sounded gruff, but there was a decided twinkle in his eyes that he tried to conceal as he waited to hear the worst.

"Well, of course Settle will want to come to town occasionally and make sure that we're all right," she told him, patting her blond curls into place as though expecting her husband to arrive at any moment. "And Agatha did say that she might spend a week or two with us and give us a hand."

Denby almost groaned aloud. So that was their little scheme, he suddenly realized. They meant to make a concerted effort, once more, to find him a suitable wife, but from his point of view they could hardly have picked a worse time for it. He was committed to helping Lord Liverpool with getting the Corn Bill in shape and through the House before they recessed next year, and there was bound to be a great deal of opposition to it.

"You needn't think that you'll have anything to do other than joining us at Almack's sometimes and, of course, hosting a small dinner and ball here, so that Josephine won't be quite so nervous later. Mama and I will, of course, send out all the invitations and take care of absolutely everything else.

"However, I'm sure that the first thing Mama will want to do when she gets here is to give this place a thorough going-over, for I've noticed that it's not nearly as well-cared-for as it used to be. Mrs. Horsfall has not been keeping as sharp an eye on the staff as a lady of the house would."

Denby was all too sure that his sister was correct, and that the whole house would be turned upside down as soon as his mama got here, a state of affairs that he had always found unreasonably abhorrent.

He was also quite certain that she and his sister would make sure that a bevy of lovely young ladies was invited to their ball, and a couple of their particular favorites would attend the dinner, in the hope that one of them might tempt him to seriously contemplate taking a wife. Why could they not leave it alone for a little while longer? After all, thirty was not such a great age. But he knew from past experience that there was little use fighting it at this time. It was far better to let them go ahead with all their plans, and then, when the time came, he would do entirely as he pleased.

"Very well," he agreed, still exhibiting a token reluctance, "but please don't be surprised if, after you have included me in your plans, I find I cannot be there at the last minute. I've much to do, and unexpected problems have had a way of spoiling quite a few of my good intentions of late."

"That's what comes of becoming too involved with the government since you came back from France," Lady Settle averred. "Lord Settle has always said that it's a mistake, and takes far too much time from your other pursuits. He was remarking only the other day that you've turned down his last two or three invitations to go shooting."

Denby nodded. "I'm afraid shooting will have to wait a little longer, but you may tell him not to worry, I'll make up for it later. Now, just let me know when everyone will be arriving, and I'll do my best to see that Barbara has a good come-out.''

''It's Josephine we're bringing out this time, Denby,'' his sister said sharply. ''Barbara is Agatha's girl, and she came out two years ago.''

''Of course she did,'' Denby agreed, ''and made a most successful match. We'll do no less for Josephine, I'm sure.''

Lady Settle rose then, beaming. ''I knew I could count on you, Broderick,'' she said, kissing his cheek in an unusual display of affection. ''You've always been most helpful with your nieces and nephews. When are you going to get married and have a few youngsters of your own?''

He grinned as he escorted her to the door. ''If Mama is as energetic as usual, it may be sooner than I think. You know, it's not that I don't like to see the young ladies flocking to town each Season. It's just that they seem to get younger every year.''

''Of course they do,'' Lady Settle said, laughing, then added, ''and they'll seem even younger still if you wait much longer before you decide to wed.''

When she had departed, he returned to his study, but he did not at first resume the work he had been forced to abandon when she arrived so unexpectedly. Instead, he considered the things he would have to give up if his mama and sisters should succeed in finding him a suitable wife.

Certainly he would continue his work with the government, but this might have to be curtailed somewhat, for he had been spending an inordinate amount of time on this Corn Bill, which, though many did not yet realize it, was of the utmost importance to the country. Once it came into law, however, he could take more time for himself.

Marriage would have little effect, if any, on his sporting pleasures, he decided, for though he enjoyed hunting and fishing on occasion, and had once been known to take part in a curricle race, he had never done any of these things to excess. Nor was he a hardened gambler, though he did enjoy an occasional game of piquet or backgammon, and invariably came out the winner.

Pressure of work had caused him to neglect his estates of late, however, and, like this one, most of the houses themselves were sadly in need of a woman's touch. But that was all to the good, for it would give a new bride something to do before she could even think of starting the interminable round of entertaining which he so thoroughly disliked but knew to be inevitable.

As for the other kind of women in his life, he had owned several mistresses over the years, and his present relationship with Mrs. Alice Whitehead was just about the most comfortable arrangement he had ever enjoyed, quietly satisfying rather than one of passion. He would very much regret having to forgo this pleasure, but he could not in all conscience think it fair to whomever he might marry if such a relationship were to continue.

With a sigh he turned back to his work. He had no doubt that his mama would be arriving momentarily, so he had best be at least mentally prepared for the resultant upheaval. Fortunately, all the servants were old friends of hers, so he need do nothing about arrangements for her arrival except to let them know.

Reaching for the bell rope, he gave it a tug and was surprised when it came apart in his hand. Lydia had been right, he decided, when she told him the place needed a woman's touch. He had best have a word with Mrs. Horsfall right away and find out what else might be in need of immediate attention before his mama got here and soundly berated him for neglecting her old home.

2

Unfortunately, the gown Melanie had asked be completed first was for evenings, so when she was required to accompany her mama on an afternoon call on Lady Settle, she had no choice but to wear one of her old gowns, much to Lady Somerfield's complete disgust.

Martha, however, was looking particularly lovely in a sprigged muslin gown of the palest green, with a bonnet that framed her face delightfully, and a matching parasol, and when the Earl of Denby joined them and made a point of sitting next to her, she positively glowed.

Although he was, of course, introduced to Melanie, she knew at once that he had not really noticed her and would not recognize her again if he met her in the street tomorrow. Her old blue bombazine suddenly appeared to her to be terribly faded, and she had never realized before that her blue bonnet was not at all becoming.

Until they entered Denby House she had not been in the least concerned about her appearance, but now, as she watched her sister and the earl converse, she wished she had asked the modiste to make up one of the afternoon gowns first. But it was too late now to think of what she might have done, and it would probably have been useless in any case, she realized.

With the two older ladies engaged in a quite animated discussion, and Lord Denby smiling and conversing with her sister, Melanie had, at least, an opportunity to sip her tea and watch the others without distraction.

There was no doubt that the earl was a very good-looking gentleman, and he appeared to be not at all bored by her

18

sister's conversation. But he did seem to Melanie to be a little too old for Martha, who was quite obviously extremely flattered by the interest he was taking in her, and gazed up at him, her long lashes fluttering over her lovely eyes.

This did not last long, however, for within a few minutes several other people arrived, including two much younger gentlemen, who immediately began to vie for Martha's attention. After a moment or two Lord Denby rose, excused himself to all present, pleading pressure of work, and left the drawing room.

"Did you enjoy yourself, Martha?" Lady Somerfield asked as they returned home after paying two more calls that afternoon.

"Oh, yes, Mama," Martha told her. "I was almost sorry that we couldn't have stayed longer at Denby House, but I suppose it would not have been as much fun with Lord Denby having retired like that. Do you suppose he went into his study to have a nap, as Papa often does?" she asked, giggling.

"Oh, no," Lady Somerfield said seriously. "Rumor has it that he was engaged in something very important during the war. At least Lady Settle always hinted as much, but one can never tell with people like them. He is the head of the family now, and it's entirely possible that they feel anything and everything he does is of the greatest importance. It is a pity that Lady Denby, his mama, has not yet come up to town, for I would have liked to meet her."

"The house was so lovely, Mama," Melanie said, "that I was hoping someone would suggest showing us around. The paintings were exquisite, and I would have dearly loved to try out the grand piano that I saw."

"There was no piano in the drawing room," Martha declared. "And I don't recall your leaving us at any point of the visit."

"When Mama was saying good-bye to Lady Settle, which, you must admit, was rather lengthy, I peeped into the room next to the drawing room and saw what I think must be one of Sebastian Erard's pianos," Melanie said a little sheepishly.

"It may have been this Sebastian person's at one time, but

I'm sure that it must belong to the earl now," Lady Somerfield said emphatically. "There is not a thing in that house that is not of the finest quality."

"Did you see the statues in the hall, Mama?" Martha put in quickly. "Some of them did not have any clothes on at all."

Lady Somerfield sniffed. "Just don't let anyone see you looking too closely at statues of that sort, or they might get a completely wrong impression about you, my girl," she said forcefully.

Melanie smiled, for she had noticed the statues also, and thought them quite beautiful. It would seem that their mama was becoming a little overprotective of her and Martha.

Lady Settle and her daughter made a return visit several days later, but the earl did not accompany them. Lady Settle explained that her brother, who, she said, worked very hard, always made it his custom not to pay calls either in town or in the country.

"At least he quite willingly puts in an appearance these days when we have callers," she told them, adding a little ruefully, "There was a time, not long ago, when he refused to do even that."

However, a few days later, Lady Settle was proved incorrect, for the Earl of Denby paid a call at Somerfield House, and he was not accompanied by either his sister or his mama, who had now come up from the country and was in residence in London.

It seemed as though a hush fell on the drawing room when Masters announced him, and Denby looked around and found, apparently to his dismay, that the visitors consisted mostly of either contemporaries of Lady Somerfield's or gentlemen in their early twenties.

He paid his respects to his hostess first; then, before he could turn around, a beaming Martha was at his side, dropping him a curtsy and expressing her pleasure at seeing him once again.

"The pleasure is all mine, my dear," he murmured. "I was passing, and noticed by the number of carriages outside that you were receiving today. Naturally, I could not forgo the opportunity to see you once again.''

"May I offer you a cup of tea, my lord, or would you prefer a glass of wine?'' Lady Somerfield asked, quite beside herself with delight at this unexpected honor.

"A cup of tea, I believe, my lady,'' he responded, "with a little milk only.''

If he noticed that Melanie was sitting at the tea urn, pouring, he gave no indication, but seemed to be listening with great interest to something Martha was telling him as she steered him to a sofa.

Lady Somerfield hurried over to take the cup of tea from her older daughter and place it solicitously in Denby's hand; then she deliberately left him alone with Martha, hoping that he might become even more attracted to her.

Not to be outdone, however, first one and then another of the young men joined them, until Martha was in the position she enjoyed most, sitting there surrounded by a group of gentlemen who were all listening attentively to every word she uttered.

But it was Lord Peterson, and not Denby, who finally asked Martha if she would care to go for a drive in the park. Irked that Denby had not asked for the honor, she excused herself to him rather coolly and ran upstairs to fetch gloves and a wrap.

A few minutes later she allowed herself to be helped into Peterson's curricle, then put up her parasol and turned to wave to the gentlemen looking through the window. She was quite conscious of the delightful picture she made as they set off in the direction of the park, but could not be sure if Denby had been one of the watchers.

In fact, he was not, but he did not stay long once the object of his visit had departed. Thanking Lady Somerfield for her hospitality, he left the house without appearing to have even noticed her other daughter.

Melanie felt a strange sense of loss once he had gone, but promptly gave herself a silent scold for ever expecting that he might remember her. She could not put the blame on her gown this time, however, for she was wearing one of her prettiest new ones, and even her mama had remarked how very well she looked today.

As the weeks went by, it became quite obvious that Martha had taken very well. She was seldom seen without a half-dozen or more of the most eligible gentlemen of the *ton* in attendance upon her, and if it went to her head a little, no one blamed her, least of all her sister.

Denby continued to call, but to Martha's disappointment, he never invited her to go for a drive with him.

"I can't understand him," she told Melanie. "All the others almost fight for the chance to take me for a drive, but Denby has never even broached the subject. All he wants to do is sit and talk to me here, or take his two dances at a ball. I've even tried to make him jealous by profusely thanking anyone who asks me out in his curricle, but it doesn't seem to have the slightest effect."

"He's probably not a very competitive person, Martha," Melanie suggested.

"What do you mean?" her sister asked, frowning. "They call it the Marriage Mart because it is competitive, don't they?"

Melanie smiled. "Not exactly, my love," she said. "It's called that because young girls are brought up to London to get husbands, just as if they were being sent to market. It seems to me that Lord Denby much prefers to sit and talk to you rather than take you to the park to show you off, as the other gentlemen do. What does he talk to you about?"

"Nothing terribly interesting," Martha admitted, pouting a little. "He never makes any remarks about my hair or my gowns, as all the other gentlemen do. And the other day he said something about a Corn Bill, but I had not the vaguest idea what he was talking about."

"I hope you did not let him realize that," Melanie said, her eyes twinkling, "for even Mama has some knowledge of it, and knows why it is so controversial."

Her sister glared at her for a moment, then said, "I did what Mama told me I was to do in such an event. I opened my eyes wide and smiled up at him as though he had said something wonderful.''

"It quite obviously works, or he would not continually show so much interest in you," Melanie said rather ruefully. "Do you really like him enough to want to marry him if he asks you?"

"Of course I do, silly. He is the most eligible of my suitors, isn't he? He's very handsome. Can you imagine how beautiful our children would be? And they say he's one of the richest men in England and has dozens of estates all over the country," Martha said, exaggerating not a little. "And I've come to quite like the way he doesn't ever call me by name, but uses an endearment such as 'my pet,' or 'my dear,' or something similar."

"It's much more important to admire the man than the number of estates he might own," Melanie cautioned. "You never need worry that anyone Mama actually brings over to meet you might be penniless, for I know it to be a fact that Papa checks all the callers out very thoroughly," Melanie informed her, "and I'm quite sure that if such a person did slip past Mama the first time, he would not be encouraged to come again."

"How would Papa know, for he's never here during the day?" her sister asked. "And he never escorts us when we go out of an evening, as some of the fathers do."

"Didn't you know that Mama tells him everything that happened each night before they go to sleep?" Melanie asked, chuckling. "You're seldom up for breakfast with him, but I am, and I can assure you that he really is aware of everything of importance that takes place."

"Not everything, surely?" Martha asked, looking quite horrified.

"Perhaps not everything," Melanie agreed, "but certainly all of the important things which might seriously affect our lives."

Denby had thought the very fact that he was spending quite a lot of time at Somerfield House would satisfy the women in his family for the time being. Instead, however, it seemed they would not permit the matter of his marrying to take its course.

His mama was even worse than his sisters, if that was possible, for she made a point of seeking him out each morning, at a time when he always ate breakfast and studied the newspapers intently. She then plied him with questions as to what he had done the day before, whom he had called upon during the afternoon, and whom he had danced with in the evening.

He had begun to avoid her as much as possible, by having breakfast earlier than usual, but then she started coming to talk to him of an evening, when he was just finishing dressing, causing him to ruin many more neckcloths than usual. It was becoming so intolerable that he determined, one night, to get it over with as soon as possible.

It so happened that he was at his club that evening, and noticed Viscount Somerfield move away from one of the card tables. Without a second thought he decided there and then to ask him for the hand of his daughter, and have done with it. He had little doubt that he would be accepted, for it was obvious that the chit liked him, and he was under no illusions as to his eligibility.

"I say, Somerfield," he began, "do you think you might have a minute to talk about something rather personal?"

The viscount seemed a little surprised, for this was the first time the earl had said more than "Good evening" to him. It had to be about one of his girls, he was sure, but he could not help but wonder which one, for Martha seemed a little young for a man of Denby's years and experience. Lady Somerfield had told him that the earl was paying frequent calls, but he could not remember for the life of him which one she had said he seemed interested in, for by now there were quite a few fellows hanging around Melanie also.

"Of course," he said jovially. "Why not now? It's as good a time as any, I suppose."

The earl led him toward a quiet table at the back of the room, ordered drinks, and exchanged pleasantries until they arrived, for he could not tolerate constant interruptions.

"I've never done this before," Denby said a little sheepishly when they were at last comfortably settled with their drinks, "but I suppose it's best to just get it over with. I'd like to ask for your daughter's hand in marriage."

Somerfield nodded encouragingly. "I heard you'd been coming to call quite frequently," he said. "Which of my girls are you interested in, Melanie or Martha?"

For a moment Denby experienced a feeling of panic, for he could not for the life of him remember her name. This had happened before, when he was in her company, and he had taken to calling her things like "my dear" and "my pet" rather than embarrass himself by calling her by the wrong name. Now he wished he had not. Then he realized how foolish he was being. It was Melanie, he was sure. Had to be, for a pretty little thing like her could never have been called "Martha."

"Why, Melanie, of course," he said quickly, vaguely recalling meeting the older sister, Miss Grenville, and supposing that she was called Martha, for the name did seem to fit her admirably.

Surprised and vastly relieved to get his older daughter off his hands at last, Somerfield beamed. "I cannot think of a better match," he told Denby, "and of course I know that Lady Somerfield will agree with me. I also knew that Melanie will be delighted. She'll make you an excellent wife, and you can look forward to a brood of youngsters, if that's what you want, for she's always been strong as a horse."

Both of his girls had indentical dowries, and after discussing this briefly they shook hands on the deal and the viscount excused himself to hurry home and tell the good news to Lady Somerfield, who, he had assured Denby, would take care of everything.

She was, of course, delighted. "I never dreamed it was Melanie he was after, and not Martha. They've just retired for the evening," she said, trying not to show her relief, for she was quite sure Martha would throw a tantrum, and Melanie would say she did not want to marry him. "We're attending a late ball at the Chathams' tomorrow night, so I would like them to get their sleep this evening."

Suddenly she had an idea that would prevent either Melanie or Denby backing out of the betrothal.

"Wouldn't it be wonderful if we could get the announcement into tomorrow's *Post*? Everyone at the ball would know about it, then, and would be congratulating us," she declared. "And having Denby for a brother-in-law is bound to increase Martha's chances of making an excellent match."

Though the viscount felt she was being hasty, he made no demur, for he also had an odd feeling about Martha's reaction.

It took no more than fifteen minutes to write out the announcement and then direct one of the footmen to take it at once.

"It is very important, so just be sure they know it must go in tomorrow's edition," Lady Somerfield directed as she handed the young man the signed and sealed document.

But though the footman returned not a half-hour later to inform his employers that publication had been definitely promised for the next day, Lady Somerfield still slept badly that night, for she would not quite believe it until she saw it for herself in print.

The first person in the household to read it was, of course, Viscount Somerfield, and once he verified that the announcement was correct, he left the breakfast table and took the newspaper upstairs for his lady to see.

"I believe you had best leave it to me to tell the girls," she said, flushing a little at what they both knew she had done. "I'm sure that Martha will throw a tantrum, but I can deal with that, I think, better than you could, and I do want her to appear at the ball tonight."

He returned to the breakfast room, only to find that in his absence his older daughter had come down to join him, as she so often did.

"Good morning, Papa," Melanie said, smiling warmly.

She was one of the few people he had ever known who came down to breakfast with a happy smile on her face, he thought as he returned her greeting and resumed his seat at the table.

"I was looking for the *Post*," she told him, a puzzled

frown on her face, "but it does not appear to have arrived as yet."

"It's here," he said briefly. "There was something in it that your mama wanted to see, so I took it up to her. Have your breakfast first, then go up to her so that she can tell you about it."

The words were scarcely out of his mouth, however, when they both heard a loud shriek that could only have come from a most distraught Martha.

With a look of alarm on her face, Melanie quickly asked to be excused, then raced from the room and up the stairs. The screams were coming from Lady Somerfield's chamber, and Melanie hurried toward the open door, stepped inside, and closed it quickly behind her.

As she looked first at her mama and then at Martha, the latter ran toward her shouting, "You stole him from me. You knew I wanted him, for I told you so, but you went behind my back and stole him."

Despite her smaller stature, Melanie was considerably stronger than Martha, however, and she grasped her sister's wildly flailing arms and pulled her firmly into her own, clasping her close and murmuring softly, "Hush, my love, do calm down or you'll have the whole house in here to see what's wrong."

As Martha's screams changed into quiet sobbing, Melanie looked over at their mama with eyebrows raised, waiting to find out what had caused her sister's hysterical outburst, and Lady Somerfield involuntarily glanced down at the copy of the *Post* that still lay at the foot of her bed.

"Your betrothal to Lord Denby is in the newspaper," her mama said firmly.

"My betrothal? What can you mean, Mama?" Melanie asked, a look of horror on her face. "Surely there must be some mistake. There'll be a retraction in tomorrow's edition, you'll see."

"There is no mistake," Lady Somerfield told her. "He asked your papa for your hand in marriage last night, and I sent it to the *Post* myself."

"But he's never spoken above a dozen words to me,"

Melanie protested. "Why did Papa not tell me about it last night, and ask me if it was what I wished?"

"Because Denby is the catch of the year, and you should be jumping for joy instead of looking at me as though the world is about to come to an end," her mama snapped, finally rising from her bed and coming toward her daughters. "Give Martha to me, then go down and talk to your papa if you think there is something wrong with marrying the wealthiest lord in England."

As though in a trance, Melanie allowed her mama to take Martha back to the bed; then she went slowly toward them and picked up the copy of the *Post*.

The announcement seemed to leap out at her from the page, and after staring at it for almost a minute, she turned around and went out of the chamber and down the stairs to the breakfast room, the paper still clasped in her hand.

"Now, don't you look at me like that, my girl," her papa told her sternly as she walked toward him. "You quite obviously don't appreciate how fortunate you are, for Denby is known as one of the most amiable gentlemen in London, as well as the wealthiest."

"But he doesn't know me at all," Melanie protested, though she could see from the expression on her father's face that he did not believe her. "I don't think he has ever exchanged more than a few words with me."

"How girls of your age exaggerate," exclaimed Lord Somerfield. "He wouldn't be asking for your hand if he didn't think he knew you well enough. Now, would he? Instead of pulling that long face, you should be delighted that at last someone has offered for you, for I was beginning to think we'd have you on our hands for the rest of our days. Get your breakfast and then go back upstairs and change into something a little more attractive. He'll be here to see you in less than an hour."

"Good," Melanie said firmly. "Perhaps he can give me a more sensible explanation of this idiocy than either you or Mama seems able to."

Before he could voice the angry retort on the tip of his

tongue, she had swung around, stalked out of the room, and was on her way up the stairs to her own chamber, still clasping the newspaper.

She slid the bolt on the door and went to her armoire to select something suitable for the occasion, but everything seemed to be in bright, sunny shades, and in her present mood she deeply regretted allowing her mama to get rid of all the black gowns that had comprised her entire wardrobe for a couple of years.

After pondering the situation, she selected a carriage dress in a deep green bombazine, but her arms suddenly felt like lead, and taking off one gown and donning another seemed to be almost too much effort. Finally, however, she had the gown in place, and was just considering sending for her abigail to fasten it up for her when a sharp rapping came on the door, and she heard Lady Somerfield's voice.

"Open this door at once, Melanie," her mama called. "As if I don't have enough with Martha throwing a fit of the megrims, without you following her example."

"I am changing my gown, Mama, and was just about to send for Bridget to fasten it and dress my hair," she said, going over to the bell rope and giving it a strong tug. "I understand from Papa that Lord Denby is expected this morning, and I should like to be ready when he arrives."

To her surprise, her mama made no further attempt to make her open the door, and a few minutes later she let Bridget into the chamber, then turned so that the abigail could fasten her gown.

"Word downstairs is that you're betrothed, Miss Melanie," Bridget said as her fingers worked busily down her mistress's back, "and if it's true, I'd like to wish you happy, but surely that's not what all the rumpus is about?"

"Oh, yes, it is," Melanie said sadly, "and it has to be a mistake, but please don't tell them so belowstairs. See if you can make my hair look a little neater, and find me a bonnet and shawl to go with this gown, for if we are to talk about it in any degree of privacy, I'm afraid that the earl will have to take me for a drive."

Bridget also added a touch of color to her mistress's cheeks, for, as she told her plainly, if she looked any paler the earl might think her about to faint.

When she finished, it was almost time for the earl to arrive, but Melanie did not go downstairs to wait for him. Instead, she stayed in her chamber until her mama came to tell her that he was here.

"And don't you forget. You tell him that you're honored to accept his offer," Lady Somerfield warned.

Melanie nodded, then walked down the stairs as slowly as if she were going to her own funeral.

Had she not been watching Denby's face as she entered the room, she would not have detected the flicker of surprise in his eyes, which was there for only a second, then disappeared at once as she dropped him a curtsy.

The only other person present was her papa, and he said, a little too quickly, she thought, "Melanie, my dear, as I know there's been no time for you to discuss your plans, I'll leave the two of you together for a few minutes."

She waited until the door closed behind him, then said quietly, "I am indeed honored by your offer, my lord," almost as her mama had instructed, then added, "but rather surprised, for I must confess that I had thought it was my sister, Martha, upon whom you have been calling these past weeks."

Only an utter cad would have told her that she was correct. Denby was an officer and a gentleman, however, and though he might confess to his mistake, years from now, when they could both laugh about it, this was decidedly not the time to do so.

He cleared his throat carefully, if a little louder than usual, then said gruffly, "Your sister will have a dozen offers before the Season is out, if she has not done so already. But I would not want to rush you into an early wedding if you feel that we should first, perhaps, get to know each other better."

As he spoke, he led her toward a sofa, and once she was seated, he took his place beside her, but at least a foot away.

She turned sad eyes toward him, and there was a faintly discernible note of bitterness in her voice as she asked,

''What difference would it make? As Mama has already put the announcement in the *Post*, it is too late for either of us to back out of it without causing a great deal of unpleasant gossip.''

He took one of her small hands in his large, well-kept one, and she noticed a slight roughness in the palm of his. Quite irrelevantly, she decided that he must be accustomed to performing at least some harsh tasks with his hands, and somehow it made her warm a little toward him.

His voice was stern, however, as he inquired bluntly, ''Are you accepting my proposal against your will, then?''

She looked up at him sharply, and could not have lied to him, no matter how angry her mama might be. ''Shall we say, my lord, that I was given no choice in the matter,'' she murmured. ''The first I knew of it was when I saw the announcement in the *Post* this morning.''

''I'd not want a reluctant bride,'' he warned her. ''If you do not wish to marry me, say so now and I'll speak to your parents on your behalf.''

Listening to the tone of his voice, she wondered if he had seen, for a moment, a possible way out of his predicament, but she knew, however, that there was none. Smiling ruefully, she shook her head. ''Mama would never permit me to turn you down, my lord, and if you should be the one to break the betrothal, I would never be able to show my face in London again.''

There was little doubt that she was right on that score, Denby thought; then he heard the rustle of skirts in the hall and he said quickly, ''My curricle is waiting outside. Let's go for a drive so that we can talk it over in privacy. Go fetch your bonnet and a wrap while I ask Lady Somerfield for permission.''

He caught the look of anxiety on her face, and wondered why he had never noticed how expressive it was. Then he added, ''Don't be concerned. I'll say nothing of consequence to your mama until you and I have had a chance to talk.''

Lady Somerfield gladly gave her permission for him to take her daughter out alone in his curricle, and the two set off at a steady pace. Not for the park, however, as that good lady had expected, but along Knightsbridge and into Kensington Gardens, where there was little chance of running into any of the *ton* at this time of day.

He had dropped off his tiger a short distance from the house, so that they could have complete privacy, and when they came to a more secluded spot, he jumped down and tied his horses loosely to a couple of trees, and then helped Melanie down. He was surprised somehow at how very light she felt.

"We'll not go far, for I want to keep my eye on my horses. They seem a little skittish," he told her, thinking how their behavior closely resembled her own. "That bench over there will do, I believe."

He was much kinder than she had thought him capable of when she first met him, Melanie thought, for she was acquainted with a number of gentlemen who would not have paid any regard to her feelings. They would, she knew, have declared outright that there had been a mistake made by her parents, and washed their hands of the whole affair.

But no matter how long they talked, they still came back to the same thing each time. She would have to marry him or be forced to leave, in shame, for the country. There was also a strong possibility that such a thing would do considerable damage to her sister Martha's chances of making a good match, for no matter how popular a young lady might be today, it could change overnight by just a few well-chosen hints and innuendos.

There was nothing for it, as far as either of them could see, but to go through with it and try to work things out as they went along.

"Do you think there is any chance that we might have a quiet wedding in the country?" Melanie asked. "I always wanted to be married in the village church, with all the people who had known me all my life to witness it."

He shook his head ruefully. "I would like nothing better," he told her, "but I can promise that when our respective mothers get together they will not be satisfied with what we want at all. I should imagine nothing else will do for them but a large society wedding at St. George's in Hanover Square.''

"Oh, no," Melanie moaned at first, but she soon realized that, under the circumstances, it was the only kind of wedding that would dispel rumors and stop gossip, and she would just have to face up to it.

The discussion had become quite animated at times, and as Denby had watched Melanie's face he realized that she was far more attractive than he had thought when he had first met her. It was a most expressive face, and she would never be good at gambling, but within the space of a half-hour he had watched humor, sadness, mischief, and joy show clearly in her lively features. He had a feeling that life would never be dull with her, and thought that perhaps his mistake in names had been a fortunate one after all.

As he drove her back to Somerfield House he could feel her tense perceptibly and go quieter, and he realized that she was a little fearful of what the next few days would bring.

"Won't you come inside and have luncheon with us?" Melanie asked him. "I can assure you that you'll not have to meet with my sister, for she usually retires to her chamber for the day when she is upset. Mama will probably have given her a strong sedative.''

"But I do not believe that I gave your sister any reason to think that I might propose marriage to her," Denby said gravely. "I did pay her attention, but then, so did a great many other gentlemen.''

It was probably quite true, Melanie felt sure, for it was not quite the thing to speak to a young lady before a gentleman assured himself that he had her father's approval. But she did not at all look forward to facing her parents alone.

She was not aware, however, that her face was expressing her deep concern, until Denby smiled at her reassuringly.

"Your parents are bound to ask what decisions we have reached," he said gently. "I think that, perhaps, I should join you, and we can tell them together what we have decided.''

He helped her alight, then gave her his arm, and they entered the house together.

The Somerfields expressed their delight that he was joining them for a simple meal, and while they were enjoying a glass of wine, Denby told them of their wish for an early wedding. He did not, of course, indicate that he had really meant to offer for the younger sister. It was not discussed today, and as far as he was concerned, it would never be mentioned.

"I am sure, Lady Somerfield," he said, "that my mama will be in touch with you to see what she can do to assist with the wedding preparations, and Melanie and I will be guided by what you and Mama think best."

Lady Somerfield could scarcely believe how gracious Denby was, and how gentle in his dealings with his betrothed.

He did not proffer the ring that he had brought with him, for it was, he felt, too ostentatious and not at all in Melanie's style, though he did not say no. Before he left, however, he made a commitment to return the very next morning with a betrothal ring that he was sure Melanie would like.

3

As Denby had predicted, nothing would do for the
wedding but St. George's Church in Hanover Square,
and the date was set for December 24, Christmas Eve.
Melanie's sister, Martha, and Denby's niece Josephine were
to be the two bridesmaids, and the ordering of the wedding
gown had been taken completely out of Melanie's hands when
she tentatively suggested using the little Frenchwoman who
had made her gowns for the Season.

In the weeks ahead, she saw little of Denby, which was
in some ways a considerable relief, for she was not yet at
her most comfortable in his presence. He had brought a
betrothal ring around to the house the morning after their
drive, as he had promised, and placed it upon her finger,
but then he had begged to be excused at once, as he had a
very important appointment—or so he said.

The ring was very beautiful, consisting of diamonds and
emeralds in an old-style setting, and she felt strangely
comforted, when wearing it, by the fact that Martha had made
it clear that she did not care for it at all.

After he gave it to her, however, she had not then seen
Denby for more than a fortnight, and then he had time enough
only to drink a cup of tea before hurrying off again. He told
her that most of his time at present was divided between
visiting his country estates to take care of emergencies and
attending meetings with the prime minister and others. But
he did make a point of putting in an appearance, at least,
at the balls given to introduce Martha and Josephine to
society.

He had little option but to be present at the dinner parties given by the Somerfields and the dowager Lady Denby, honoring the two of them, but there was little opportunity for private conversation on either occasion.

It was her brother, Michael, who inadvertently let slip to his younger sister that Denby kept a mistress in town.

Martha was, of course, delighted, and brought up the subject with Melanie at the very first opportunity.

"I think that it's so considerate of Denby to continue his relationship with Mrs. Alice Whitehead, Melanie, don't you?" she asked, adding, "It's most sensible of him, for she's been his mistress for years, you know, and once you're in a family way he'll not need to bother you again until after the baby is born."

"And just what do you know about such matters, young lady?" Melanie asked sharply. "Even at my advanced age I know very little, but I am quite sure that Denby will do whatever is the accepted thing."

She would never have let Martha know how she really felt about such an arrangement, for she was fully aware that her young sister was still feeling considerable anger toward her. Though Denby had given not the slightest hint that he was serious about her, Martha still considered that Melanie had stolen her most eligible suitor, and she showed it by making frequent unpleasant insinuations.

"You know, it's probably for the best anyway," Martha went on airily, as though she had not heard her sister's response, "for once he's made sure of an heir, he'll not need to bother you at all. Then you'll be able to have your flirts and cicisbeos to take you about."

"What a lot of nonsense you talk, my love," Melanie said a little wearily. "I hope to have more than one son and at least a couple of daughters, and I'm sure that Denby feels the same way. As for cicisbeos, I'll have enough to do looking after my brood without bothering about men of that sort. Who told you about his mistress, anyway?"

"I got it from a most reliable source," Martha said firmly, "but I cannot, of course, reveal it or I may never be told anything again."

"So it was just a rumor, was it?" Melanie said, looking

considerably relieved, for she really did not want it to be true.

Her sister's eyes flashed. "It's much more than rumor, for it was our own brother who told me, and he swore that he'd actually seen Denby going up the steps to the woman's house. She lives on Seymour Place, you know."

Melanie barely shrugged, pretending that it was not at all important to her, but she quietly decided to speak to Michael and suggest that he cease telling her sister such stories. Martha could never keep anything to herself, and it was quite probable that, by now, all her contemporaries would be talking about it.

However, Melanie was determined not to live the life of a sadly neglected wife whose husband went his own way, and she started to work out a scheme which would make Denby eventually realize that he had taken a wife, not just a female who would dutifully produce a son or sons for him.

He was at present in town, she knew, for some important parliamentary discussions, so she sent a note around to Denby House, telling him she wished to speak to him and asking that he let her know when it would be convenient for him to call.

His response came early the next morning, before her mama and Martha were abroad, and she excused herself from the breakfast table to go to her chamber and read it in privacy.

The note was brief, stating merely that he would call on her that afternoon between four and a quarter after, and take her for a drive.

She was glad that he had thought of going for a drive, for she had not mentioned it, but now wondered how she would have been able to talk to him at all had the family been sitting there watching them the whole time.

He was greeting Lady Somerfield when Melanie came down the stairs, completely unaware of the serious look on her face, and her mama was being most insistent.

"But I am receiving today, Denby, and some of my guests are still here. You must at least come in and have a cup of tea or a glass of wine," she protested, then noticed her daughter's bonnet and parasol.

"Oh, what a sly puss you are, my dear, for you knew he

was coming and never told me. Well, I'll excuse it this once, for I know you have not seen each other for some time and must have a great deal to talk about. I really should send someone with you, but I won't do so this time, for I have every trust in you, my lord," she went on, "and I know that my daughter is in the best of hands."

"You may certainly be sure that she will come to no harm in my company, Lady Somerfield," Denby said quite sternly, then offered his arm to Melanie and escorted her to the waiting curricle.

As before, he dismissed his tiger a couple of streets away from the house and then continued toward the park, but took the way that would be quietest at this time of day.

"I am afraid that I have been neglecting you somewhat during what must be a very trying time for you, but I can assure you that it has been absolutely necessary," he said seriously. "I am pleased, however, that you felt free to send word, for I assume there is something you wish to discuss with me."

Now that he was here beside her, and there had been not the slightest difficulty in persuading him to call, Melanie felt a little more kindly toward him. She still meant to let him know how she felt, however.

"Yes, my lord, there is," she began quietly, but he raised his hand to stop her.

"Before you proceed," he said, a firm note in his voice, "allow me to request that you call me either Denby or Broderick, for I do not find 'my lord' to be acceptable from your lips unless you are extremely angry with me, which I sincerely hope you are not."

"If not quite angry, I am a little annoyed," she said, turning her head to look at him, and noticing how he raised just one eyebrow.

"Then tell me what you are annoyed about, for I detest women who pout and sulk," he told her calmly enough.

She took a deep breath. "When we last went for a drive some weeks ago," she began, "you were all amiability, and I felt then that we would be able to rub along reasonably well. Since then, however, you have scarcely spoken a word

to me except to politely ask after my health when we met
at the two dinners we attended—''

"And you are beginning to have some doubts, I assume,"
he said sternly, finishing her sentence for her. "Are these
doubts severe enough to make you reconsider your decision
to marry me, because if so, for God's sake say so now before
any more plans are made."

She shook her head, glad that he could not completely see
her face because of the wide brim of her bonnet.

"Then let me tell you something, which I have on the very
highest authority," he said, a gentler tone in his voice. "It
is a fact that most brides, and an even greater number of
bridegrooms, as a matter of fact, experience considerable
doubt during this period as to whether they are doing the
right thing."

He reached over and unfastened her bonnet, lifting it off
her head and placing it on her lap.

"That's better," he said, his smile still a little grim. "Now
I can see your face, which, by the way, as I have noticed
before, is extremely expressive."

"I cannot conceive how you could possibly have noticed
anything about me," she snapped, "for the only occasion
when you have really looked at me at all was when you
realized that I was Melanie and not Martha."

To her chagrin, his eyes twinkled and his mouth twitched
before he finally broke into a wide grin.

"I'm not going to deny it," he told her, "for that would
not be fair to you, but I must tell you that I had no special
feelings for your sister, and have come to realize that you
are a far better choice. She's a nice-enough youngster, to
be sure, but having listened to her absurd attempts at serious
conversation, I realize I would have been driven to drink
in less than a sennight."

Secretly pleased at his remark, she did not show it,
however, but retorted sharply, "Then am I to assume that
you find my reticence much more to your liking?"

"I have already noticed that you are far from reticent, my
dear," Denby said ruefully, "but as I said before, I abhor
pouting and sulking above all things, and your sister has

frequently displayed both since you and I became betrothed. I'll tell you now that I would not tolerate such behavior in a wife.''

"Pray tell me. What else would you not tolerate, sir?" This conversation was not going at all as Melanie had hoped, but she felt that she might as well know the worst now.

It was fortunate that they had reached a quiet spot, for Denby was able to pull the carriage over and let the horses stand for a moment. They had not been moving at all fast thus far, and were in little danger of catching a chill.

He reached over and took one of her hands in his, marveling at how small it was compared to his own.

He looked directly at her, a smile twitching at the corners of his mouth, and all of a sudden she had a ridiculous desire to touch his lips with her fingers and see if they felt as soft as they looked. Once they were wedded she would be free to do so, she realized, and found herself, for the first time, looking forward to the opportunity.

"I don't think you will find me an intolerant husband, my dear," he told her gently. "Tell me honestly, do you enjoy people who pout and sulk?"

She shook her head. "I'll try to be the kind of wife you would like, Broderick, and I'm sure we will rub along at least as well as most couples do," she told him, then gasped with surprise as she felt him slip a strong arm around her and draw her close.

She felt instinctively that if she started to pull away from him even slightly, he would release her, but those blue eyes seemed to mesmerize her as she allowed him to tilt her chin upward.

His kiss was gentle, as if he did not want to frighten her, and knew instinctively that she had never been kissed before. Melanie, however, had no wish for that lovely warm feeling to stop. When he did finally release her, she felt strangely bereft.

"Your mama would be horrified, I know, my dear, but I do not believe that you are, are you?" Denby asked softly.

She shook her head, and he realized that there was no need

for words, for her eyes were shining in a way he had never seen them before, and there was a very special glow about her.

He heard a carriage approaching and withdrew his arm from around her shoulders, then gave a small tug on the reins, and the horses responded immediately, moving toward the road at once. By the time the carriage passed them, it appeared as if they had merely slowed for a moment, and Denby was relieved, for he had no wish to give cause for gossip.

"Tell me," he said, when they were moving once more at a slow pace, "is there anything you really wish to discuss further with me before I take you home? I give my word that I will try to see you more often. If I cannot do so, you must realize that once we are married we will be away from London for quite some time, and I have much to accomplish here before I can leave for so long."

Melanie shook her head. "I think you must have been correct, and I was simply becoming nervous and wondering if I was really doing the right thing. I'm all right now, though, and I promise to be a little more patient."

It was not until later that evening, when she saw her face in her pier glass and noticed how much happier she looked, that she realized she had forgotten all about his visits to his mistress. For some reason she no longer felt quite so angry about it and, not the first time, wondered if, perhaps, her sister had been telling the truth.

But Martha would not let well alone, and the very next morning, having been told of Denby's visit by their mama, she waited until she and Melanie were on their way to the lending library before bringing up the subject again.

"Mama told me that Denby called for you yesterday and that you went for a drive alone with him," she began. "Did you ask him how Mrs. Alice Whitehead was?"

"I'm not at all sure that Mrs. Alice Whitehead is not just a figment of your decidedly vivid imagination," Melanie told her sister coldly. "In any event, what Denby does or does not do should not be any concern of yours. If Mama knew that you were even hinting at such thing, she would box your ears.''

Martha's expression was decidedly smug. "So you didn't mention it to him, did you? You wouldn't dare, just in case he decided not to marry you after all.''

"You know, Martha, I never realized what a very unpleasant young woman you have grown to be,'' Melanie told her quietly. ''If you continue to be as nasty and spiteful as this, you'll lose all your friends, for no one will want anything to do with you.''

She knew her sister well enough, and should have realized what would happen next, for Martha burst into tears and continued to sob so loudly that they finally had to turn around and go back home.

Melanie left her in their mama's charge and went upstairs to remove her cloak and bonnet. After she heard them come up the stairs and go into her sister's bedchamber, she slipped out of her own room and went down to the library.

It was here that her mama found her a half-hour later.

"I've just come from giving your sister a soothing powder and putting her to bed,'' she said angrily. ''You know quite well that Martha has always been highly strung, yet you still go out of your way to upset her. She told me that you said she was nasty and spiteful. Is that true?''

"Quite true, Mama, for she is,'' Melanie said calmly.

"And what, pray, occurred during your ride yesterday to make you decide to take it out on poor Martha?'' Lady Somerfield asked, glaring at her older daughter. ''Or did you just get up in a bad temper?''

"As you must recall, I don't tell tales,'' Melanie reminded her mama. ''If Martha has not told you what occurred, then I will not.''

"You're not too old for your papa to thrash, young lady,'' an angry Lady Somerfield declared, ''and I'll see what he has to say about this when he returns for nuncheon. I shall be glad when you're away from here, for you've always been jealous of Martha because she is prettier than you are. Go to your chamber and stay there until Lord Somerfield returns.''

Picking up the book she was reading, Melanie silently left the room and did as her mama ordered, telling herself that it really didn't matter, for she could read just as well in her room as in the library.

But once there she could no longer concentrate on the book, but dwelt on what her mama had said. It was quite true that Martha had always been by far the prettier of the two, but Melanie had never been jealous of her sister's looks, which came from their mama, for Lady Somerfield had always been a good-looking woman.

Martha had been a sickly child, however, and because of this and her pretty face, she had been spoiled abominably by their mama. If she found the right husband, however, one who would love her but not let her have all of her own way, Melanie was quite sure that her sister would grow out of her petty lies, for she was not a bad person at heart.

As for herself, she did not for a moment believe that her father would lay a finger on her, but he would scold, she knew, and that was something she was not looking forward to.

But as it turned out, he was not even cross with her, for Michael had spoken to him on her behalf, having guessed what the quarrel was all about.

"I'm sure the thought of your husband keeping a mistress does not appeal to you, my dear, for you know very well that I have never followed such a practice," he said to her. "But I will give you a word of advice, for you to take or not, as you choose."

Melanie was most surprised that her papa was willing to talk about it at all, for she knew that her mama would not, and she gave him her complete attention.

"For the most part, a husband who is well-satisfied with his wife quickly finds that he does not need a mistress. Make Denby happy in your marriage, and I promise you that this Mrs. Whitehead will quickly be sent packing—if she hasn't been already," he assured her. "That's all I have to say, except to ask you to try to be patient with your sister. You have to put up with her for only another month. I know quite well that you love her, so surely you can turn the other cheek for so short a time, my dear, can't you?''

Now she was the one in tears, and she hugged him and promised to do her best.

''I'll miss you,'' he told his favorite daughter, his arms still around her, ''but Denby is a fine man and you could not have done any better if you'd been really trying. Just don't underestimate him, though, for he's his own man, and not the sort to let a woman wrap him round her little finger.''

She hurried up the stairs, passing her mama, who gave a nod of approval when she saw the tears in her daughter's eyes, and duly carried the information to her younger daughter.

The four weeks prior to Melanie's marriage went remarkably quickly, and Denby kept his promise to try to see her more often, though they were never again alone together. Then, after a final week of endless fittings for the elaborate wedding gown, not to mention all the other clothes that had been ordered, the wedding day arrived and her mama, Martha, and various aunts buzzed around Melanie like bees as they assisted her with her toilette before the wedding.

Martha was looking particularly beautiful in a gown of palest green. It matched her eyes, which were glittering even more than usual, for earlier in the day she had managed to see Melanie alone and pass along what she called a little tidbit of information. She had it on the best authority, she told her sister, that Denby had actually visited his Mrs. Whitehead as recently as two nights ago, and had stayed a considerable length of time. And if Melanie did not wish to believe her, she had added, she could always ask their brother, Michael, about it.

Prior to her sister's visit, Melanie had been feeling much happier about her wedding, for Denby had called on her unexpectedly the night before and presented her with a lovely necklace that matched her betrothal ring. After her sister's disclosure, however, all her trepidation returned. She felt almost as though she had stepped outside of her body and was watching it go through the necessary ritual.

She heard both of the questions the ladies who were helping

her asked, and her own replies to them, as though she was just an onlooker, but only her papa seemed to notice anything wrong. And of course he put it down to bridal nerves, covered her cold hand with his own, and whispered words of encouragement. As she began to walk down the aisle toward Denby, she could not help but remark to herself how very handsome he looked, standing there in morning dress.

His smile was warm and encouraging, but she heard the service as though it was in the distance, happening to someone else. At least she was alert enough to make her responses at the right times. Then she was walking back down the aisle, on Denby's arm this time, a fixed smile on her face, as if she was enjoying herself.

The smile did not slip when she was handed into the waiting carriage for the drive to the Somerfield home for the reception, but it did turn to one of secret amusement at times as she recalled the little surprise she had planned for her groom—in fact, several surprises, for she did not mean to allow him to forget that he now had a wife.

Denby felt only relief that the worst was over, or so he thought. If his bride did not appear to be quite herself, at least she was smiling instead of crying, which he had heard many young ladies in the same position were inclined to do. Then he recalled that he had not yet told her where they would be going once the wedding breakfast came to an end.

"Are you not at all curious where you will lay your head this night, my dear?" he asked her, smiling at what he thought to be her completely calm assumption that he would take care of everything.

"I know myself to be in the best of hands, Broderick," she murmured, "and so do not need to concern myself about it, but by all means tell me if you wish."

"We shall be setting out first to my principal estate, which is in Sussex, within walking distance of the sea, where I will need to spend at least a couple of weeks in order to catch up on some of the bookwork with my bailiff," he told her. "After that, we will commence a tour of the lesser estates so that you will be able to familiarize yourself with them and, perhaps, come to a decision as to which you like the best. I shall be very interested in what you decide and why.''

"How many lesser estates do you own?'' Melanie asked, by now feeling some curiosity about them.

"Just four more, not counting the London town house, of course,'' he hastened to add. "They are in Devonshire, Derbyshire, Yorkshire, and also in Kirkcudbrightshire in the Southern Uplands of Scotland.''

"It seems that we might easily be journeying for a six-month, Broderick,'' she said lightly, "and I should, I suppose, be grateful that these five estates are all you own.''

He gave her a warm smile that wrinkled the outside corners of his eyes in the most charming way, and she found herself gradually thawing and responding to him.

"If you wish me to be absolutely accurate, I must add that I also own shooting boxes in Devonshire, Derbyshire, and Scotland, which can easily sleep a couple of dozen men and their servants,'' he added.

"Then by all means let us be absolutely accurate,'' Melanie said, her face serious but with the tiniest of smiles playing at the corners of her mouth, "for it sounds as though one of your shooting boxes would almost sleep a whole village if the size of the chambers is what I imagine them to be.''

"I am pleased to note that you seem somewhat easier of mind than before,'' he told her gently. "When I turned and saw you coming down the aisle, you looked as though you might shatter into fragments at the slightest touch.''

"I felt dreadful,'' she admitted, "and I think if Papa had not held me so tightly I might have turned and run. But now I feel much better, my lord, thanks to you.''

"If you had turned and run, I can assure you that I would have run right after you and hauled you back,'' he assured her. "I can think of nothing more dreadful than being left waiting at the altar.''

A servant refilled Melanie's champagne glass, for toasts were about to start. Feeling thirsty, she took a sip, then laughed, feeling her eyes water as the bubbles tickled her nose. She was about to reach for a handkerchief in her reticule, then realized that today she did not have such a thing with her.

"Here, take mine," Denby told her, seeing her problem and placing a large white kerchief in her hand.

The trouble then, however, was that once she had used it, she still had nowhere to put it, and her cheeks went pink at the thought of returning a used kerchief to him. Then she heard him chuckling at her dilemma.

"Come along, give it to me," he said, grinning at her embarrassment. "You're learning very quickly all the quite splendid things husbands can do for their wives."

When she made no move to do so, he reached over and took it from her, slipping it into one of his pockets.

"Have you any idea how embarrassed I would be if you walked out of here with a large kerchief in your hand? Our guests would be quite sure that I had already reduced you to tears," he teased.

Just then her papa rose and proposed a toast to the health of the bride and bridegroom, and all eyes turned toward them. This was followed by a toast to the parents of the bride, the mother of the bridegroom, and then a long line of people, many of whom neither Denby nor Melanie had even heard of, as the glasses were refilled time and time again, and some of the guests began to appear quite light-headed.

"I think it's high time we departed on our wedding trip," Denby said, fearing that if things got any worse, Melanie would find it exceedingly embarrassing. "I just caught my mama's eye and she has slipped out through the door on the left. When we stand for the next toast, just step behind me and go out the same door. I'm sure you'll find her waiting for you. I'll meet you in the hall in half an hour."

She followed his instructions exactly, and was pleased to find that Denby's mama was indeed waiting to go with her up the stairs to her bedchamber and help her change into a warm carriage dress and wrap. The dowager Lady Denby explained that Melanie's mama thought it would be best if the family did not suddenly disappear to help Melanie, or some of the guests might decide to play last-minute pranks on the bride and groom. Bridget had already started out for Sussex with Denby's man, Godfrey, and the remainder of Melanie's clothes.

Lady Denby glanced out of the window at the heavy gray sky, then turned back, shaking her head.

"I'm not sure that it's wise to even start for Sussex today," she said, a worried frown on her face. "It's been getting colder as the day goes along, and if that sky is anything to go by, we'll have snow before the day is out."

Melanie shrugged. "I'm sure that Broderick will know what is best for us," she told her new mama-in-law. "He said he would meet me downstairs in half an hour, and it's almost that now."

"Yes, my dear," Lady Denby agreed. "He'll probably have the carriage outside by this time and ready to leave. Don't worry about anything, for I know that you'll just love Denby Downs when you finally get there."

They hurried down the stairs to where, as was expected, Denby was waiting impatiently, but he still had time to thank his mama and give her a big hug before he and Melanie stepped outside and into the waiting carriage, which had been heated to a comfortable temperature with hot bricks.

"I should think there'll be some disappointed guests when they find we have already left," Melanie suggested, "but our mamas thought that this was the best way to leave."

"They were right, and I frankly have little patience with the pranks people play when they've imbibed a little too much of the grape. They're usually aimed for the most part at the bride, and I particularly did not want you to experience any unpleasantness today of all days," Denby explained, taking her hand in his and squeezing it gently.

Melanie gave him a grateful smile, then peered out of the carriage window, noting that the sky looked even worse than before.

"It doesn't look at all good," Denby told her, "and I'm afraid we'll just have to stop somewhere on the way if snow actually starts to fall. I suppose that most of your clothes have already been sent ahead with your maid, haven't they?"

She nodded. "I'll manage somehow, though, but I do hope we'll not have to stay longer than overnight."

"So do I," he agreed ruefully. "Why don't you put your head back in the corner and rest for a while, for you must be feeling exhausted after such a hectic day. I doubt that I'll doze off, but if I do, and the snow starts to come down, my driver knows to inform me at once.''

To Melanie's surprise, he reached over and carefully removed her bonnet, then moved the squabs around until she was in the most comfortable position possible.

"Let yourself relax, my love," he told her, "for there's nothing much we can do about the weather.''

To her surprise, she actually did fall asleep, and awoke a couple of hours later to see Denby with his face to the window, peering out.

He heard her stir, and turned around to see if she really was awake. "I believe the first flakes of snow are starting to fall now, and they're large enough to quickly cover the ground. I think we'd best stop at the first decent inn we come to and see if they can put us up for the night," he told her.

He rapped on the roof, and the second coachman slid back a small door and called, "Yes, milord?"

"I don't like the look of it," Denby said. "Tell Tom to stop at the first reasonable-sized inn we come to and we'll see if they can accommodate us for the night.''

There was a murmur from above, and then the small door opened again and the previous voice said, " 'E says there's naught of any size for another ten miles or more, milord. Do you want to try the first one we come to?"

"We'll have to, I suppose, even if it's only to get information. Tell Tom not to take any chances, no matter how slowly he has to go," Denby added, then closed the small door once more.

"Are you sure you're warm enough, my dear?" he asked most solicitously.

"I am at the moment, Broderick, but I do hope we find an inn before the bricks cool down altogether, or we'll both feel the cold," she said quite calmly. "Now I know why June is such a popular month in which to get married.''

"You'll like Sussex even if everything is covered in snow for the first day or so," he told her. "The house is built on quite a high hill, so the view is truly delightful and the sea is but a short walk away, so the snow never lasts long.''

He sounded almost homesick, she thought, and wondered how much time he had been able to spend there in recent years, for she was aware, of course, that he had served with Wellington throughout the Peninsular Wars.

The coach was slowing down now, and through the window they could just make out the outline of a small building, and someone was approaching who looked a little like a walking snowman with a lantern in his hand.

"I'm sorry, milord." The voice was gruff but respectful. "The only thing we 'ave left at all is a small room on't top floor, but it's clean and dry and we've plenty of wood for a fire. It's only meant to sleep one, though, and a maid p'raps."

"Can you give us some supper, my man?" Denby asked.

"That I can, milord, an' a good one too, but I've no private rooms like you're used to," he warned. "An' you'll find nowt else of any size for another nine or ten miles."

Denby smiled grimly. "We'll take what you've got, and be glad of it on such a day," he told him. "See that the fire in the room is lighted right away, if you please, and I'd best carry my wife in, I think, or she'll have wet feet."

Ignoring Melanie's protests, he stepped down, then reached into the coach and gathered her up in his arms as though she weighed no more than a child. It was only a few strides to the front door of the small inn; then he set her down in the hall and they followed the innkeeper toward the staircase and up the stairs.

The room was exactly as the innkeeper had described, but it was better than trying to reach a larger place and getting stuck on the road, Melanie decided. There was no question but that it must be the smallest chamber either she or the earl had ever slept in, she thought, then remembered that he had probably become accustomed to sleeping wherever he could when on the Peninsula.

A maid was busy lighting a fire, and the innkeeper told her to put hot bricks into both beds at once.

"If you'll come downstairs and have a bit of supper, we'll have this place as clean and toasty as can be, I promise," the man told them. "My wife's just roasted a fine piece of pork, and she's got Yorkshire puddings in t'oven already, if that'll suit you, and you'll find that 'er apple pie can't be bettered even in London.''

An hour later, both Denby and Melanie were in agreement that he had just cause to brag, for they had consumed a meal that Prinny himself would have been happy to sit down to. There were no fancy wines to drink with it, but the home-brewed beer was pronounced excellent by Denby, while Melanie sipped cider made from the inn's own apple trees. It was a delicious brew, but a little too potent for her to have very much of it.

With some reluctance they slowly climbed the stairs to the small bedchamber, but even here they received a surprise, for sheets and spreads had been changed since their arrival, and the room was warm and inviting.

Nothing could change the size of the beds, however, and in the end Melanie had her way and took the maid's bed, while Denby climbed into the slightly larger one. They were both prepared to sleep in their undergarments, and though Denby's feet still hung over the end of the bed, they were closest to the fire, which was well-banked-up, and there was not the slightest chance of his feet being cold.

''This must be one of the strangest wedding nights ever recorded,'' he told Melanie when they were settled between their separate sheets. ''And I must tell you how proud of you I feel for the way you have accepted what is, at best, a most uncomfortable situation.''

Had she told him the truth, that she was not at all unhappy to retain her virginity for one more night, he would not have been at all surprised. For him, however, it was extremely difficult to spend the night in such close proximity to his bride, yet not be able to even kiss her good night, for he feared that were he to do so, he would not be able to stop at just a kiss.

''There was surely little point in making a fuss about something that could not be helped,'' Melanie said in a practical tone. ''At least you made certain that we were not stranded overnight in the coach, as, I have to admit, I feared might happen.''

She wished him a good night and then closed her eyes and pretended to sleep. But the events of the day, followed by the most satisfying meal and potent cider, quickly took effect, and she fell into a sound, dreamless sleep.

4

When Melanie opened her eyes, the first thing she became aware of was the complete silence. Accustomed as she had become these last few months to living in London, where some street sounds almost always penetrated the interior of the most well-built houses, the lack of noise was quite eerie, and it took a moment or two before she realized where she was.

She glanced toward the other bed, only to find it empty, and could hardly believe that Denby had arisen and put on clothes just a few feet from where she lay, without her sensing his presence.

Now she slipped out of bed, wrapping a blanket around her, for it was quite cold in the room, and went over to the small window. It had a lovely, delicate design traced upon it in frost, and through it she could see a sky of the brightest cerulean, above a carpet of pure white snow that stretched as far as the horizon. The branches of nearby trees that had long since lost their leaves now looked as if they were topped with fluffy white pillows, and even the song of the birds was hushed for now.

She swung around at the sound of a key turning in the door, and was relieved to see Denby entering, holding a morning tea tray in his hand, just as if he performed this task every day of the week.

"Good morning, my dear," he said, smiling warmly. "I don't have to ask what kind of a night you had, for you were asleep almost before your head touched the pillow, and I don't believe you stirred all night."

Melanie wrapped the blanket more tightly around herself

and stepped over to the bed she had just abandoned, feeling decidedly embarrassed that he should find her in such a state of undress.

She had no idea how lovely she looked to Denby, for her hair fell below her shoulders in delightful disarray, and her face had just now turned a rich rosy pink. To add to the effect, though she would have been horrified had she been aware of it, the blanket that she clutched around herself so tightly served not only to cover but also to emphasize all the more her delicious curves.

"I won't ask you to take the tray from me," he said, grinning, "for your hands appear to be otherwise occupied, but if you can just move a little to the left, I will be able to put it down on the bed beside you."

She carefully did as he requested, and once the tray was in place he poured a cup for each of them, then sat on the edge of the other bed, sipping the deliciously strong brew and nibbling one of the biscuits he had just watched the innkeeper's wife take straight from the oven.

"Is there any prospect of our leaving today?" she asked him, once she had made herself a little more comfortable.

Denby nodded. "I believe so, for the sun is quite strong and has already begun to melt some of the snow. By early afternoon I should think we might be able to make a start, so I have ordered a light breakfast in half an hour, a midday dinner, and a picnic hamper just in case we should meet with any further trouble before we reach Denby Downs."

"If the food is at all like the dinner we ate last night, we shall not need any more for a week," Melanie said with a chuckle, having now recovered her equanimity to some extent.

"I cannot but agree, and have been finding out exactly where we are so that I may stop here by intent next time, rather than by accident," Denby told her. "The innkeeper's wife is one of the finest cooks I have ever had the good fortune to come across."

"I agree, but what on earth will we do with ourselves this morning?" Melanie asked. "I would seriously doubt there

is a book to be had in the whole place, and I do not even
have a piece of needlework with me to occupy my time."

"I'll not lack for work, for I have some of my bailiff's
recent reports to go through," Denby told her quite shortly,
"and this is an excellent opportunity for me to catch up on
such things."

All of the pleasant feelings that Melanie had started to
entertain toward her husband disappeared with this last
remark, and she determined that as soon as breakfast was
over she would see if she might borrow a pair of pattens from
the landlady and take herself off for a walk in the countryside. If that was the way Denby intended to spend the
morning, and probably all the rest of the mornings away from
London, she meant to find her own means of entertainment.

"Did you arrange for breakfast to be brought up, or are
we to go down to the dining room?" Melanie asked coldly,
adding, "though, in either case, I need to dress, so I would
appreciate it if you would allow me some privacy to do so."

"Of course," he murmured, frowning slightly at her tone,
and moving toward the door. "I'll come back for you in ten
minutes, and if you need any hooks fastened, I'll attend to
them then."

He was puzzled by the quick change of mood in Melanie,
but as his mama and sisters were occasionally abrupt for no
reason that was apparent, he decided she was probably of
a similar temperament, and went downstairs to see how the
coachman was faring with the cattle.

Of course, once he became involved in a discussion of the
possibilities of reaching Denby Downs that day, he completely lost track of the time, and was most surprised that
Melanie had not waited for him in the small chamber as he
had suggested, but had somehow handled the hooks on her
gown by herself. She was sitting at a table in the dining room,
sipping a cup of hot tea and conversing with the innkeeper
when he came back down the stairs.

He found himself quite irritated at the thought of her
wandering around the inn alone, but since his own tardiness
had been the cause, he decided to refrain from bringing up

the matter with her at this time. After all, the circumstances were unusual, and they would be leaving in a very short time now.

When they were finished with what few would have called a light breakfast, Melanie told him she wished to go through to the kitchens to compliment the innkeeper's wife.

"That's a good idea," he said, nodding. "I'll be working in the small room to the left of the bar, called a snug, when you're finished."

If he thought she was going to sit in silence watching him work for the rest of the morning, like a good little wife, he was very much mistaken, Melanie decided, and made her way along a corridor to the kitchens.

Once she had told the good lady how excellent the meals had been thus far, she asked about pattens, and a pair that were only a little too large for her were brought out at once. Then it was only a matter of slipping up the back stairs to their chamber to get her warm cloak and bonnet, and returning the way she had come.

She had been told by the innkeeper's wife that the walk to the village was a most pleasant one, and been given directions on how to get there, so she set out at a good pace, enjoying the feel of the sun on her face, but though it might melt the snow, it had little real warmth at this time of the year.

There were not very many people about, for everyone in the whole of England, she felt sure, would be busy today preparing for Christmas dinner, and she wondered if they might reach Denby's home to find that his cook had a holiday meal waiting for them.

She had found the village easily enough, where she had browsed in some of the small shop windows for a while, and was just starting back the way she had come when she saw Denby approaching at rather a quick pace.

Just for a moment she felt like turning around and running as fast as she could, for the great strides he was taking seemed to presage trouble. But instead, she went forward rather more slowly, and finally just stood and waited for him to reach her.

As he came nearer, he called angrily, "Have you no sense at all in that pretty little head of yours? Or were you deliberately defying me?"

"I quite frequently go for walks alone when I'm in the country," Melanie began, then gasped as he took hold of both her arms and gave her an impatient shake.

"You're hurting me, Broderick," she said weakly, and he relaxed his grasp at once, then pulled her into his arms instead.

"You silly girl," he murmured, his breath close to her cheek. "When you didn't come through to the snug, I went looking for you, and finally the innkeeper's wife told me where you'd gone. It never occurred to her, of course, that it was dangerous for a lady to be out walking alone."

"Why would it be more dangerous for a lady than for any other female?" Melanie asked, puzzled.

For answer he reached over and slipped the glove from her left hand, revealing her emerald and diamond rings.

"There are many ex-soldiers roaming the countryside close to London, most of them looking for work, but a few trying to get anything that is available, and not caring whom they hurt to get it."

"I'm sorry," she said softly, now completely remorseful. "I never meant to make you worry so."

She could feel his warm mouth moving against her forehead; then he lifted her chin with a finger and touched her lips with his own. He was gentle at first, but gradually more and more demanding, until she found herself clinging to him and responding eagerly to his kisses.

When he finally raised his head, neither of them moved at first; then a slow grin formed on his stern features, softening them and making Melanie smile gently back.

"I swear that if you ever frighten me like this again, I'll either thrash you soundly or lock you in your chamber," he told her.

"And throw away the key?" she suggested.

"Oh, no," he said, his eyes twinkling, "I'm not that much of a fool. I can think of a great many things for the two of us to do behind a locked door."

Her cheeks turned a deep pink, and she tried to look away, but he turned her face toward him.

"I didn't mean to embarrass you, but I've a feeling that, in time, you'll completely enjoy the things that happen between a man and a woman," he told her softly.

Then she recalled another woman, Mrs. Alice Whitehead, and her body automatically stiffened.

He noticed her change in expression right away, and wondered what he could have said to cause it.

He waited a moment, thinking she might say something, but when she remained silent, he released all except her left hand, and set off at a rapid pace at first, then a few minutes later he shortened his stride to accommodate her shorter legs.

"Is it close to twelve o'clock yet?" Melanie asked, remembering the beef that had been roasting on a spit in the kitchen of the inn.

"It will be in a half-hour," Denby told her, and asked, "Did the walk give you an appetite?"

"I believe it did, but I also smelled the beef roasting in the kitchen before I left, and I can't wait to try it," she told him.

As they strode along, Denby suddenly said, "When I think about it, I really cannot blame you for wanting to take a walk on a day like this, but would you please tell me what you mean to do next time, so that I can point out any dangers, and at least know where you are?"

"But if you had said I couldn't go, what then?" she asked.

He stopped and turned to look into her face. "I would expect you to comply with my wishes," he said quietly. "I do have the right to insist on this, you know."

He was not demanding, nor at all aggressive in his manner toward her, but there was something in the quiet voice that made her want to do as he asked.

"I wouldn't have gone if I had known how worried you would be as to my safety," she told him. "But I felt too cooped up, and the thought of having to sit with nothing to read or do but stare into space disturbed me."

He smiled as though he now knew what had happened, and he touched her cheek lightly with his fingers. "You felt that I had no right to disregard you so, when we had not been married even twenty-four hours, didn't you?"

She nodded, unwilling to lie to him.

"On this occasion you were right, my love, and I was being very thoughtless," he admitted. "But you must remember that I am no more used to being leg-shackled and having to think of someone else than you are. I promise to try a little harder if you will do so also."

When she nodded once more, he took her chin gently in his hand, then bent his head to place a tender kiss upon her lips.

They resumed the walk back to the inn, and on arrival hung their outer garments on a rack in the hall, then went into the dining room, where several of the other stranded travelers were already seated at tables and quite obviously ready for the meal. The table they had occupied before was being held for them, and they were just in time, for a moment later the innkeeper entered with the large cut of beef, surrounded by baked potatoes.

His lady followed with a large tureen of cream-of-turtle soup, and while she served this, her husband began to carve the beef, the juices flowing with every cut of the knife, and causing the mouths of the watching guests to water in anticipation.

Even had the roads cleared overnight, the meal would have warranted staying a few more hours, Melanie decided, for she could not recall when she had partaken of anything quite so delicious. She ate far more than she had meant to, but it was just too good to forgo a single mouthful, and as she stepped into their carriage an hour later, she overheard the two coachmen marveling at the meal which they, too, had just eaten in the kitchen.

Then the carriage started to roll, and they were on their way at last to Denby Downs.

"Do you think we might reach your home while it is still light?" Melanie asked, more in an effort to make polite conversation than with an eagerness to get there.

"I would say that all depends upon the kind of weather we encounter," Denby began rather ponderously; then he suddenly noticed the decided twinkle in her eyes and went on, "for if we should meet up with heavy snow again, I might be tempted to drop you into it as a reprisal for daring to mock someone so very much older than you are."

Her reaction to his mild teasing was quite surprising, for her expressive eyes positively danced with fun, and she eventually failed completely in her efforts to hold back her outright laughter. It occurred to him that she had not known he possessed even the slightest hint of a sense of humor, and that she was vastly relieved to find that he did indeed.

When she recovered somewhat, he answered her original question. "I believe we will be there by nightfall or thereabouts, for it's dark by five o'clock at this time of year. Coach travel does not appear to tire you unduly, from what I have seen thus far, but if you feel the need to get out and stretch your legs at any time, please let me know and I'll be happy to stop the carriage."

"I doubt that I will need to do so, my lord," she told him, her eyes still twinkling, "but I thank you all the same for your offer. Will there be anyone else in residence when we get there?"

He shook his head. "My mama stays there quite often, but I know she would not think of disturbing us at this time. She is a quite surprising romanticist by nature, you know, and she is most anxious to have some Denby grandchildren to make a fuss over and spoil dreadfully, as she did with my sisters' children."

He waited for the pink flush to spread across her cheeks, as he knew it would at his remark, then went on quietly. "I'm sure you must realize I want an heir, and I most sincerely hope that you share my feelings."

Melanie nodded, then tried to hide her embarrassment by making light of the subject. "I had quite supposed that you already went through all of this with Papa, checking my bloodlines, state of health, average life expectancy, and so on. You surely could not do less when choosing a wife than you would were you buying a horse at Tattersall's?"

"Of course not," he said with a straight face, "but I don't

think I was able to check out the teeth at the time. Open your mouth and I'll take a look now.''

Had she known him just a little better, she might have done so and displayed a pink tongue, but realizing that this might be going a little too far with him, she laughed instead, showing her pretty white teeth to advantage.

Denby was delighted that she was becoming a little more familiar with him, and did realize that his own rather serious manner was as much at fault as anything for her slowness to relax in his company.

"Tell me if I'm right in thinking that you and your sister are not quite the best of friends,'' he said a few minutes later. "An age difference of four years is hardly enough to account for it.''

Melanie sighed, then looked directly into his eyes. "Considering that we are sisters, I suppose that we have never really been very close since we were quite small, but it wasn't too noticeable until quite recently. I'm afraid that you had something to do, quite unwittingly I am sure, with our present complete lack of affection.''

He raised an eyebrow. "I know that I did pay her some attention when we first met, but only as one of a crowd of other gentlemen,'' he protested. "I never offered to take her for a ride in the park or anything of that sort.''

"But you were still paying her some attention by being one of the crowd of young men always surrounding her, Broderick,'' Melanie said softly. "At no time did you ever realize that I was even present in the same room. I'm sure that neither Papa nor Mama told her that you had mixed up our names, though they must certainly have realized it. But she had been watching you very closely, you know, though it may have just been because you never did offer to take her riding in the park.''

He did not attempt to deny it. "That confusion of names was the most providential mistake I ever made, my dear. It was almost as though fate intervened and stopped me taking the wrong sister. I'll not lie about it, for you deserve better than that, but all it took was that one ride in Kensington

Gardens with you for me to realize how extremely fortunate I had been.

"Did she never discuss it with you? Ask if we had been seeing each other away from the house or anything of that sort?" he suggested, and when Melanie shook her head, he went on, "I may not have spoken to you, but I know I had given your sister no reason at all to believe that I wished to marry her. There's nothing to be done at the moment, however, until she meets a man she cares for, he proposes, and they get married. No doubt when that happens there will be a corresponding improvement in the relationship between you."

Melanie smiled. "I'm very much afraid that will happen only if this fictional hero considerably outranks you, sir," she told him dryly, and he smiled a little grimly at that.

Although she had not realized that she was at all tired, it was not long before the rocking of the carriage put Melanie to sleep. When she awoke, it was to find that it was almost dusk and they were within just a few miles of Denby Downs.

She struggled to make herself a little more presentable in the short time left, then turned to her husband, who appeared to have been working with the same papers the whole time, and asked him if her bonnet was on straight.

"Straight enough," he told her. "No one would expect you to look your best after spending a couple of days traveling in the same clothes. The very first thing I mean to do when we get inside is to send for hot water and take a bath."

It was not quite the very first thing he did, however, for it had simply not occurred to him that the entire staff would be lined up in the hall waiting to be presented to their new mistress.

He glanced quickly at her face as they entered, and was both surprised and pleased to notice that she did not seem at all disturbed. She smiled pleasantly when he introduced the very proper butler, Withers, to her, and that austere person then made sure that every single one of the forty or more upper servants were duly presented to their new mistress.

While Withers was doing what he felt to be his duty, Mrs. Birkett, the housekeeper, told Denby that there was plenty of hot water whenever they might want it, and that her ladyship's abigail had all her mistress's clothes unpacked and ironed already.

Melanie returned in time to hear the good news, and said quietly, "If you will excuse me, my lord, I'll seek my chamber now and put myself in Bridget's most capable hands."

"What time should we serve dinner, milady?" Mrs. Birkett asked her as she turned to leave.

Looking across at Denby, Melanie raised her eyebrows. "Will seven o'clock be all right, my lord?" she asked.

Denby nodded. "And we'll meet in the drawing room at half-past six for a glass of sherry, I think," he told her.

Bridget was waiting at the top of the stairs, ready to show her mistress to her chambers, and once inside, she threw her arms about Melanie and said, "I've been so worried about you, milady, traveling all this way in that snowstorm."

"We found a small inn when it became clear that we could not go much further," Melanie told her, then chuckled. "You cannot imagine the size of the chamber we slept in last night. I was on the maid's bed and the earl was on one not very much larger. But it was worth all the discomfort to waken and find the countryside so quiet, and so very beautiful."

"Beautiful for them that doesn't 'ave to get up first and light the fires and shovel the paths," the abigail said practically. Then she hurried to answer the knock on the door and let in white-aproned maids with a huge copper tub and large jugs of steaming water.

After Melanie was clean once more from head to toe, Bridget rubbed her hair dry, brushed it until it gleamed, then piled it high on her head, with just a few wispy curls framing her face.

"Now, which gown is it to be, milady?" Bridget asked. "They're all freshly ironed and so lovely it's difficult to decide which is nicest."

"I'll wear the first one from the left," Melanie said,

without looking, for the time seemed suddenly to have flown, and she did not wish to keep Denby waiting on her very first evening here.

Bridget groped inside the armoire and drew out a quite simple but very elegant gown in ice blue. White ribbons spanned the high waist and tied in a large flat bow beneath the breasts, the ends left to dangle almost to the floor.

It took but a few minutes to don the gown and let Bridget fasten it, then pull on long white gloves that reached almost to the hem of the gown's small puff sleeves.

White slippers and a small white reticule completed the outfit except for some form of hair ornament, and Bridget frowned, as if not quite sure what would look best. Then she opened a drawer and took out a length of narrower white ribbon and made a small bow in which she inserted a pearl-and-diamond pin.

A string of matching pearls completed the effect; then the meticulous abigail finally gave a nod of satisfaction and Melanie was free to hurry down the stairs and into the drawing room, where Denby was waiting, a glass of sherry in his hand.

He set it down on the mantelpiece as she came across the room, and went toward her, his hands held out to clasp hers.

"You look delightful, my dear, and almost rested," he told her, "but I cannot think that there was enough time to close your eyes for even a minute."

"There wasn't," Melanie said ruefully, "not with Bridget insisting that everything had to be absolutely perfect for my first dinner here."

Releasing her with obvious reluctance, he took a fresh glass of sherry from a nearby tray and placed it in her hand. Then he went over to take his own glass from where he had left it on the mantelpiece.

"To your first dinner at Denby Downs, my dear. May you always look as lovely as you do tonight," he said, raising his glass and taking a sip.

"Thank you, Broderick, and I must also thank you for your excellent suggestion that my abigail journey a day ahead of us. I think it must be the first time in my life that I have arrived somewhere to find all my clothes already pressed and put away.''

Denby looked surprised. "I'm amazed, for Lady Somerfield appeared to me to be a most efficient organizer, particularly as far as the wedding plans were concerned."

She grinned. "Oh, Mama is very good at organizing things when she travels. What she does is send someone ahead, such as her older daughter, to make sure everything is in order for her arrival," Melanie told him.

"Does she not employ a caretaker to look after a place in the family's absence?" Denby asked in surprise.

Melanie nodded. "Yes, of course, but the couple who looked after the London town house have grown old, and this year the wife had become quite feeble and needed constant care, so I found that nothing had been done when I arrived. Bridget, my abigail, is a gem beyond price, for she is willing and able to do just about anything, including keeping me in order."

Denby grinned. "How very interesting. I'd best have a talk with this paragon and see if she can give me some helpful suggestions."

Melanie glared at him for a moment, then had to smile. "I shall try my best to keep the two of you apart, for she's known me since I was little, and might tell too many of my secrets."

There was the sound of a throat being cleared to get their attention. "Dinner is served, my lord, my lady," Withers intoned.

5

The Earl of Denby had been sitting at the desk in his study ever since his bride had excused herself and gone to her chamber more than two hours before, and, to be perfectly honest, he had not the slightest idea that it had been so long a time since she had left.

He had been concentrating on his smaller estates of late, and had not realized how far behind things had been allowed to slip since he was last at Denby Downs. He would have to spend less time with his bride and more time in this room, he decided, if things were to be brought up-to-date within the two weeks he meant to stay.

But now he was very tired, for he had slept little the previous night, and he had before him the distasteful task of initiating his young wife into the so-called art of making love. It was something he had never done before—that is, breaking the so-called barrier—and he had not the slightest idea of how to go about it other than by causing her pain, which he had no wish to do.

He had meant to ask Mrs. Whitehead about it at the time he had told her he was marrying and had given her a substantial final farewell present, but at the last minute he had felt too embarrassed to ask such a question.

The ridiculous thing was that last night he could have gone ahead with it without any worries, for their proximity and her odd state of undress had made him more than a little aroused. But tonight was a different matter, and in any case, she would probably be fast asleep by now and he would be forced to waken her.

With a heavy sigh he put out the candles downstairs and

made his way to his own bedchamber, which was next to that of his bride. There was not a sound from that chamber, however, to make him think she might be awake and awaiting him.

His valet, Godfrey, was waiting for him, however, and he allowed himself to be helped out of his evening dress and into his nightshirt. Then he dismissed the man.

The turned-down bedcovers looked so very inviting that he almost decided to forget his obligations and slide between the sheets; then he determinedly walked quietly to the adjoining door and entered his wife's chamber.

A lamp burned not far from the bed, and from the light it cast he could see her lying there, her hair spread out across the pillows and a delicate lace gown covering all but a very small portion of her chest. It was quite obvious that she was in a deep sleep, so he turned quietly around, slipping through the adjoining door and closing it silently behind him.

The very last thing he wished to do was hurt her and then leave her lying awake for the rest of the night, wondering if it was always going to be so painful.

He must have made the right decision, he decided the next morning, for he had fallen immediately into a sound, dreamless sleep, and had awoken completely refreshed.

He had left word with Withers that he would require an early breakfast, and leaving a message for Melanie that he would be back for luncheon, he went off to keep his appointment with his bailiff.

When Melanie awoke and realized that her husband had never been near her all night, she was not quite sure whether to feel relieved or angry.

She was, of course, glad that he had not awoken her and done whatever awful thing he was supposed to do to make her no longer a virgin, but on the other hand she felt insulted that he had not treated her the way he ought to treat his bride on the first night of what was at least supposed to be their wedding trip.

As she had suspected, Denby was nowhere to be seen when she went downstairs to the breakfast room, but Withers

handed her a note from her husband, informing her that he
had an important appointment this morning but that he would
return in time for luncheon.

This was the moment, Melanie decided, to put her first
plan into action and to make sure he was fully aware that
he really was now married. After nibbling on a piece of toast
and sampling some of the bacon and eggs, she sent word
to Mrs. Birkett that she wished to see her in the study.

Denby had spent a rather unsatisfactory morning with his
bailiff, for it appeared that the man, to whom he paid a high
salary, had neglected to take care of a number of important
matters. As a consequence, the estate was now suffering,
and he intended, after having luncheon with Melanie, to retire
to his study and go through most carefully all the records
which had been made of improvements to the estate in the
last year.

If it should take him the whole afternoon and evening also,
he was determined to find out who else might be at fault,
and the full extent of the errors.

Before entering the dining room, where Melanie would
be waiting, he went in the direction of the study to put down
some papers that would facilitate the necessary checking.

He paused to listen for a moment at the study door, for
it was most unusual for any sounds to be heard from the
room, which he considered his own personal domain. He
was quite sure, however, that there was more than one person
inside at the moment.

Grasping the knob, he flung the door wide and was
astounded to find a half-dozen or more belowstairs servants
there, armed with pails and mops, quite obviously intent on
cleaning the room from the oak floors to the molded ceiling.

Rugs, pictures, and books that had been there the night
before were nowhere to be seen, nor was there any sign of
the ledgers which he had left open on the top of the desk
when he went out, firmly believing that no one would have
the audacity to touch them in his absence.

Crossing the room at a rapid pace, he tugged on the bell
rope for Withers, then realized that it would be better to send

one of the footmen to find Mrs. Birkett, the housekeeper, and bring her here to him at once.

He gave the necessary instructions and, while he waited, glanced at the empty bookshelves, which were thick with dust, and at the clean places on the oak floors where the rugs had lain. There was no doubt whatever that this work should have been performed some time ago, but, thinking about it, he recalled how he had given instructions to his mama that the study must not be touched in his absence.

He glanced outside, noticing for the first time how dirty the windows had become, and how dull were the oak frames around them.

Mrs. Birkett came bustling into the study, a big smile on her round, jolly face.

"It's so gratifying to have a mistress in the house again, milord, and to be able to really take care of things when they're needed. I'll wager you had no idea just how dirty this room had become until you saw it with all its trimmings removed," she said, obviously most excited at being able to do something about it at last.

"This is, of course, on Lady Denby's instructions, I imagine," he said quietly enough.

"That it is, milord," the good woman confirmed, "and it'll take the best part of a week before it's all finished, but it will be worth it, for I wager you'll hardly recognize it when it's all done. The carpets are hanging on clotheslines at the back of the house, and all the dust will be beaten out of them before they are brought back."

"And the books?" Denby inquired. "Do you know where they are?"

"All put into boxes, milord, and they're up in the attic now. The shelves have to be cleaned and waxed before they can be put back," the housekeeper said proudly. "And her ladyship put the things from the top of your desk into a box with her own hands, and had a footman take it up to your bedchamber."

"Did she, indeed?" Denby said a little grimly. "Do you have a list of any repairs which will be necessary to the chairs or other items in the room?" he asked curiously.

"I made one, milord," Mrs. Birkett said, beaming, "and her ladyship is sending out for the things that will be needed to fix everything."

He managed a smile. "I suppose that luncheon is still being served at one o'clock, Mrs. Birkett?" he asked, and when she nodded, he took out his watch and said, "Good, I will see Lady Denby in about ten minutes, then."

"Her ladyship won't be back in time, I'm afraid, milord," the housekeeper said, "for she's had Tom drive her into East Bourne to pick out some new fabric to cover the worn chairs with. She took the chair you've always used at the desk with her, to be sure the fabric would look right on it."

"Did she say when she might expect to return?" he asked in deceptively quiet tones.

"Why, yes, milord, that she did," Mrs. Birkett said happily. "She said I was to be sure and tell you that she would be back in time for tea, and hoped you might join her then."

He nodded. "Tell Withers to serve luncheon for me in my bedchamber today, then, and I will work on some papers there at the same time."

As though to emphasize his purpose, he picked up the documents he had brought back with him and took them upstairs with him.

The longer he thought about it, the less angry Denby became with his bride, for after all, she was only being housewifely. And there was no question but that the work in the study had needed to be performed several years ago.

Some hours passed before he heard Melanie's voice in the next chamber, and what sounded to him suspiciously like a conspiratorial giggle, but he decided that he must be mistaken. It was the worst possible time for him to have had his study turned out, but Melanie could not be expected to have known that.

He thought of opening the connecting door and greeting her, but decided to wait until they met over tea—a far more civilized place in which to speak to her about the way she had inconvenienced him—if, indeed, he should decide to mention anything at all about it. That would depend entirely on her own behavior when they met, he decided.

She was all smiles when he joined her in the drawing room for tea, and looked particularly elegant in a morning gown of pale blue muslin sprigged all over with tiny cornflower-blue flowers. A tailored ribbon bow in the same deeper blue emphasized the high waist, its ribbons almost touching the floor. Looking at her now, he did not understand how he could possibly have missed seeing her when he had been calling on her sister.

"I had such a delightful ride to East Bourne this morning, Broderick, and must say how much I enjoyed visiting the surprisingly well-stocked shops. I took Bridget with me, of course, for I knew you would not like me to wander around in a strange place without anyone in attendance," she told him. "And Bridget has a good eye for colors, so she was most useful in helping me make my selections."

"I hope I'm not going to see my study done up in pale, feminine shades," he grunted, adding, "and I would have liked to have my say in what changes were to be made."

"Would you really, Broderick?" Melanie asked him in surprise. "I'm afraid that I didn't give a thought to your wishing to help with the minor decisions, for I cannot for a moment imagine you going in and out of the shops and making selections of fabrics and styles."

"You could have brought samples back here for me to see," he said rather gruffly.

"But that would have meant having the study uninhabitable for a dreadful length of time, and I didn't think you would care for that very much," Melanie said, turning her head as if to look down at the hem of her gown, though really trying to hide her amusement.

He took a sip of his tea and reached for a maid-of-honor tart. "And just how long do you estimate my study will be uninhabitable now that you have selected the fabrics?" he asked.

"I really don't know for sure," she said thoughtfully. "If you should wish to use it before the chairs are newly reupholstered, it would not be more than about a sennight, I would say. Mrs. Birkett told me that you were working in your bed-chamber after luncheon, which I suppose is as good a place as any, if you do not wish to be disturbed by workmen going in and out.''

Her last remark decided the matter for him. He would stay out of the study until it was finished, for otherwise there'd not be one iota of privacy.

That night, after dinner, he went up to his bedchamber to work, for there was no longer even a chair for him to use in the study. But he could hear the soft murmur of voices in his wife's chamber, and it was proving impossible for him to concentrate on anything while he tried to imagine what she looked like in a state of undress.

Without waiting for Godfrey to arrive and assist him, he removed his evening attire and put on a nightshirt and robe, then knocked on the door between the two rooms and entered.

Melanie seemed completely taken aback, and Bridget, who had just helped her mistress into a deep green velvet robe, took one startled look at Denby's face and quickly excused herself.

''Did you wish something, my lord?'' Melanie asked as coolly as she dared.

''Yes, as a matter of fact,'' Denby told her, looking deeply into her lovely eyes. ''I believe it is past time for our marriage to be consummated, and the sooner we get it over with, the better it will be.''

It was just about the most unromantic way of putting it that Melanie could ever have imagined, and her displeasure of this morning was greatly increased.

''Very well,'' she said stiffly, ''just tell me what you wish me to do and we will, as you say, get it over with.''

''Take off your robe and get into bed, then,'' he told her, turning his back toward her in case she felt in need of privacy, ''and then I will do the same.''

When he heard the bedsprings creak, he knew she must be in bed already, and found when he turned around that she was indeed in bed, and lying quite rigid, with her back toward him.

There was no question in his mind but that she was frightened, though she offered no resistance, complying with his every request without once looking at him directly, and he wished with all his heart that he did not have to hurt her in this way.

"Try to relax a little, my dear," he said softly. "I cannot tell you that it will not hurt this first time, and if there was any way I could prevent causing you pain, I assure you that I would do so."

"Please, just do whatever you must, and let's be done with it," she told him in a strained voice.

He tried stroking her back gently, but she visibly shuddered at his touch, and he asked her, "Didn't your mama tell you anything about this, and what you should do?"

"She tried, but I wouldn't let her," Melanie whispered.

"What she would probably have told you," he said quietly, "was that it would hurt the first time, because there is a barrier which has to be broken through. After that it is much easier, and you will, I hope, eventually find it most pleasurable."

When there was still no response, he reluctantly decided that the best thing he could do was what he had said at first, get it over with as quickly as possible. He would try to arouse feelings in her some other time, when she was a deal less frightened than at the moment.

He could not entirely understand how he himself could still be aroused under the circumstances, but he was, so he did what he had to do, then put his robe on again and went over to the nightstand, returning with a damp washcloth in his hand.

Without a word, she took it from him, and he wished her a good night, then returned to his own chamber.

The whole business had been distasteful to him to such a point that he knew he would not sleep for some time, so he settled down to do some of the work he had meant to take care of earlier that evening.

In the next room, Melanie was also having difficulty in sleeping, but not for the same reasons as her husband.

She decided, not long after Denby left, that, first, she had allowed herself to become unnecessarily frightened, second, that he had not hurt her any more than he could help, and, third, that she had behaved like a ninnyhammer. After all, it was not as though she did not wish to have children, for this was what she would like above all else, and it was, in her opinion, the only sound reason for getting married. At least, that's what she used to think, but now she was not quite sure about it. There was much to be said for the warmth and comfort of his arms around her; and that kiss in the snow had been most exciting.

However, she had expected to be taken on a wedding trip on the Continent at the very least, before he had made it clear that the most she could expect was a visit to each of the country estates he owned, so that he could oversee the work of his various bailiffs.

Because of this, disrupting his plans in the way she had done gave her a good deal of satisfaction, as well as ingratiating herself with the upper staff. It would take a sennight at least for his study to be completely usable again; and before then she must think of some other disturbance she could cause him that would jolt him out of his completely unstudied indifference to his bride's needs.

"I believe that most of the books and things could be moved back into the study tomorrow," she told him some days later, when they were sitting at the breakfast table. "Your desk chair will not be ready yet, but I'm sure you could make do with another until the reupholstery is completed."

"What a relief that will be, for my bedchamber is not exactly the most suitable place to use as an office," Denby remarked, reaching for a second piece of toast, "though I have to admit that the study is already looking a hundred percent better than it did before.

"Oh, and by the way, I forgot to tell you that I ran into my Great-Aunt Adelaide in the village yesterday. She's quite a character—drives a pony and cart because at her age it's the only vehicle she's allowed to handle on her own. She's giving a dinner party in our honor this evening."

"And you only just tell me, Broderick?" Melanie said in an exasperated tone. "It's a good thing I don't know many people as yet, or I'd be bound to have made some other plan, you may be sure."

"Oh, I don't know about that," he said calmly. "Most of my friends have the good sense to leave a newly wedded couple to their own devices for the first three months or so."

"But to give a party in our honor, and not tell us until the very day, is a little strange, don't you think," she suggested, "even for a great-aunt?"

He gazed at her, a lazy grin on his face. "Not to anyone who knows my Great-Aunt Adelaide, my dear. We're in the country now, so dress is a little less formal than in town. And, by the way, if she has dancing, which she always does, just be sure that you keep dodging my Great-Uncle Charlie, because I don't want to see you tightly clasped to his bosom. He does it to all the ladies when he first meets them."

Melanie looked askance. "What does he do on the second occasion?" she asked dryly.

"There's rarely a second time," he told her, his eyes sparkling with amusement, "for the ladies, who are always much faster on their feet than he is at his age, get quickly out of his way when he appears to be coming directly toward them to ask for a dance."

"You'd better tell me what he looks like," Melanie said, not sure how much to believe about this old gentleman, "for I mean to keep out of his way before the first dance."

"It's a good idea, though I'm not sure that it isn't being a little unfair to the old fellow. After all, you're no size really, but you could make two of him," Denby murmured, then added, "He does have long arms, though."

This was too much for Melanie, and she started to laugh merrily; then, when she was a little more controlled, she asked, "Do you happen to have any more strange relatives living in the neighborhood?"

He nodded his head slowly. "Of course, for this is my official country seat, and you surely did not think that the family would let two such dear old people live entirely alone, did you? All the older ones on both sides of the family live around here, and the ones who are a little younger keep a careful eye on them.''

They were expected at half-past five, for they kept country hours, and because of this Melanie felt that she should not wear anything too ornate. But in this she was mistaken, for Great-Aunt Adelaide, who stood no more than four and a half feet tall, wore a bright green gown that could only have been in fashion some fifty years ago, for it had panniers under a wide skirt, the front of which was decorated with ruched and pleated silk. Above a high powdered wig was a head-dress of feathers and flowers, which threatened to poke out her guests' eyes as she turned from side to side to greet the newcomers.

"Delighted to meet you at last, my dear Melanie," the little lady said, "and I do hope you are keeping a close watch on our young nephew. Always one for the ladies was Broderick, until he went and volunteered to serve under Wellington."

Of her husband, Denby's Uncle Charlie, there was as yet no sign, and Melanie could not help but wonder if he, too, would be dressed in clothes of another era. Then she saw the little man, and for a moment she had a difficult time keeping a straight face, for Denby had told her the absolute truth: he was very small, with long, rather monkeylike arms—and he did, quite obviously, have his eye on all of the ladies present.

A neatly dressed older woman seemed to be everywhere at once, for to Cousin Margaret fell the unenviable task of keeping the old couple happy and making sure that nothing serious ever came from their little idiosyncrasies.

They set an excellent table, with so many courses and removes that Melanie quite lost count. Broderick had been seated so far away from her that she was a little nervous at first, but then she gave her attention to the food, and soon found herself thoroughly enjoying tasting the excellent dishes and just listening to the various conversations going on around her.

She had almost been lulled into actually enjoying the party when the music started with a waltz, a number of couples took their places on the small floor, and Great-Uncle Charlie was coming straight toward her!

"May I have the pleasure, my dear?" The deep voice in her ear held a decided note of amusement, and it was fortunate that as she hastily rose, her chair was quickly rolled back from the table and Denby's strong hand firmly clasped her elbow.

"That was a narrow escape," he murmured, "and I shall expect to be appropriately rewarded later this evening."

She looked up quickly, startled by his words, but was relieved to find that his eyes were twinkling merrily down at her. "Only if you continue to protect me until we leave, for your uncle looks like a very determined gentleman and may try again later."

As she spoke, she glanced around the small floor, then gasped as she saw that Uncle Charlie had indeed found himself another partner and was holding her in a clasp that left his victim almost unable to move.

"Don't feel too sorry for Lady Craven, for she's a little shaky on her feet," Denby informed her, grinning, "and has told me that he is the only partner with whom she feels secure."

"How long do we have to stay?" Melanie asked, wishing they could make a previous commitment an excuse for an early departure.

"At least another half-dozen dances," he told her, "but I could invite Uncle Charlie to give me a chance to beat him at cards. It's the one thing he enjoys even better than dancing."

Five minutes later Melanie smiled with relief as she watched him take his eccentric uncle through a door at the end of the room.

"Such a dear boy." The gently modulated voice was that of a white-haired lady who had been sitting across from Melanie at dinner.

"You've probably forgotten my name, my dear, as I always used to when I met so many people at once. I'm Gertrude Londsdale, and I'm one of your closest neighbors," she said, adding, "but don't go thinking you have to call at once, for we all know you're newly wedded, and don't expect to see you about very much for now.''

"I doubt that we'll be here much longer than another week," Melanie told her apologetically, "for Lord Denby wants to show me a little of each of his estates and says that we must then return to London.''

"Ah, yes," Lady Lonsdale murmured, "the Corn Bill, I'm sure. What a shame, for Denby Downs must need a great deal doing to it by this time. The late earl traveled constantly, you know, and the house has not been really lived in by the family for years, except for occasional visits by Broderick's mama. It's a pity, for it was once such a beautiful place.''

"It will be again," Melanie said confidently. "I've already started Mrs. Birkett giving the study a good cleaning and refurbishing, and I mean to leave instructions with her for some of the other rooms.''

"The study!" Lady Lonsdale exclaimed. "How on earth did you persuade dear Broderick to make changes in there? I don't believe anything has been even moved around in it, or more than just surface dust disturbed since his grandfather's days.''

"It wasn't easy," Melanie said, smiling, but she had no intention of telling Lady Lonsdale, or anyone else, what she had done—or what she intended to do first thing tomorrow morning, after Denby left with his bailiff for an all-day tour of his lands.

6

"Good morning, my dear," Denby said, peering around the edge of his newspaper. "I trust you had a good night's rest."

"A very good one, thank you, Broderick," Melanie replied, watching the earl's blond head disappear once more behind his copy of the *Times*. "And you?"

The lack of response was not deliberate rudeness, she had concluded, but rather that he had acquired the habit of closing his ears the minute he had his favorite newspaper in front of him.

"Did you also have a good night, Broderick?" she asked, raising her voice a fraction.

"What was that? Did you say something?" he asked, his face appearing around the newspaper again, and a slight frown now gathering on his well-shaped brows.

"I asked if you had a good night also," Melanie repeated.

"Oh, but of course I did. It's rare indeed that I have difficulty sleeping," he affirmed.

He went back to his newspaper and Melanie gave her attention to Withers, experiencing some minor difficulty in deciding whether to have a little ham or one of Cook's home-made sausages this morning.

She was halfway through the meal when Withers came in once more to tell the earl that the bailiff had arrived and was awaiting his pleasure.

At this Denby carefully folded the newspaper and asked Melanie, "Do you wish to read this, my dear?" before placing it on the table at her right hand.

"Thank you, Broderick. Do have an enjoyable day," she murmured, a rather naughty half-smile playing on her face as she thought of how differently he would feel when he returned to the house later this afternoon.

After he left the room, she allowed Withers to pour her a fresh cup of tea and then said, "I will see Mrs. Birkett when she is ready."

With a murmured, "Yes, milady," he left the breakfast room and a few minutes later the housekeeper came hurrying in and dropped her a curtsy.

"Good morning, Mrs. Birkett," Melanie said, smiling. "Today is going to be another busy one, for I have decided that the earl's bedchamber is sadly in need of refurbishing. We'll do the same thing we did with the library. Get all the cleaning staff together, then, first of all, take down the draperies and bed hangings and see if they're worth saving— which I seriously doubt—then check the mattress for any needed repairs and give it a good cleaning. The carpets will go outside, of course, for a sound beating and the removal of stains. I'll join you in about an hour to see how everything looks and if we will need to have new hangings made, chair seats covered, and the like."

"Oh, my lady," Mrs. Birkett said, "I'm so glad, for it's needed doing these twenty years and more. Will you be going to East Bourne to look for fabrics?"

"Yes, I'll do that immediately after luncheon, for I want to be back before the earl returns, of course," Melanie said firmly.

But it seemed that there were too many items to look for in East Bourne, and she did not arrive back at Denby Downs quite as early as she had hoped. Denby preceded her by ten minutes, and though he said not a word to the staff, he was in a rare mood by the time she entered the house.

"I was told by one of the servants that I am to use a guest room, which you have designated, until my own chamber has been refurbished, madam," he said sternly. "Why was I not consulted in a matter that concerns me more than anyone else?"

"But, Broderick," Melanie began, "surely the upkeep of this house is one of my principal duties as your wife." She put a hand on his arm. "Come, let me show you something that I think will amaze you."

She led him through the house and past the kitchen gardens to where several servants were beating a carpet for all they were worth. Huge clouds of dust were rising into the air.

"Do you recognize the carpet, Broderick?" she asked him quietly.

"Of course I do," he muttered angrily, "but how on earth did it get into that state?"

"It was just an accumulation over the years, I suppose," Melanie suggested.

"Couldn't Mrs. Birkett have done this once we left?" he asked.

Melanie quickly thought of an excuse.

"I'm afraid that she could not, for the chair coverings are quite worn, and new ones must match the carpets," she explained carefully. "Until the carpets have had all the dust and dirt removed, it is simply impossible to tell what the color used to be. I brought fabric swatches back, and must undertake the matching myself, of course, unless you would care to do so. Would you like me to accompany you to your temporary bedchamber and see what I can do to make it more comfortable for you?"

He nodded, then slipped her hand into the crook of his arm and escorted her to the upper floor.

"Is this chamber big enough for you for now?" Melanie asked.

"It's big enough for a short time," Denby reluctantly admitted, "but it has just a writing table instead of a desk with drawers in it. And the wing chair isn't large enough for a man to stretch out in comfort."

"I'll ask Mrs. Birkett to find a footstool to match the chair, and I know exactly where I can lay my hands on the desk that will be just right for you," she said, smiling. "Of course, your own desk will be brought in here just as soon as it has been cleaned up and polished."

He gazed around the chamber, trying unsuccessfully to find something else wrong with it.

Finally he said, ''I'd no idea you meant to go to East Bourne today, or I believe I would have put the bailiff off a day and accompanied you. Mention it to me next time you decide to go, and perhaps we can make an outing of it together.''

''I'd like that very much,'' Melanie told him, almost shyly, for she had not expected him to make the offer.

There was a knock on the door, and after Denby's call to enter, his valet came in, followed by servants with the bathtub, steaming jugs of water, and several big towels, which were placed on the other side of the hearth from where they sat.

''Can I persuade you to join me?'' Denby whispered in Melanie's ear. ''There's room in that big bathtub for two.''

Her cheeks turned a rosy pink, and she shook her head, though she suddenly wondered what his warm, soapy hands might feel like as they caressed her bare skin.

''Very well,'' he said softly, ''some other time, when we know each other a little better, I'll show you just how delightful the sharing of a bathtub can be.''

She rose quickly, more than a little embarrassed in case any of the male servants, who were just leaving, had caught his words, and Denby chuckled quietly to himself.

''When that time comes, and you have learned to relax and trust me not to hurt you, we can see how you enjoy a number of things you've probably never heard of, my dear,'' he told her, and she was surprised to see a tenderness in his face that she had never noticed before.

''You must be tired, also,'' he went on. ''Why don't you have an early bath and lie down for a while before supper? I don't want you to become exhausted with all these changes, for if most of them have waited so long, a few more months won't make much difference. I'll see you in the drawing room at the usual time, and I shall hope to find you much refreshed,'' he warned.

He was right, of course, Melanie realized, for she did feel

tired this afternoon, and was wondering why, for it was seldom that she had any indispositions.

To her surprise, when she stretched out on the chaise in her chamber she fell asleep, and had not Bridget come in at the customary hour, she would have slept longer and been quite late going down for dinner.

As it was, she arrived exactly on time, but Denby was there before her and had already poured her sherry.

"That's better," he said as he placed the glass in her hand. "You look much more refreshed than you did earlier. I hope it was not my scolding that upset you, and assure you that I seldom allow myself to become so aggravated."

She could hardly tell him that she'd rather have the scolding than be ignored completely, so she gave him a decidedly weak smile and said nothing.

"When would you like me to look at the fabric swatches you brought back?" he asked, so obviously trying to make up for his earlier bad temper that she felt a little guilty—but only a little.

"Tomorrow morning, I think, for daylight would be best," she said thoughtfully. "I'll have the carpets rolled and placed in the conservatory, which must be the lightest place in the house, and then we can compare them with my swatches."

"We'll look at them after breakfast, then," he said in a most agreeable tone, "and then in a couple of days, when the fabrics have all been ordered and the work is in progress, you and I will travel to Derbyshire and visit Tideswell Manor, in the Peak District."

It was Melanie's turn to be taken aback, and she gazed at him for a moment in complete surprise before saying, "But I thought we were to remain here at least another week. Didn't you say that you'd need at least that much time to complete your business with the bailiff?"

His wide grin made her wonder if perhaps he was beginning to understand what she had been doing, but she soon realized he most certainly did not.

"I think that he, also, can take care of some of the orders I have given him, and then when we return I will be able to check on his progress and see if, by then, some of the work that has been neglected in my absence has been handled the way I want it. If not, then I may have to make other arrangements,'' he told her.

He had until now given Melanie no hint that he was dissatisfied with the bailiff, though she had not liked the look of the man at all, and thought he had a decidedly sly expression on his face.

"How far away is Tideswell Manor?" she asked. "Is it more than a day's drive?"

"It's more like three or four days' drive, provided we do not run into snow again," he murmured thoughtfully. "On second thought, I think we'll head for Moorland House in Devonshire next, for though it's just about the same distance from here, we're much less likely to run into bad weather on the way. In fact, it's sure to be a good deal pleasanter, for currents of warm water traveling across the Atlantic pass relatively close to Devon and Cornwall, and sometimes result in quite balmy weather in the wintertime."

"Oh, do let's go there, Broderick," Melanie said eagerly, "for it sounds heavenly, and quite perfect for a wedding trip."

He found her enthusiasm most appealing, and sent orders to his coachmen that they would set out for Devonshire two days hence.

Over dinner he told her how much he and his sisters had enjoyed Moorland House when they were children, and was much amused by her horrified expressions when he mentioned some of the ghosts that were supposed to haunt houses in that particular part of the country.

"You don't have a family ghost, by any chance, do you?" Melanie asked. "Even for warm, balmy weather, I'm not sure that I would like to share my bedchamber with a ghost."

"Should you ever waken in the night and feel scared, I promise that you could always come to mine, whatever the hour, and would receive a very warm welcome," Denby told her with a distinct twinkle in his eyes. "I cannot recollect, offhand, any actual ghost stories at the moment, but I do remember that there was once supposed to have been a magic beer barrel in the cellar of the home of a certain family, which flowed for many years without needing to be replenished,'' he said.

"Did it stop for some special reason?'' Melanie asked, quite curious so long as it wasn't the ghost of a person.

"Oh, yes, it did.'' There was a sly grin on his face as he paused for effect. "A woman, a maidservant at the house, was sent down into the cellar where it lay and, like many of her sex, she was possessed of, shall we say, an inquiring mind, and she pulled out the bung to have a peep at what was inside the barrel.''

"Well, what happened? Surely there wasn't a body inside? You said it wasn't a ghost story,'' Melanie told him.

"It's not, and there was no body,'' Denby said. "All that she saw inside were cobwebs, but from that day the beer ceased to flow, and it was said that the pixies were offended. The family who owned the house, no longer in possession of such an unusual attraction, gradually lost all their money, and the place had to be sold.''

"If I meet any pixies in your house in Devonshire, I'll be very careful, I promise, not to offend them in any way, for I would not want to be the cause of your losing all your money,'' Melanie assured him.

"As my wife, it's your house too, my dear,'' Denby said quietly. "I sometimes have the distinct impression that you do not yet feel that my property is also now yours.''

"But it isn't mine.'' She said it quietly, and looked directly at him as she tried to explain. "If it were, then I'd be able to make housekeeping decisions without causing you to go into a rage, even a well-controlled one.''

"Oh, I don't really know that you would. For instance, you have your own bedchamber, but I would never think of making the changes to it that you ordered made in mine today,'' he said softly, "without at least consulting you.''

"But cleaning isn't changes, Broderick, and you admitted later that it was high time the chamber was redone. To be honest, I didn't think you would have let anything be touched if I hadn't presented you with a *fait accompli*,'' she admitted a little self-consciously.

By this time they were sipping coffee, and Denby was pouring himself a brandy.

"Would you care for a glass?" he asked. "Have you ever tasted it?"

Melanie shook her head and almost shuddered at the thought of it. "We used to be made to drink it when we were feeling faint or something, and I don't really know how anyone can like it. I suppose you have to develop a taste for it."

"When you're made to drink anything as a medicine, I admit that it is difficult to take a liking to it," he agreed, "but though I was finding our conversation most enjoyable and did not want it to end, I'm afraid I must now get back to some work. However, I'll join you upstairs later, if I may."

It was not so much a question, but a statement he made deliberately, for he had now joined her in her bedchamber a couple of times since the first night, and though it seemed no longer painful, she had shown not the slightest response to his lovemaking. Now he regarded it as a challenge and was determined to try his best to arouse warm feelings in her, even if it should take weeks to achieve.

Her smile was somewhat enigmatic, but she simply inclined her head and said, "Certainly, Broderick."

She was almost asleep, however, when he finally came into her chamber and slipped under the covers, for he had decided to glance at some farming figures and forgotten the time, as he was frequently inclined to do.

To say he had outstanding success on this occasion would be somewhat of an exaggeration, but he was painstakingly patient, stroking and touching what he knew to be the most sensitive places, and he was quite sure, by the time he left her, that he had finally succeeded in arousing her to some extent. All he had to do now was be patient but persistent, and he felt satisfied that she would turn into a warm, loving partner.

Melanie had fallen fast asleep almost before the door closed behind Denby, and she slept soundly most of the night, wakening only once, when, to her surprise, she found that she missed her husband's body beside her in the bed.

The next morning she felt unusually serene, and she greeted Denby in the breakfast room with a bright smile and a cheerful good morning, and was all ready to take him to the conservatory afterward to select the upholstery colors for his bedchamber.

He, however, was not quite so cheerful, for he had found some difficulty in getting to sleep last night after retiring to his own chamber. He had been so anxious to give his wife pleasure that perhaps he had not fully satisfied his own needs. Had he been still in London, he might have been tempted to visit Mrs. Whitehead just one more time—and been sorry afterward, for it was against his better feelings.

And he had to admit that Melanie looked very well this morning. There was a glow about her that he had not noticed before, and he thanked God for the mistake he had made in the two sisters, for he now knew he could never have been happy with the empty-headed one.

He smiled at her as he allowed Withers to help him to some more of the scrambled eggs and ham steak, and as soon as they were alone again he said, "I'm sure you must have slept well, my dear, for you have a radiance about you this morning."

"Thank you, my lord," she said, smiling warmly. "I had an excellent night and woke unusually refreshed."

"When we're through in here, shall we go and look at the carpets and swatches?" he suggested. "I'm quite eager to see them and thus get this business of refurbishing my bedchamber over and done with."

When she agreed brightly, he turned his attention back to the *Times* and was just pondering the financial news when Withers came in to announce that Mr. Crawford, the bailiff, had arrived.

"If you'll excuse me, my dear," Denby said to Melanie, "I'll set him to work on his own right away, and then rejoin him when you and I are finished."

"By all means, Broderick," she murmured. "I'll just go

and see that everything has been set out in the conservatory, and you can join me there when your business with Mr. Crawford is finished.''

She left as the bailiff was being shown into the room, and quickly satisfied herself that they could make a suitable selection from the swatches she had brought home. She knew at once the one she would have chosen, and secretly hoped that Denby would feel as she did. But she would not try to influence him, for it was, as he had said, his bedchamber that was being refurbished.

She waited for him for almost an hour before deciding that he must have forgotten about her again; then she left everything in place and walked through to the hall. There was no sound of voices coming from any of the rooms, so she sought out Withers and asked him where the earl was.

''He and Mr. Crawford went out half an hour ago, milady,'' he told her, ''and he didn't say when he'd be back.''

Melanie smiled weakly at Withers, then went in search of Mrs. Birkett.

She ran the housekeeper to earth in the kitchen, and, after explaining that she did not want the swatches and carpet now in the conservatory to be moved until Lord Denby had made his selection, she went back to her bedchamber and changed into something more suitable for a winter's walk.

She went first toward the cowshed, where a small girl was sitting on a stool and most efficiently milking a placid-looking cow, and Melanie was quite fascinated by the deft movements of her dainty fingers.

Then she strolled into the chicken coop, and watched yet another girl going around and gathering up the eggs. The hens squawked loudly in protest, and one or two tried to peck at her, but she was most skillful in avoiding them.

Next she went into the dairy and saw a large woman skim cream off some milk, put it in a churn, and begin the process of making butter.

Just as Melanie walked over to the door, Denby came in.

''I was told that you were seen headed in this direction, my dear,'' he murmured. ''You must learn, when you leave the house alone, to let someone know where you are going, you know.''

"It would have been impossible," she told him frankly, "for I had not the slightest idea where I was going when I left the house. Then I saw this place and came over to watch what they were all doing so industriously."

"Did they give you some samples?" he asked.

She shook her head. "Apart from the milkmaid, I don't think they realized who I am," she told him. "No one has said a word to me unless I asked a question."

"They know who you are," he said assuredly. "They probably didn't want to say anything to you in case they said the wrong thing and lost their jobs as a result."

She suddenly remembered that she had waited for him, only to find he had gone off with the bailiff without a word to her. Denby, more alert to the rapid changes in her facial expression than she realized, recognized at once that he was in for at least a scold, and tried to forestall it.

"I'm sorry that I left no message for you, my dear, but when Crawford arrived, he had such important news for me that, I must admit, everything else went out of my head. Will you forgive me and take me to where you have the swatches laid out?"

"Of course," Melanie said coolly, heartily disliking his admission that she had been completely forgotten. "Everything is in the conservatory, for it seemed to be the room with the most daylight. Do you wish to go there now?"

He nodded. "Yes, let's go quickly before anyone else gets a chance to stop me and put me in your bad graces again."

"You're not in my bad graces, Broderick," she said with a smile that did not quite reach her eyes. "I can fully understand how easy it is to forget your wife when you have so many more important things to think about."

"I did apologize to you, my dear," he reminded her quietly. "Shall we repair to the conservatory while we still have morning light?"

His clasp on her arm was gentle but firm as he directed her in silence past the main house and into the huge, high-domed glass house that had been his own contribution to Denby Downs when he inherited the earldom.

"They are at the north end," she told him, sorry now that she had made such a fuss, for, she told herself, she really wanted his cooperation in making the selections of fabric.

Had she been more truthful, however, she would have admitted that, for the first time, there had been something about his lovemaking last evening that she had actually enjoyed, and he had left her with a feeling of warmth and comfort. She had been really looking forward to seeing him this morning and working together with him on redoing his bedchamber. Now she had the feeling of rejection with which she was becoming only too familiar.

There were no gardeners around, and just before they left the rows of large orange trees in tubs, he paused, turning her toward him.

"Pax?" he asked softly. "I did beg you to forgive me, you know."

It was quite unexpected, and Melanie swallowed hard, her anger melting at once. She gave him a rather tremulous smile as she nodded her agreement.

There was something in his eyes that told her he was going to kiss her a moment before he drew her into his arms, and she instinctively raised her face toward his.

As kisses went, it might not have received high marks for passion, but she was not ready for that yet, and he was unwilling to go too quickly with her. His lips were gentle and undemanding, but they left her with a feeling of warmth and a strange longing for more, which was exactly what he had intended.

As he drew away from her he took her small hand in his and said, "Come, let me see to what extent you mean to change my life."

The carpets were folded to reveal a portion of the pattern and colors of each, and he looked at them in astonishment.

"I cannot believe it, but this must be what they looked like when they were put down for my father," he said, "and they're really quite lovely."

"They must have been much brighter when new," Melanie told him, "for a considerable amount of fading takes place over the years, but I think they're still most attractive, and it would be a shame to replace them at this time."

"It most certainly would," he agreed. "Let me take a look at the swatches you have."

She handed him a bundle of fabric pieces for covering the chairs, and he went carefully through them, squatting on the floor and putting each one by the side of the carpets.

It took quite some time, and he placed on one side the ones he preferred.

"Before making a final choice," she said, "you must now put the drapery-fabric swatches to both of them, for everything has to blend together, you know."

When he had selected a number of these also, she put aside the ones not suitable, and together they picked out what they both agreed was the perfect combination of fabrics.

He rose, then helped Melanie to her feet.

"I feel a little guilty," he told her, "for I had the distinct feeling that you were making me as uncomfortable as possible because of certain misdeeds of mine of which I was unaware. Now I see how wrong I was, and I must tell you how much I appreciate the time and effort you've put into making more attractive the rooms I call my very own."

Unwittingly Denby had just said the thing that irked Melanie once more. Had she not been aware of his very recent visits to his mistress, she might have felt a little guilty herself for deliberately making him so uncomfortable. But when he spoke of "misdeeds of which I was unaware," as though he was innocent of any wrongdoing, she was once more glad that she had caused him inconvenience.

She accepted his words of appreciation with a smile, however, and told him, "I really must hurry away now, for these swatches have to be returned and the fabrics ordered. I'll probably not be back until late this afternoon."

Holding in her hand the swatches he had selected, she went off to find Mrs. Birkett and ask her to pack up the rejected ones so that she might return them that day when she went to East Bourne to place her order.

Denby sighed as he watched his wife's rapidly retreating form, and wondered what he could possibly have said to cause her to go off in such a hurry. He would never understand women, he decided.

7

They set out on the journey to Devonshire on a day that was cold and crisp, but with a sun so bright and a sky so blue that the very air itself seemed almost to sparkle. Denby had elected to ride alongside the carriage with the outriders this time, so Melanie had only the company of her abigail, and, fond though she was of the maid, Bridget was hardly the companion she would have chosen for a journey of such a length.

By the time they reached Arundel, a bustling little town where a substantial luncheon had been ordered, Melanie was feeling decidedly irritable.

"If you mean to ride on horseback the whole way to Devon, Broderick," she told him as they sat down to luncheon, "I'm afraid you will think me but poor company of an evening, for I find traveling all day with just a maid most tedious."

"Am I to understand that you are feeling anxious for my company, my dear?" he asked, teasing a little. "Wasn't the ride with me to Denby Downs tedious for you also?"

"You did not hear me complaining," Melanie said quietly. "In fact, had the weather not been so bad, it would have been a most pleasant ride."

"Should there be a storm, I will join you," Denby promised, "but I generally enjoy riding beside the carriage at least half of each day. Could you not have brought a piece of needlework to keep you occupied, or a book to read and pass the time, for we will not be traveling after dark."

"The jolting of the carriage and the lack of good light make it impossible to do needlework unless you wish to have to pull the stitches out again every night,'' she said, smiling at his ignorance of such matters. "And as for a good book, much the same applies, for the print becomes blurred with the carriage's constant motion.''

Denby shrugged slightly. "I am exceedingly sorry, my dear, but I doubt that I would be much better company than your maid were I forced to ride in the carriage for long periods.''

Melanie had an idea. "I have a riding habit in one of my trunks,'' she said. "Is there any reason why I should not ride alongside also for part of each day?''

He shook his head. "The best of reasons, my dear, for you are much safer in the carriage, with enough outriders to completely surround it in an emergency, than if you were riding alongside. I'm afraid it's out of the question.''

They ate in silence for some time; then Denby offered, "If you are becoming stiff, I'll be glad to massage the worst places and apply some liniment this evening. It would be my pleasure and, I hope, yours. And don't look so startled, for this time all the best inns have been reserved in advance, and we shall be most comfortable unless we run into extremely bad weather.''

He placed his large hand over her smaller one on the table. "Please believe me,'' he said persuasively, "when I tell you that you will enjoy the journey when we are a little further away from the coast and can move a little faster. The countryside in these parts is beautiful at any time, but with the stark bare branches of so many of the trees, it takes on a rugged magnificence all its own.''

He was right, of course, and Melanie realized, before they finally reached their destination, that at the pace they set, she would never have been able to ride on horseback for more than a couple of hours at a stretch. Having them stop for her to get in and out of the carriage each time would have also meant further delays.

As it was, she found the eight hours of travel quite tiring that first day, and was glad to arrive at the ancient city of Winchester, where they were to spend the night at an excellent inn right in the city itself. As Denby had promised, the best rooms in the place had been reserved for them, and though the sounds of the street could be faintly heard in her chamber, she found it comfortingly like the sounds outside her family's London house.

Having passed through the city on many an occasion, Denby was a little amused that his bride found it so interesting.

"But Winchester might easily have remained the capital of England instead of London," she protested. "Couldn't we leave just a little later in the morning so that I might visit the cathedral?"

She looked so very appealing, as though asking for a treat, that Denby had not the heart to refuse.

"Very well," he told her, a smile of amusement softening his face. "I'll take you over to the cathedral myself immediately after breakfast, but we'll have to ask for a packed luncheon to take with us in the morning, or we'll not reach Exeter before dark."

"Would it be an imposition?" she asked, for she at least wanted to see something other than the inside of the coach on this journey.

"Not at all," he assured her, his eyes twinkling, "so long as we don't find ourselves eating in a heavy snowstorm."

She looked alarmed, and asked, "Are we likely to run into one, then?"

He grinned. "I was only teasing," he told her. "The skies don't look at all heavy, and the further west we go, the less likelihood there is of snow.

"I've ordered dinner to be served in here tonight," he went on, "for I thought it time we saw a little more of each other. While I was riding alongside the carriage today, I was thinking of what you said about traveling alone, and I can fully understand how uncomfortable it must be for you in such a confined space, with only Bridget for company."

Melanie felt quite touched, for she had not thought that Denby could so clearly understand her point of view. She began to wonder if perhaps she had misjudged him, and to look at him a little differently than she had before. For instance, to have dinner *tête-à-tête* was really most romantic, and he had seldom shown himself to be of such a disposition. He was certainly more than handsome enough for young girls to lose their heads over, and hearts also, but she was forced to admit that he seemed completely unconscious of it.

She suddenly realized that he was saying something, and murmured, "I do beg your pardon, my lord. I'm afraid I was dreaming for a moment."

"Were you, my dear Melanie?" he said, smiling. "It would be interesting to know what young ladies of your so advanced years dream about."

She felt her cheeks go hot with embarrassment, for she could hardly tell him that she had been admiring his looks, and was for once quite unable to think of something else to say on the spur of the moment.

"I shouldn't tease you so, I know, but I simply couldn't resist the impulse. You look so delightful when you're embarrassed, but you need never be uncomfortable with me, my love," he assured her. "I was actually asking you about your family. You appear to be quite close with your father, not quite so much with your mother, and to have little in common with either your brother or your sister. I could be wrong, but that was the impression I received on the occasions when you were all together."

Melanie was amazed at so astute an assessment. "I don't think the relationships are quite as bad as they sound," she said thoughtfully. "Papa and I have always been close. Mama also, though she was a little irritated with me for not actively seeking a husband; and my brother and I are still fond of each other, as were Martha and I when we were younger. When she began to realize how very pretty she was, I'm afraid Martha changed considerably. I've sometimes thought it a good thing that I have never been pretty, or I might have grown up that way also."

He shook his head, smiling. "Quite frankly, I have begun to wonder how I could ever have not noticed you when I came to call. You'll never be a conventionally pretty woman, but there are times when you are strikingly beautiful, and you'll eventually learn to emphasize your looks in your choice of clothes. I know you're fond of Bridget, but I'd like to find you an abigail who has the knack of bringing out your beauty to the best advantage.''

"I couldn't let Bridget go." Melanie was horrified at the thought, for she was extremely fond of her.

"You don't have to, and I wouldn't want you to, for I feel she would make a wonderful nanny for our children." He noticed her cheeks turn pink, but continued. "She's a sound, practical woman and quite devoted to you."

He drew out his watch and glanced at it. "I believe we should now get ready for dinner, for it will be here in a half-hour. I shall wear a maroon silk dressing gown, and I hope you can find something equally suitable."

He turned and went into one of the bedchambers while Melanie, feeling not a little shocked at this unusual dinner attire, went into the other one to discuss what she should wear with Bridget, who was not nearly so disturbed about it as her mistress.

Thirty minutes later Melanie stepped out of her bedchamber wearing a deep gold brocade dressing gown with puff sleeves that came down to slender points at her wrists. Her hair was piled high on top of her head and secured there with a gold clip, and several curls had been deliberately allowed to escape to form an uneven frame around her face, giving her a decidedly waiflike appearance.

Denby, who had been selecting the wines that the waiter had suggested that they have with dinner, turned and looked at her in amazement.

"I take back everything I said about Bridget," he murmured. To Melanie's chagrin, he walked over to her so that he could see her from all angles. "We'll have to find someone else for a nanny."

"You like it, then?" She had been afraid that he would not, but Bridget had been more insistent than usual.

"The gown is lovely, and the coiffure makes your eyes look huge. Of course, it's not for every day, and it gives a gentleman an urge to . . . look after you. Don't ever wear it like that when I'm not with you," he warned.

He took a glass of sherry from the waiter's tray and handed it to her, then raised his own glass, "To you, my dear, a very lovely lady."

They sat on the sofa in front of the fire while the waiters went back and forth, bringing what Melanie thought must be a ten-course meal, and though Denby said little, she felt that she would now always be grateful to him, for he was the only person who had ever made her feel beautiful. She could readily imagine what her sister would say if she could see her now, but her opinion was not important anymore.

The following morning Denby was as good as his word, and after an early breakfast he took her over to see the great Winchester Cathedral, and, wanting her to see as much as she was interested in, he got a booklet for her to read, and allowed her to lead the way while he trailed behind.

"Which school did you attend, Broderick?" she asked, turning away for a moment from the effigy of William of Wykeham with three small figures sitting at his feet.

"I went to Eton," Denby said, "and I am aware that Henry VI modeled it after Winchester College."

"I don't know how anyone can even think of sending sons to schools like these. Do you know it says here that a Latin inscription on the wall of Winchester College warns, 'Learn, leave, or be licked.' Did they flog young boys at Eton when you were there?"

Denby grinned. "Of course they did," he said, "and it doesn't seem to have done any of us much harm. If you and I are fortunate enough to have sons, my dear, I can assure you that they will go to Eton."

Melanie turned and frowned at him, then continued her tour of the cathedral. Denby took out his watch and looked at it meaningfully, then glanced at his wife.

She sighed. "I suppose we really must start out now, but I hate to leave this place. There's so much to see here. Will you bring me back sometime?"

"Most certainly, if you still want to come. I'll even take you over to see Winchester College if you'd like to go there at some later time,'' he told her, taking her arm and leading her out through the great door.

"I don't think I wish to see a place where they flog little boys,'' she told him, "so perhaps you'd better not take me.''

He turned away to conceal his broad grin. Before they married he had been completely unaware of how strongly she felt on certain subjects, but he was rather enjoying a wife who voiced her opinions—that is, as long as they didn't become too emphatic, of course, for he was not the sort to put up with a shrew.

It was after dark before they stopped that night, and everyone was feeling tired and cross, though the servants, of course, did not dare to show it. Denby had hoped to be in Devonshire by this time, and privately blamed their tardiness on traveling with women, completely forgetting that this was supposed to be Melanie's wedding trip, and should have been a pleasant, leisurely one. But he had left behind him a great deal of work, and it weighed heavily on his mind. He had also noticed one of the proponents of the Corn Bill in the public rooms of the inn, and hoped that he might get a word with him later and see if he could get some idea of the feelings about it in this part of the country.

Melanie could scarcely keep her eyes open and, unlike last evening's dinner, this one was eaten in comparative silence, after which she and Denby retired to their respective bedchambers without so much as a good-night kiss. She was a little piqued at this, however, and even felt somewhat neglected. She would never have let him notice that she minded, but because of it she did not fall asleep as quickly as usual that night.

When she heard the door of his bedchamber open a half-hour later, she thought he was coming to her. Then there came the sounds of the outer door closing and his quiet but distinct footsteps as he walked along the corridor toward the stairs.

It was a couple of hours before she heard him return, during which time she had imagined all kinds of things. At first she told herself that he merely wished to speak to one

of his servants. But as time went by and he did not return,
she could not help wondering if he had perhaps made a secret
assignation with one of the women who could be seen in the
public lounge when they entered the inn.

"What on earth have you been doing all night, milady?"
Bridget asked her when she brought her a morning cup of
tea. "You certainly don't look as if you got much sleep,"
she went on, then suddenly realized what she had said, and
was instantly horrified at her forwardness.

"I'm sorry, milady," she said quickly. "I just don't know
what I was thinking of, and you a new bride and all."

"It wasn't what you're imagining, Bridget," Melanie said
dryly. "I just had one of those nights when I couldn't seem
to sleep for more than a couple of hours at a stretch. I'll be
all right once I've had this cup of tea, you'll see."

But she wasn't all right; she was tired and impatient, and
she took her irritation out on Bridget as she tried to help her
dress, and then on Denby as they ate breakfast together.

He felt annoyed at first, knowing he had done nothing to
warrant her display of bad manners. Then he remembered
that he had been so intent on meeting the local gentleman,
and sounding him out about the Corn Bill, that he had
neglected her last evening. Could she be hurt because he had
not come to her bedchamber? he wondered, smiling to himself. If so, then he must really be succeeding in his campaign
to arouse her feelings.

"Have we very much further to go, Broderick?" Melanie
asked rather plaintively. "Is there any hope of being there
before luncheon?"

He smiled reassuringly. "It will take at least another three
hours, for we have to go around Exeter and then onto Dart-
moor. Moorland House is not too far from the village of
Widecombe, which is quite famous hereabouts for its local
fair, and I believe you will enjoy the surrounding countryside,
which is mostly moorlands, hence the name. We'll not be
able to do much walking at this time of year, however, but
we'll come back in the summer when the heather is in bloom,
and you can appreciate it more."

She had to smile despite herself, for it sounded most attractive, and she started to look forward even more to their arrival.

"I'll send outriders ahead to let the housekeeper know we are coming and will expect a late luncheon," he told her, pleased to see her looking more cheerful.

"I know that it has been a tedious journey for you, my dear," he said gently, "but once you get there you'll find much to occupy your time, I'm sure. A word of warning, though. It will be more than your life is worth to touch a single thing in my study this time. In fact, I think it best to forbid you to even set foot in there without my permission."

His wide smile softened his words, but there was a note in his voice that made Melanie realize he was not joking at all, but deadly serious this time.

"But really, my lord," she said, smiling also, "what can you possibly have in there that you do not wish your wife to see?"

"Old furniture that could use a cleaning in the far-distant future," he pronounced a little grimly, "and a great many dusty books and bookshelves which I prefer to remain in that condition for now."

"Oh," Melanie said; then, unable to hide her amusement, she put her napkin to her mouth and chuckled.

"You can laugh now," he said, smiling also, though his eyes told her that he meant what he was about to say, "but please do not disregard my wishes, my dear, or neither of us will find it amusing."

Her breath seemed to catch in her throat at the veiled threat, and she wondered what he might do should she defy him, then decided she had no wish to find out.

This time the journey seemed to be too short, for Melanie soon discovered that she loved the rugged moorland, bleak though it was on this winter's day. As they drew near to their destination, they slowed to go into the old village of Widecombe-in-the-Moor, passing a tiny village school, a lovely old church, an old farmhouse, and a small smithy.

But they were through all too soon and climbing once again

toward a lengthy copse through which Melanie could just make out what appeared to be extensive gardens surrounding a large stone house.

A moment later they entered the driveway, and as the coach came to a halt a few minutes later, footmen came hurrying from the house toward them.

The earl appeared at the door of the coach and Melanie stepped down and into her husband's outstretched arms. Suddenly, in this lovely setting, it seemed so very good to feel his arms around her and his warm breath upon her cheek.

"Come, my dear," he said softly, "let us go inside and see if that luncheon is almost ready to be served. We made excellent time, however, so we may have a few minutes to linger over a glass of sherry first."

He half-walked, half-carried her into the great hall, where once again the entire staff awaited them.

"I can't believe that I'm already growing accustomed to this sort of thing," Melanie murmured. "How large a staff do you have here?"

"To be honest, I don't really recall," he told her a little guiltily. "I would think there are about thirty upper staff, and about as many again who work in the scullery, laundry, stables, and so on. It's not a very big house, actually, so you're most unlikely to get lost in it."

Just as she made to step forward, however, there was the sound of rather uneven footsteps on the upper landing, as though someone was limping toward the stairs, and they both looked up when a voice, quite gruff but decidedly female, called to Denby.

"Is that you at last, Broderick? Wait right here and I'll be down as quickly as these legs of mine will permit."

"Go ahead and let Wallace introduce you to everyone," Denby said quietly. "I'll see if I can give her a hand down the stairs."

The small ceremony of meeting the staff was performed with efficiency, Melanie murmuring a few words to each of them; then she allowed Wallace to take her to the drawing room to join her husband.

Denby was standing with his back toward the fireplace,

listening to what appeared to be an older lady, gowned in black, who was seated on a settee facing him.

He came quickly across the room to Melanie, took her arm, and drew her forward as he said, "I'm sorry to leave you to perform that chore alone, my dear, but my aunt can't negotiate the stairs very well on her own."

The lady turned her head slightly as Denby said to Melanie, "I'd like to present my Aunt Matilda, or Mrs. Broadwith. Aunt Matilda, my bride of just a couple of weeks, Melanie."

She was not at all an attractive woman now, though she might quite easily have been some years ago. But there were harsh lines around her mouth and eyes, and an expression of discontent on her face.

"Pardon me for not rising to curtsy, my lady," she said with a smile that did not reach her eyes, "but I'm too old for that sort of thing now, and in any case I understand that you've not been accustomed to it until just recently."

The remark was so surly that Melanie, who would never have been rude to an older woman in the normal course, could not help retorting, "Perhaps not, but I have always been aware of what is and is not good manners."

She turned to Denby, who was looking at her with his eyebrows raised in an unspoken reproach.

"If you will excuse me, my lord," she said, "I will have Wallace show me to my bedchamber, for I would like to wash my hands before luncheon, and I understand that it will be served momentarily."

He stepped forward and took her arm in a firm grasp. "There's no need to ask Wallace. If you'll excuse us both, Aunt Matilda, I'll remove a little of the dust of the road also, and we'll meet you in the dining room in, say, fifteen minutes."

He led Melanie up the stairs and along the corridor in silence, then opened a large double door and took her into an enormous bedchamber furnished with huge pieces of rather old-fashioned furniture.

He released her but said nothing until he had closed the door firmly behind him, then walked over to where she was standing, looking out of a window onto the gardens below.

"I know she was rude to you, my dear," he said a little sternly, "but was it necessary to make an enemy of her right away?"

Melanie swung around. "I have a quick temper, I know," she admitted, "but I don't regret one word of what I said to her. She was deliberately rude to me, and if I start allowing that kind of behavior, I know it will go on. Who is she, anyway?"

He led her over to the dressing room, where water and towels had been placed for their use.

"We may as well do what we came up here for," he said, reaching for a piece of soap. "She's my mama's maternal aunt; she's a widow, and lives in a house some miles away. Frankly, I've no idea what she is doing here, for I doubt that she came to welcome us, but she was crippled from a bad fall many years ago, and is now inclined to be somewhat outspoken."

"Just because she sustained a disabling injury does not mean her mind was impaired also, unless she wanted it to be," Melanie said firmly. "I will gladly help her in any way I can, but I will not permit her or any other of your relatives to be deliberately rude to me."

They were glaring at each other in the mirror; then suddenly Denby chuckled.

"For goodness' sake don't let's quarrel over her, for I've never been able to stand her either, but I put up with her out of pity for her condition," he admitted a little ruefully.

She turned to face him, taking a grip on his arm, her face very serious. "Let me tell you something now, Broderick. If anything like that should ever happen to me, don't you dare pity me. Shout at me, slap me if necessary, do anything it takes to make me behave like a normal human being in every way possible, but never, ever pity me."

He nodded slowly. "I give you my word of honor on that, my dear, for I cannot but agree with you. However, I believe that it is too late now to do anything about Aunt Matilda. Let's go downstairs and try to find out just how long she means to stay."

The luncheon was not quite a disaster, for the food consisted of plain well-cooked local dishes and was most delicious. But Aunt Matilda constantly complained—about the weather's effect on her bones; about the manners of young people these days (being careful to generalize and not be specific); about the quality of service having severely deteriorated; and, finally, about the food that was put before them.

Both Melanie and Denby refused to be drawn into an argument, Denby simply smiling blandly and changing the subject each time, and Melanie maintaining an aloof manner except when she and her husband playfully teased each other.

"What brings you to Moorland House, Aunt Matilda?" he asked genially. "You could not have known that we were coming here so soon, for we did not originally mean to arrive for another week yet."

"The cold weather is what brought me," she said, scowling out of the window as the wind bent the bare branches of the trees. "There seemed little point in staying in my drafty place in wintry weather like this, when you keep this place cozy just for a lot of servants."

Melanie looked across at her husband's shuttered expression and waited with some impatience to hear what he would do. Then she watched him send a silent message to Wallace, who left the room at once, closing the door quietly behind him.

"Do you mean that there was no emergency? That you just came to stay here, without invitation, so that you could economize upon *your* fuel bills?" he asked dangerously quietly.

"I knew that my niece would be only too glad for me to enjoy the comfort of Moorland House in the cold months, as I have done for the last few years," Mrs. Broadwith asserted.

"Your niece, my mama, does not own this house," Denby informed her, "nor did she advise me that she had given you permission to stay here each winter, as has apparently been your practice."

"Well, she didn't exactly say I could do so every winter," Mrs. Broadwith blustered, "but you were away in the war, and the pipes in my house burst, so she told me to come over here. I can't go back now, for that house of mine will take days to warm through at this time of year."

"I'll send someone over there today to see that the fires are lighted and kept burning," Denby told her. "It should be habitable in four or five days, when my coach will take you back."

She stumbled to her feet, accidentally knocking the chair over as she did so, and clasping the table edge for support. Denby rose also, picking up the chair and offering his arm to escort her out of the room.

"I never thought a nephew of mine would throw his old aunt out of his house in the dead of winter," she snapped, glaring at him fiercely and ignoring the proffered help. "But if that's the way you feel, I'll go, and gladly. I know when I'm not wanted, and whose fault this really is. You always could be twisted around a woman's little finger."

She reached for her cane and went limping to the door, where Denby waited to open it for her. Then he closed it behind her and returned to his seat.

"It rather sounded as though she means to leave right away," Melanie said. "Do you want me to go up later and persuade her to stay until her house is in readiness for her return?"

Denby shook his head. "She'll not go one hour before she absolutely must," he told her quietly. "Can you imagine anyone having the audacity to move into someone else's house in order to save on her own fuel bills?"

"I feel sorry for her, in a way," Melanie said. "If she had been a pleasant person to have around, I'd have been glad of her company, particularly as you will probably spend a considerable amount of time away from the house."

"Isn't 'sorry' the same as pity?" he asked.

She shook her head decidedly. "No, it's not at all the same thing," she asserted. "Not in my mind, anyway. Would you like me to go up to her chamber after a while and make my peace with her?"

He shook his head. "If you do, she'll never leave, I'm afraid. And I would like the place to ourselves for a while.

Leave it alone, Melanie. I dislike playing the villain who throws the old lady out into the cold, cold snow, but she has a perfectly cozy home, with a half-dozen or so servants to look after her. As they're not here, I can only assume that she's sent them to their homes for a holiday so that she doesn't have to pay their wages while she is here.

"I've no doubt she'll write my mama a sad little letter telling her how cruel I have been to her. Mama knows what she is like, but I'll apprise her of what happened, and that will be the end of it."

"Won't the whole countryside be told a similar story," Melanie asked, "and think badly of you?"

"They've probably already decided what a fool I must be for allowing her to play such a trick on me," he said quietly. "Country folk are much brighter than city dwellers, as a rule, and they're likely to be chuckling if they've ever felt the rough side of her tongue. In any case, she's not out of the house yet."

8

They heard no more of Aunt Matilda that day, and a quiet inquiry to Wallace, when Melanie found that no place had been set for the old lady at the dinner table, revealed that she was already eating dinner from a tray she had requested be sent to her bedchamber.

There was no question that it was a relief to both Denby and Melanie to have the dinner table to themselves, but when her husband settled back with his port and cigar, Melanie excused herself and went up to the chamber Mrs. Broadwith was using, knocked on the door, and entered.

"And what do you want, pray?" the old lady asked gruffly. "Haven't you done enough to me for one day, without coming to my chamber to make more trouble?"

"I knew you were not exactly starving to death," Melanie said dryly, "and to be frank, it was a relief not to have you at the dinner table, constantly grumbling. If you were a pleasant person to have around, I would have put in a good word for you to stay, but no one wants to be with a constant complainer day in and day out."

"Well, it's too late now, isn't it? My nephew didn't sound to me as though he'd go back on his decision," Mrs. Broadwith asserted, but there was a slight question in her voice that Melanie did not fail to notice.

She nodded. "You're quite right, for I'm sure he'll not go back on it," she said flatly. "But if you ever want to come here again, I would advise you to leave here on a friendly note and not with a list of grievances."

"So you're threatening me now," the old lady averred. "You're not content to have me thrown out. You're telling

108

me that if I don't go all smiles as I leave, you'll make sure I never get back in here again. That's it, isn't it? You don't like to have to look at an old crippled woman.''

"Don't be ridiculous. I've looked at people who were crippled much worse than you are, but they weren't as sorry for themselves as you seem to be.'' Melanie gazed at her coldly. "If you'd stop thinking only of yourself and take an interest in other people, you'd live a much happier life.''

"Why, you're nothing but an upstart yourself,'' Mrs. Broadwith almost shouted at her. "How dare you speak to me like that? As I heard it, Broderick wanted your sister, not you, and I must say that I'm sorry for him.''

Melanie smiled coldly. "You really are a nasty old lady, aren't you? You're wrong, however, for he didn't really want my sister either, and I certainly didn't want him. But I do now, and if I hear that you're spreading any tales about us in the village, I'll go down there and tell everyone exactly what happened here today.''

"You wouldn't, would you?'' the old lady asked, looking quite horrified. "I'd not be able to get any more credit from the shops, and then what would I do?''

"Pay your bills, I suppose,'' Melanie said bluntly, "for you've no doubt been using Broderick's good name to get unlimited credit, haven't you?''

There was now a rather sad look on the old lady's face, and she seemed quite defeated. "If I keep my mouth shut and don't tell any stories about either one of you, will I be invited to come back here sometimes, for tea or perhaps dinner?''

"If you're prepared to be pleasant when you come, and not complain all the time,'' Melanie told her, "I'm sure that when we're in residence, my husband would wish you included on guest lists occasionally, as well as having you here for tea. You are family, after all.''

"Very well,'' Mrs. Broadwith said almost agreeably. "I'll leave just as soon as my house has been warmed through again, and I'll take all my meals in here until then so that you two can be alone.''

Melanie smiled. "There's no need for that, if you'll just

stop grumbling so much when you're with us. By all means join us for lunch and dinner, but I imagine it's easier for you to eat breakfast up here, so that you can take your time in getting washed and dressed.''

The older lady smiled, much to Melanie's surprise, and asked, "How do you know so much about cripples? It's not often anyone as young as you will even look at me straight in the eye. They glance sideways, as a rule, and then edge away, thinking I won't notice them doing it.''

Memories had come flooding back to Melanie, private ones that she rarely shared, but she decided it might perhaps do a little good to tell the old lady about them.

"Not long after my grandmama died,'' she told her, "Grandpapa had a seizure, and for the year before he also passed on, I looked after him much of the time. He had been such a fine-looking man that Mama couldn't bear to see his twisted face and useless arm and leg, but deep inside he was still the grandpapa who had picked me up each time I fell off my pony, and kissed and hugged me, and put me right back on again.

"I saw the lifeless limbs that had once been so strong, and was sorry for what had happened to them, but it was only the outside that was damaged. He was still the grandpapa I loved, and who loved me, and in the year that remained to him, we had many happy hours together that I wouldn't have missed for anything.''

Mrs. Broadwith nodded, then reached over and patted Melanie's hand. "I'm glad you came up to see me,'' she said in her gravelly voice. "I didn't think you'd bother making sure I was all right after what I said to you earlier. And I will try to stop grumbling so much, though I don't think it'll be easy.''

"Just try, and you may be surprised how pleasant everyone else is.'' Melanie was smiling broadly now. "Have a good night's rest, and I'll see you at luncheon tomorrow.''

She swept out of the room and along the corridor to the bedchamber next to Denby's, which was much more feminine, as befitted the lady of the house, and it had an adjoining door.

She felt tired and wondered if she had done the best thing in telling the old lady something that was so very private and precious to her, then decided it couldn't have done any harm and might even have done some good.

It was somewhat of a relief to open the door of the chamber and find Bridget waiting inside, with warm water, and her nightgown airing out in front of the cozy fire.

"I saw you go into that old witch's room, and you were so long that I almost came looking for you, just in case she'd cast one of her spells over you," the abigail told her, chuckling.

"She's just a frightened old lady, that's all, and she tries to cover it up by being nasty and belligerent. I don't think we'll have much trouble with her for now, though I'm not saying she'll be all sweetness and light either," Melanie said with a sigh. "But you've no idea how wonderful that bed looks to me. I didn't realize how very tired I was. Are there hot bricks under the covers?"

"Of course," Bridget said soothingly as she helped her mistress out of her gown and into her nightclothes. "Just sit here while I brush out your hair, or it will be all tangles in the morning."

Melanie almost dropped off to sleep as the strokes of the brush soothed and relaxed her, and she was just stepping into the warm bed when the door between the bedchambers opened and Denby came in, having already changed into a maroon silk robe.

Bridget gave a little bob to him, and hurried from the chamber.

He did not slide into Melanie's bed immediately, as was his usual practice, but sat down on the edge of it, facing her. As she lay there with her dark hair spread over the pillow and around her shoulders, he could not help but realize how much more lovely she seemed to him now. Much lovelier than her younger sister had ever been.

He smiled at her, and brushed her cheek lightly with his fingertips, then let his hand move slowly down to her slender throat, over the lily-white chest, and under the neckline of her gown to caress a softly rounded breast.

Her eyes had never left his from the moment he sat on the bed, and he now heard her slight intake of breath as he stroked the rosy pink bud hidden beneath the gown. He was convinced that her gray eyes had turned a deeper shade, and that her pulse had quite noticeably quickened.

She had been very still and obviously frightened the first night he had come to her, and he knew he had hurt her, though she had not made a sound. But he had persevered, trying to be as gentle as he could with her and seeking, in very slow stages, to arouse the feelings hidden deep inside of her. She had changed considerably in just this short time, and the fact that she had been his, and his alone, made him feel slightly overawed, in a way he had not felt since he was a stripling.

As he continued to tease her breast gently, he asked quietly, "Did you go to see my great-aunt tonight?"

She looked, for a moment, as though she hadn't heard him, then said slowly, "Yes, and I think we understand each other much better now. But let me tell you about it later, please."

This was the first time she had ever shown so clearly that she did not want him to stop what he was doing to her. He nodded, well pleased, and continued to arouse her gently until he was finally able to gain the satisfaction he desired, and he knew that, to a lesser extent, she had also. It would not be long, he was quite sure, before she would bloom into a very loving, sensuous wife, something virtually unknown in *ton* marriages, and he knew that he was a very fortunate husband.

Over breakfast the next morning she told him briefly what had transpired in his aunt's bedchamber the previous evening, and his first remark was to the effect that he wished he did not have to spend the entire day out with his bailiff.

"I am most anxious to see," he told her, "if the changes in my aunt can survive so much as one night's sleep, for she has forever been known for a grumbler and pinchpenny."

Melanie was pleased by his tone of approval, which she wished for more than anything—or at least more than she had believed possible. But she could still not put Mrs.

Whitehead out of her mind for long. This morning, when she awoke and remembered the way he had made her feel last night, she found herself wondering if he did the same things to that woman he had done to her.

Denby did not fail to notice the shadow that came over his wife's face, and was puzzled as to what could have brought it about, for she had seemed happy enough a moment ago. He was due to meet his bailiff in just a few minutes, however, so he put the matter from his mind for the time being.

At his request, the servants had left the room after serving the meal and now, putting aside his napkin, Denby rose, saying, "I'm afraid I may be out most of the day, so if I'm not back by one o'clock, please don't wait luncheon for me, my dear," and to her surprise, as he came beside her chair, he raised her chin and placed a gentle kiss on her lips.

It was such an unexpected gesture that she flushed a deep pink, then saw his eyes twinkling at her embarrassment.

"Don't get into any mischief while I'm gone," he reminded her, grinning, then strode from the room, leaving Melanie, for once, at a complete loss for words.

She heard his voice in the hall, asking if his horse had been brought around, and then the front door close behind him, and she went to the window and watched him mount and ride off to meet a heavy man coming up the driveway on horseback, who she assumed must be the bailiff.

Now she had all the morning to herself, for she felt sure his aunt would take her advice and not come down until luncheon. First, of course, she wanted to meet with Mrs. Jackson, the housekeeper, and discuss today's meals, and also those for the next few days.

There was a knock on the door, and Mrs. Jackson came bustling in, as though she had read her mind. She had a notebook in her hand, and a cheerful smile on her round rosy-cheeked face.

"Would you like to go over a few things with me now, milady, or would you rather wait until later?" she asked.

"By all means, let's go over them now, Mrs. Jackson," Melanie told her. "My husband does not believe he will be back in time for luncheon, so it will be just Mrs. Broadwith and myself, and I'd like to keep it as simple as possible.''

Together they planned not only that day's meals but also those for a few days ahead, since it was Melanie's hope that Denby would take her with him early tomorrow or the next day to see some of the lands he owned. The countryside appeared harsh and rugged now, but promised to be very beautiful in the summer when the heather and gorse were in bloom.

"Perhaps after luncheon, if his lordship is not yet returned, you'd like me to show you around the house, milady,'' the housekeeper suggested. "There are one or two things needing to be attended to that I didn't feel I should do without his lordship's or your orders.''

"Of course,'' Melanie agreed, glad to put it off until later in the day, for it would be a good excuse for not spending the whole afternoon with Denby's aunt.

As soon as the housekeeper left, Melanie made for Denby's study, for his refusal to allow her to even enter that room had made her all the more anxious to do so. She dared not disturb anything there in case he carried out his threat, but at least she could find out what he might have in there that he deemed worth hiding from her.

It was a beautiful room, kept in a much better condition than the study at Denby Downs, and she could see at a glance so very many books she had been anxious to read for some time. She dared take only one at a time, however, in case he should miss them if she borrowed several.

Having made her selection, she took it down from the shelf, and separated the rest of the books slightly to hide the fact that there was one missing. Then she turned and glanced at the plans spread out on the desk. She surmised that he must have been going over them before breakfast, for they called for extensive improvements to this particular property, and she found it very interesting indeed.

She would like nothing better than to ride with him across all the lands he owned throughout the country, and listen to what he meant to do to make sure they would still be there for their children, for by now, though she did not know him as well as she would have liked, she certainly knew him to be the most astute person she had ever met.

With all his properties and monies, he could quite easily have sat back and lived in extravagant idleness on what he had inherited. But instead, between his efforts in Parliament and what she had seen of his care both in Devon and here, it seemed that he worked harder than most of those who had to do so just to keep food on the table.

After a while she left the study, making sure there was no telltale sign of her ever having been there, and went up the stairs, instinctively hiding the book she had borrowed in the folds of her skirts.

Luncheon that day was a great deal more pleasant than Melanie had anticipated, and dinner was even better, for Aunt Matilda was, it seemed, determined to show them that she could be good company when she chose to be.

To Melanie's delight, though she had put her head around the door of the study when she was retiring for the evening, and left Denby poring over his papers, he came into her bed-chamber a short time later.

"Did you have a good day?" she asked him as he poured a drink from the decanter he had brought with him, and settled into one of the chairs in front of the fire. "It became dreadfully cold after lunch, I know, and I worried about what you would do out there on the moors if it started to snow."

"You needn't have, my dear," he said, finding himself inordinately pleased that she had been concerned, and also that she had pulled her chair quite close to his. "Our land is spread out, and borders the moors in certain areas, and we have to cross them, of course, but the paths are well marked and there are small huts at intervals to provide shelter in inclement weather."

He was wearing a deep blue dressing gown tonight, and she flushed a little as she thought of him removing it very soon now, and doing things to her that she had begun to enjoy a little more each time.

"It would seem that you have worked wonders with Aunt Matilda," he told her, watching her expressive face as the dancing flames from the fire cast interesting shadows across

it. "My mama will never believe me when I tell her how
pleasantly she behaved at table this evening."

"I told her that she was a nasty old lady. And don't smile
like that," she said, "for I hated doing it but knew that your
mama had probably tried being nice to her and it had failed.
I threatened to tell the villagers how she had behaved here,
and that she had money enough of her own, and she became
frightened the shopkeepers would start calling in all her
notes."

He did not quite believe her, for he felt there was something more to it than that, but he was content to let her keep
her secret if she wished. Then he looked into her eyes, and
what he saw there made him rise and reach out his hand to
her, then slip an arm around her waist. For this evening at
least, there was no further need of words.

It was the following morning when Denby, having risen
early and gone to his study for an hour's work before breakfast, suddenly remembered something he had noticed last
evening in his wife's bedchamber, but had understandably
forgotten about in the passions of the moment.

There had been one of the books from his study lying on
a table by the bed, and though he did not at all mind her
borrowing his books, he had made a point of specifically for-
bidding her to enter that room. As the only male of his family,
he was accustomed to being obeyed without question, and
had not thought her to be recalcitrant.

Upon giving the matter some consideration, however, he
came to the conclusion that while appearing to be mild-
mannered and obedient, she had done a number of small
things, and a couple of large ones, which were expressly
designed to inconvenience him.

Removing from his desk the plans of his estate, which he
had no doubt she had perused in his absence, he replaced
them with the rather complex outline of the Corn Bill with
which he had been assisting Lord Liverpool.

He had some doubts as to whether a female mind could
readily understand the points at issue, but it would be
interesting to find out. If he brought up the subject and she
did not seem to know what he was talking about, he would

let the matter drop. But if she appeared to be curious, and tried to find out more about it, then he would lead her on until she gave herself away.

When Melanie came down to breakfast, Denby had not yet started, and he rose quickly and seated her, dropping a swift kiss upon her forehead and smiling warmly.

"I trust you slept well last night, my dear," he said softly, but did not resume his seat at once. "I told Wallace that I would help you to breakfast myself, so what can I get for you?"

She gave him a mischievous grin. "I believe I'll have a soft-boiled egg, two rashers of bacon, and a very small piece of finnan haddie, sir," she declared, "but what would your mama and sisters think if they saw you behaving in such a way?"

He quickly prepared her plate, and brought it over to the table, placing it in front of her and sliding her serviette onto her lap.

"I very much fear that they would attempt to employ my services themselves," he intoned, imitating Wallace's solemn voice, and placing the toast and butter closer to her left hand. "May I pour coffee for you, or would you prefer tea this morning?"

"Tea, please, with just a little milk," she murmured, "and perhaps some of that strawberry jam."

He produced the items with a flourish, and then resumed his seat at the head of the small table.

"They would no doubt be highly amused, and wish to know what the occasion is," he ruefully admitted.

"And what is the occasion?" Melanie asked. "I don't recall that it's my birthday yet, and my wedding anniversary is a long, long way off."

"I'll think of something before the day is out," he told her, "and in the meantime, make the most of it, for there are times, as my mama would no doubt tell you, when I get out of bed on the wrong side and hardly speak a word for the first hour that I'm up."

"Whatever the occasion, I thank you, kind sir," she said, and as she looked directly into his eyes, she saw something in their depths that made her stomach give a funny little jump inside.

"It looks a little cold outside this morning," he remarked a few minutes later, "but tomorrow, if it's a bit warmer, I was wondering if you might like to accompany us and see something of the lands and of the moors. We'll ride, of course, for it's completely different on horseback than from the inside of a carriage."

Melanie's face sparkled with delight. "I'd love to, and must now persuade the heavens to give me a warm, sunny day for it. Will your bailiff not be with you?"

"Of course he will," Denby said, "and in any case, it's time you got to know him. He's a good countryman, and very knowledgeable."

As soon as they finished breakfast and Denby had left, Melanie hurried into the study to refresh her memory of the layout of the land, and was surprised to find that the map was no longer on the desk.

What was there instead appeared to her to be equally interesting, however, for she had heard a great deal about a proposed Corn Bill, and knew that there was much to be said for and against it. The continental blockade during the war had emphasized the fact that Britain needed to be as self-sufficient as possible, but now that the war was over, there was great fear of foreign competition.

She did not realize, however, that the price of wheat had been as high during the war as an average of 118s.9d. a quarter in 1813, and had fallen to 60s.8d. a quarter in this month, January 1815. She was interested to read that a committee appointed last year to study the matter, had concluded that eighty shillings a quarter was the minimum remunerative price for the domestic producer at this time, and recommended that the import of foreign wheat below this price should be prohibited.

Melanie could clearly recall having heard her papa say that more people were employed in agriculture in England than in anything else, and it seemed, then, that the bill must be necessary to protect both the farm workers and the owners of all those fields of grain.

She could also see, however, that to raise the cost of bread now by almost a third as much again would be a hardship to all those poor people and out-of-work soldiers who relied almost entirely on bread for sustenance.

At the sound of voices in the hall, Melanie slipped out of the study and back into the breakfast room, where the housekeeper came looking for her a few minutes later.

"You did say, milady, that you might wish me to take you to have a look at some of the unused chambers upstairs, and I wondered if this morning would be a good time to do it?" Mrs. Jackson inquired. "It'll be cold up there, though, and if you wish to go now, I think you'd best put a shawl around your shoulders, for I'd not want you to catch a chill."

"What a good idea," Melanie said, glad of the chance to see more of the house. "I can get a warm wrap from my bedchamber as we pass by."

Bridget was in the chamber when her mistress went in, and she pulled out a heavy old shawl and wrapped it around her mistress's shoulders.

"Now, don't you take that off until you get back here," she cautioned Melanie, "for I know just how cold unused attic chambers can be, and you'll not want to come down with something and be in bed for a week."

"What a pair of fusspots you and Mrs. Jackson are," Melanie scolded. "I don't believe I've ever been in bed for a week in my whole life, and I don't mean to be now. I only came in here because I could see she feared my lord would blame her if I caught a cold."

"And so he would," Bridget said firmly, "though he probably knows by now how stubborn you can be sometimes."

Anyone else who had spoken to Melanie like that would have been given an instant set-down, but Bridget had been with her for so long that she had earned the right to scold on occasion. Melanie did give the maid a fierce scowl, however, as she hurried from the chamber and into the hall, where the housekeeper was waiting patiently.

And, of course, both of her helpers had been correct, for it was icy cold in the rooms they went in and out of, but it was a successful visit, for she came across some kitchen chairs that could be put to good use now that the staff was to be increased, and a chest full of the loveliest silk fabrics, which must have belonged to Denby's grandmama.

There was also a chest of tiny baby garments, quite obviously little used, including an heirloom-quality christening gown.

"Be sure to have these two trunks brought down to my chamber," Melanie told the housekeeper, "for I'd like to go through them at my leisure. The workmanship on these tiny garments is quite exquisite, and though I have little need for them yet, I hope I will be able to put them to good use in a year or so."

Mrs. Jackson smiled warmly. "Indeed I hope so too, my lady," she said. "It's rare to find the likes of these little things nowadays."

9

Denby was waiting for Melanie when she entered the drawing room that evening. He had already poured a glass of sherry for her, and he placed it in her hand, then raised his own glass to toast her.

"And how was your day, my dear?" he asked gently. "Aunt Matilda was not too much of a trial, I hope?"

"Not at all, Broderick," she told him. "In fact she was really quite pleasant. I was telling her about my inspection of the upper chambers with Mrs. Jackson, for I came across a chest of the most beautiful fabrics for evening gowns, and also a smaller one filled with exquisitely made baby clothes that appear to have hardly been used."

His quizzical look made her turn quite pink, and she hastened to explain. "We won't need them for a long time, I'm sure, but I'm afraid that I am not nearly so talented with a needle as the person who sewed these. I've had them brought down to my chamber, and perhaps you'd like to see them sometime when you're there."

Denby could think of a great many more things he preferred to do in her chamber than look at baby clothes, but he had not the heart to tell her so when she was quite obviously very happy with her discovery. He wondered what other rooms she had inspected. His study, perhaps? If she had done so, no telltale evidence had been left behind, for he had already checked the room thoroughly.

"We'd best take them with us when we leave," he said thoughtfully, "for the fabrics would be of most use to you in London, and from there we could send the smaller things down to Devon, for that is where you would have need of them, I feel sure.''

Melanie hoped that she did not look as warm as she felt, and she said with some irritation, ''You know, I really cannot understand why I become embarrassed at the mere mention of baby clothes. It's not as if you did not wish to have a child, for I know that you are trying very hard to give me one.''

Denby almost choked, for he had just taken a sip of his sherry, and he quickly turned away to place the glass on a nearby table and reach for a handkerchief with which to dab his eyes.

It took a moment or so for him to control his laughter before turning back to Melanie, who had a look of surprise on her face. His eyes twinkled merrily.

''I'm sorry, my love,'' he croaked, pausing to take another sip of his sherry and soothe his irritated throat. ''I'm afraid your choice of topic for a predinner conversation was a little unusual, to say the least. You would have been extremely embarrassed if Aunt Matilda had entered the room at that moment and heard what you said. However, I'll be most happy to continue this conversation later this evening, in the privacy of your bedchamber, if you wish.''

Melanie had no chance to reply, for at that moment Aunt Matilda did enter the room, and Denby turned to pour her a glass of sherry while his wife greeted her.

''How nice you look, Mrs. Broadwith, Melanie told her, meaning it, for Denby's aunt was wearing a most becoming gown of deep blue, trimmed with a lighter blue satin ribbon. Even the headdress she wore was less cumbersome than usual.

''I wish you would call me Aunt Matilda, my dear, as Denby does, for we are family now, you know,'' the older lady requested.

She had a pleasant smile on her face as she made the request, and Melanie gladly consented, then watched Denby's face for some sign of what he might be thinking. He had, however, put on his inscrutable expression, and she turned back to his aunt, somewhat disappointed.

''Very well, Aunt Matilda,'' Melanie said, then added,

"I hope that you did not venture out this afternoon, for though I remained indoors, I understand it was very cold—too cold to snow was what I heard Wallace say."

Mrs. Broadwith shuddered. "I wouldn't think of going outdoors if I didn't have to," she told them, "for my old bones can't stand the cold the way they used to. When I was your age I enjoyed it, and used to go out riding when the ground was as hard as iron."

"There was a good red sky tonight," Denby remarked. "A sure sign, I am told, that there'll be a fine day tomorrow, and, according to my bailiff, it will be a little warmer. Do you still want to join me, Melanie, my dear?"

"Of course I do," she replied, delighted that he had remembered his offer. She would not have declined the invitation even if she had been out-of-sorts, for it was the first of its kind she had received from him, and she did not mean it to be the last.

He looked thoughtful. "How well do you ride?" he asked. "And please be honest, for I don't wish to put you on a horse beyond your ability."

Despite, or even perhaps because of, his explanation, she was most insulted, and snapped, "I ride extremely well, and I do not wish to be given some gentle old mare who would much rather have stayed in her nice warm stall and has no wish to keep up with you."

Denby grinned. "You'd better be telling the truth," he warned, "for the country around here is quite rough, and I'd much prefer you to remain in the saddle if it is at all possible."

She glared at him, but said nothing more, though secretly hoping that he might get his deserts instead, and have a bone-shaking, but not bone-breaking, fall.

Then she noticed that Aunt Matilda was looking from one to the other of them with a great deal of interest, and she felt an explanation was necessary.

"Our stable in London was not as large as it might have been, and in addition to the carriage horses, my papa preferred not to have to bring mounts for the ladies, as well as for himself and my brother, so Denby has never seen me on horseback," she told the older lady. "It did not quite stop me riding, however, for I still brought a riding habit to town, and sometimes helped exercise their horses—but not at a time or place where anyone would recognize me."

"Did you indeed?" Denby's expression was one of mild disapproval. "If you're trying to impress me, you may regret it, you know," he warned.

They went in to dinner then, and immediately afterward the ladies retired to the drawing room for tea, leaving Denby with his port and cigar.

"It seems to me that my nephew has met his match," Aunt Matilda remarked, "and a good thing, too, for with all those women in the family who allow him to do whatever he wishes, he was getting a little too spoilt, to my way of thinking."

"From what I can see," Melanie said quietly, "he works very hard both here in the country and, when in town, with various branches of the government. When I first met him I thought he was very much older than he is, for he did not behave the way so many young men of his age do. Under the circumstances, I believe he has a right to the respect he receives."

"That's all very well, but he needed someone to bring him down a peg or two, and if you're not just the right person to do it, then I'm a Dutchman," Aunt Matilda declared. "Be careful, though, for if I'm not mistaken, you're falling in love with him, aren't you?"

Melanie was embarrassed. "Of course I love my husband," she said stiffly, adding, "and I also admire him for the way he keeps his temper—with both you and me."

The old lady chuckled. "He'll lose it one of these days, and you mustn't be frightened when he does, for he'll never harm you. But even I can see, in this short time, that for some reason you're pushing him, and one day you'll go too far, and then you'll see him out of control. It should be most interesting."

Melanie *was* falling in love with him, of course, but could it possibly be so obvious? she wondered. She sincerely hoped that this old lady, who was much more astute than Melanie had realized, would return to her home soon. She would rather not have her around to guess at what had happened when she confronted Denby regarding his mistress—if she could ever get up the courage to do so.

To Aunt Matilda's vast amusement, Melanie quickly changed the subject, and then, as soon as the latter finished drinking her tea, she rose, saying, "I don't know about you, Aunt Matilda, but I'm somewhat tired this evening, and must be up bright and early in the morning, so I believe I will now retire to my bed."

But for once, when she was sitting back in her night rail and robe, while Bridget brushed her hair, Melanie lost all inclination to sleep, and by the time Denby entered the bed-chamber, the abigail was long gone and her mistress so completely immersed in a book that she did not even hear him come in and close the door behind him.

As was his usual way, he did not get into the large bed immediately, but sat down on the side of it and looked at his wife, who was, for once, half-sitting up, propped against the pillows, the book she had been reading still open beside her.

He picked up the slim volume and recognized it at once as one of his own.

" 'Breathes there a man with soul so dead, who never to himself hath said, this is my own, my native land?' A very promising writer, I must say. Is Scott a favorite of yours?" Denby asked casually.

She nodded, hoping he would not realize that this was one of the books that belonged in his library.

"How long is it since you were on horseback for half a day?" he asked, a hint of laughter in his eyes.

Melanie grinned ruefully. "At least six months, I'm afraid. I'll probably be very sore tomorrow night."

"It will be a pleasure to relieve the soreness for you. I'll massage you myself as soon as we get back," he promised, "and that will teach you to brag about your riding."

Just the thought of his strong hands on her buttocks and thighs, rubbing out the soreness, was too much for her, and she felt a warmth spread through her entire body, as if in anticipation. Denby seemed, in some uncanny way, to realize what she was feeling, and she wondered if it was her rapid breathing or her eyes that betrayed her.

"Bridget is very capable of assisting me, if you do not have the time, my lord," she murmured, deliberately teasing him.

"I'll make sure that I have the time," he told her with a mischievous grin, "and if she's here waiting for you when we get back, I'll inform her that I have taken over some of her duties. I know that will not be necessary, however, for she always scurries out of the chamber the minute she sees me."

"It's not out of fear," Melanie informed him. "She's been with me since I was a little girl, and as far as I recall, I have never known her to be frightened of anything. It's just that she feels very strongly about giving a husband and wife complete privacy."

He nodded, well pleased.

"Speaking of privacy," he said, as though he had just thought of something he meant to tell her, "we'll probably have only another week here for now, for I have to return to London for a time, and I will, of course, want you to accompany me."

"I know you warned me that you might have to return," Melanie said thoughtfully. "Is there some special reason?"

He nodded. "Yes, the Commons will be taking up the issue of the Corn Bill about the middle of February, and I should be there to answer any questions that might arise."

"Do you think it will pass both houses?" she asked him, not a little to his surprise.

"I hope so," he told her. "If it doesn't, the country will be in quite a mess. Do you understand anything about it?"

She shook her head. "I've heard Papa speak of it, but I don't know very much about it, I'm afraid, except that if it does not go through, and prices are forced even lower by the importing of cheap grain from Europe, our farmers will not be able to pay the workers' wages. If the government can stop wheat being imported at less than eighty shillings a quarter, the market will not be flooded with cheap foreign wheat and we can continue to grow enough for everyone, and pay the workers' wages.''

"That's rather an oversimplification, I'm afraid," Denby informed her dryly, "but you really seem to have got the gist of it. In quite an extraordinary way, too, for your father could not possibly have known that eighty shillings a quarter was the price the committee set, for they only just arrived at that figure. It was, in fact, unknown to me until I received the papers that are presently spread out on my desk in the study here.''

Melanie realized at once that she had fallen into a trap, and there was no use in her denying it. She clearly recalled the threat he had made shortly before they arrived here in Devon, that it would be much more than her life was worth to touch anything in that room. He had then forbidden her to even set foot inside.

She had been carefully studying the pattern on the sleeve of his brocade dressing gown, but realized she would have to look up at him eventually, and so she raised her head. She could not quite tell, however, the extent of his displeasure.

"I did no damage to your papers, nor to the plans of this estate when I looked at them," she protested mildly, though she was inwardly quaking, remembering what Aunt Matilda had said just an hour or so ago.

"But you will agree, I am sure, that you deliberately disobeyed me," he maintained quietly, "and wives are supposed to obey their husbands, as you vowed to do only some short time ago. Did those vows mean so little to you?''

He reached out a hand toward her, and she instinctively shrank back, but all he wanted was to take hold of the hand and turn it to expose the rings she wore.

When she made no answer, he went on, "If you felt that I was being unfair in not permitting you to enter my study, why did you not come to me and tell me so? I have no objections to your borrowing a book''—his glance slid to where the volume of Scott's *Lay of the Last Minstrel* was placed beside her bed—"nor do I mind you looking at the plans of the estate of which you are mistress. As for the Corn Bill papers, I will admit I left them there to see if you would examine them.''

He saw the tears that she was trying to hold back and decided suddenly that he had no wish to scold her further for a crime so small as entering a room he had said she might not. He had made his point, he felt, and she would obey him in the future.

Slowly, so as not to frighten her this time, he drew her into his arms and held her there while his lips traced a delicate pattern from the single salty tear that escaped from one eye, to the corner of her rosy mouth. He tasted only the soft lips at first; then he found himself demanding more until she was clinging to him and returning his passionate kisses in a way that she had never done before.

When they finally drew apart, he was reluctant to let her go for the moment it took to remove his dressing robe, and he was amazed to find that tonight Melanie seemed to be as anxious as he to feel his body close to hers. If it was comfort she sought, it would soon turn to something more abandoned, he was sure, and as it did so, he stopped thinking at all and simply enjoyed the complete fulfillment.

Nothing more was said that night concerning Melanie's transgression, and when he returned to his own bedchamber, leaving her in a deep sleep, he had completely forgotten about it.

When Melanie was awakened the next morning by Bridget, she, too, had forgotten what had happened for a moment; then it all came back to her, and she felt, once more, all the emotions and sensations of the night before.

''Now, come along, Miss Melanie,'' Bridget scolded. ''This is no time for daydreaming, or that husband of yours will go off and leave you if you're not at breakfast in fifteen minutes.''

Melanie very much doubted that he would do so, but she was not, however, prepared to take a chance on it, so she let the maid hurry her into her clothes and tie her hair in the back with a big bow.

''It'll not get blown about as much, like that,'' Bridget

told her, "and there's no question about it suiting you."

As Melanie reached for her riding crop, gloves, and the shako that matched her bright blue habit, Bridget stopped her and pushed her toward the door.

"Just leave those here, and you'll find them on the hall table when you've finished breakfast," she told her mistress, shaking her head. "When will you learn to behave like the lady of quality you are?"

Melanie ran lightly down the stairs, and was still smiling at Bridget's scolding when she entered the breakfast room, to find Denby there ahead of her. He signaled to Wallace to continue preparing his plate, and rose himself to seat his wife at the table.

"Good morning, my dear," he murmured, his lips lightly brushing her cheek as he slid the chair beneath her. "I must say that you look quite delightful in that habit."

"Thank you, my lord," she said, looking up into his smiling face, then asked teasingly, "Have you picked out a gentle old mare for me, or are you leaving the selection to your head groom?"

He chuckled. "Never fear," he told her, "you'll get a worthwhile ride on the horse I told them to saddle for you."

They made small talk while Wallace prepared a plate of ham and eggs for Melanie, and then when he had finished and left the room, closing the door behind him to give them privacy, Melanie summoned up the courage to ask the question she had been wondering about ever since she had risen from her bed.

"I realized this morning that we did not come to any definite conclusion regarding your study, Broderick," she began, swallowing hard as she raised her chin and looked directly at him. "Do I now have your permission to go in there, remove a book or so . . . and look at anything that is on the top of the desk?"

"Of course you have, my dear," he agreed readily, "and into any other room in the house, including my bedchamber. But if I ever return and find either room being turned out, without my permission, you had better run and hide. That's the best advice I can give you."

Melanie's chin went up and she shook her head firmly. "I wouldn't hide from you or anyone else," she told him. "I'm not afraid to face the consequences of my actions."

Denby chuckled. "You might be when you see the horse I've selected for you to ride this morning. I hope you weren't just bragging about your riding ability."

She looked at him curiously for a moment, then turned back to her breakfast, for she had awoken quite hungry and did not want to be forced to leave any of it on her plate if the bailiff should suddenly arrive.

Denby had, however, arranged to meet the man at a farm some distance from the house, for despite his threats, he had no intention of putting Melanie on a horse she could not handle, and seeing her embarrassed in front of an employee.

"What time is your bailiff expected?" she asked as soon as she had swallowed her last bite of toast. "I seem to recall you leaving earlier than this in the past."

"Oh, didn't I tell you?" he asked. "We're meeting him at Stonecroft Farm in about a half-hour from now. Do you need to run upstairs for anything?"

She shook her head, smiling. "Bridget assured me that if I would just come down the stairs to breakfast like a lady, I would find my gloves, shako, and riding crop on the hall table, waiting for me."

"How long did you say you had known her?" he asked, chuckling to himself.

"She was the littlest and lowest maid at the house when I was born, and was frequently given the task of watching that I didn't get into mischief," she told him, smiling. "And she still thinks it a part of her duties toward me."

He rose, then pulled back her chair as she stood up, and together they went into the hall.

"Just give me a minute to put this thing on," she begged, and attempted to fix the shako firmly on her head, but it took several tries before she finally succeeded; then she grabbed her gloves and crop and swung around, saying, "I'm ready when you are, Broderick."

He had been standing watching her with amusement for quite some time, and now he walked to the door and held it wide for her to pass through, but could not resist giving her a light swat on the bottom with his riding crop as she did so.

"Ouch!" she said, swinging around and wagging her own crop threateningly at him. "You'll get your deserts, just wait and see."

As he led her around to the stables, clasping her small hand firmly in his, Denby suddenly realized that he was happier at this moment than he had ever been in his whole life. He was quite sure that Melanie was growing as fond of him as he was of her, and decided that though he now knew the inconvenience she had put him through in Sussex had been deliberate, it was probably because she had resented so very much having to marry him at all. What a waste it would have been, he thought, had she remained a spinster for the rest of her days.

As they neared the stables, Sam, the head groom, came toward them, and behind him a couple of boys led a handsome black stallion, Denby's own horse, and a lively chestnut mare.

Denby heard Melanie's gasp. "What a beauty she is, Broderick."

"I believe she will suit you very well," Denby told her, "and if she does, she's yours, and we'll take her back to London with us."

He personally made sure that the saddle was right for Melanie and that everything was secure before helping her mount; then he mounted his own horse, talking to him softly to settle him down a little as they trotted out of the stables and into the lane that led from the house to the moorlands.

"We must keep strictly to the footpaths once we reach the moors," he called back to Melanie, "and watch out for rabbit holes."

She nodded, grateful that he was leading the way and protecting her a little, for though it was a dazzlingly sunny day, she could already feel the fierce wind blowing toward them from the moors.

The farmhouse where they were to meet the bailiff was not very far, however, and the farmer's wife insisted at once that Melanie come indoors for a moment. She wanted to find her a light wool scarf to put around her face until the sun took away most of the early-morning chill, for she could clearly tell that her ladyship's cheeks would be chapped without some protection.

Melanie was quite touched by the woman's thoughtfulness, and said as much to Denby.

"I should have thought of it myself," he told her, "for I had the deuce of a time getting accustomed to the cold again when I first came back from Spain."

"Isn't it ever cold there?" Melanie asked.

"In the mountains it is, sometimes, but nothing like the bleak winds that blow across the Yorkshire moors in the middle of winter," he said as he wrapped the scarf around her face in such a fashion that it would not blow away. "Can you still breathe?"

All he could see were her eyes, but they sparkled with fun as he thanked the good woman for her thoughtfulness. Then he threw her up on the mare, and they set off once more, Tom Barker, the bailiff, riding ahead of them.

"The broad valley that Widecombe lies in is called East Webburn, and of course the river over yonder is the Dart," Denby explained, "which meets the sea at Dartmouth. I'll take you there before we go back to London, for it's an interesting town with twin castles guarding its entrance from the sea. Dartmouth Castle is on one side, and Kingswear Castle on the other, and there used to be a chain between the two of them, known as 'Jawbones,' that was stretched tight at night between the two castles to prevent an invasion."

He could not see Melanie's pleased smile at the idea of him making a special trip there just for her enjoyment, but her eyes were most expressive just the same.

When next they stopped, all Melanie could see was a vast heap of stones, but Denby assured her that both the stones and about a hundred acres of land really did belong to him.

"There was, of course, a house here at one time," he hastened to assure her, "but it fell into disrepair about a couple of hundred years ago, and it is so far away from every-thing that none of my ancestors has attempted to rebuild."

"Are you sure that it just fell into disrepair," Melanie asked him, "or was it perhaps owned by a Catholic branch of your family to whom Cromwell took a dislike?"

He grinned. "You do know your history, don't you? The timing was right, and I must admit that I have always had a sneaking suspicion that they were either Catholics themselves or else sheltered Catholics, or anyone, for that matter, who had fought with Charles. It would have been an ideal location for all kinds of treachery and deceit."

"Do you suppose that there might be bodies still buried under that heap of stones?" Melanie asked, her voice assuming a conspiratorial whisper.

"By this time they'd no longer be bodies," Denby assured her, "but there could quite easily be some piles of bones underneath. Do you feel like digging, Tom?"

The bailiff, who had been standing a little way off to allow them their privacy, rode over to join them.

"The locals have always believed there were people inside when the building came down," he told them. "And you'll not find anyone coming this way much after dark."

"I should think not," Melanie said, giving a little shudder. "It's so terribly far from anything else, including roads."

"Oh, there used to be a road all right, milady," Tom Barker told her, "and there are still some faint tracks to be seen in places, but there's an old wives' tale of a half-dozen or more ghosts that rise up from the stones on a certain night in the late summer and dance and wail till dawn."

"Is there really, Tom?" Denby seemed surprised. "Now you see the kind of family you married into, my dear. We have not one, but a whole family of ghosts. We'd best make sure that our children never hear of this, or they'll be coming here on whatever night it is, and waiting for them to put in an appearance."

From her own knowledge of children, Melanie was quite sure they would, and she made a silent vow never to tell them anything about it.

They visited another farmhouse, and Melanie accepted a cup of tea and a fresh baked scone from the farmer's wife, while the men went to examine some of the stock. Then it

was time to go home for a late luncheon, so they turned
around and let the horses have their heads for a good gallop
on a fairly smooth piece of land.

Melanie had removed the scarf before entering the
farmhouse, for the sun had made the air quite balmy, and
now she enjoyed the feel of it on her face as they cantered
back home.

She had felt very stiff after sitting for even such a short
time at the farmhouse, and knew that she would shortly be extremely uncomfortable. She wondered if Denby remembered
his promise.

He had, for after helping her down, he slipped an arm
around her waist and asked quietly, "Do you want that
massage before or after luncheon?"

"Afterward, I think," she told him. "I'll just go to my
chamber and wash my hands, then come right back to the
dining room. If you don't have time, though, I'm sure that
Bridget can take care of me."

"But not as well as I can, I'm sure, and I wouldn't miss
the opportunity for anything," he said. "Go directly to my
chamber after you've eaten, for my man always keeps some
rubbing liniment handy."

By the time she was halfway through luncheon, however,
she began to feel dreadfully uncomfortable, and would have
excused herself from the table under other circumstances,
but she did not wish to give Denby the opportunity to gloat.
Toward the end, however, she was replying to Aunt Matilda's questions in monosyllables, and just pushing the food
around on her plate, and Denby, seeing this, rose at once.

"If you'll excuse us, Aunt Matilda," he said, "I believe
Melanie has overdone it a little this morning and needs some
attention. We'll see you in the drawing room later."

Once outside the dining room, he did not even listen to
her weak protests, but lifted her up in his arms and carried
her to his chamber.

On some other occasion she might have been jealous at
the speed with which he was able to undress a woman, but
she was now far too miserable to care. Then, as his strong
fingers kneaded the liniment into the aching muscles in her

legs and buttocks, she wanted to scream at first. But she forced her body to gradually relax, and finally let herself thoroughly enjoy the sensation—until she began to feel uncomfortably warm inside.

Perhaps it was uncanny instinct, but Denby seemed to know when the change took place, and was out of his clothes in minutes, and on the bed beside her, holding her in his arms.

Then he noticed the shocked expression on her face as she glanced toward the window, and he slid out of bed and drew the curtains before returning to finish what he had started.

10

Melanie could not believe that she had slept the entire afternoon away, but when she awoke in Denby's bed and found that it was almost time to dress for dinner, she felt delightfully relaxed despite the slight stiffness that remained.

She was wearing her own dressing gown, and felt mildly curious as to how her husband had put her into it without waking her. Yawning and stretching lazily, she lay there looking at the plaster designs on the ornate ceiling, until she heard a sound from the hall and suddenly realized that he or his man might come in here at any moment. In but a few seconds she was off the bed and through the door between their bedchambers, closing it quietly behind her.

"I was wondering where your dressing gown had got to, milady."

Bridget's lilting voice caught Melanie by surprise, and she turned around quickly to find her maid standing with her arms akimbo, an expression of delight on her face.

"I must have slept the whole afternoon away," Melanie told her, "but I feel so much better now. I was miserably stiff from my ride, but my husband took care of it."

"It smells as though he did, too," Bridget remarked dryly. "But your bathwater will be here at any minute, and a good warm soaking will take care of the rest. Did you enjoy the ride?"

Melanie nodded. "You would have loved it too, for we saw a place where one night every year ghosts are supposed to rise up from a great pile of stones and dance and moan till dawn."

"I'd have done no such thing," Bridget protested. "What poor troubled souls were they?"

"Denby thinks the house was probably destroyed by Cromwell, and I agree with him," Melanie told her. "So they were probably some of the Catholics he hunted down."

"Aye," the maid said, nodding sadly. "He was a sore trial to my people, to be sure. But come along now, milady, for I hear the maids with your hot water. Which gown did you want to wear tonight?"

Melanie made her choice from a number of gowns she had not yet worn, and in little more than an hour she walked into the drawing room, a vision in pale green sarcenet. Her rich brown hair had been swept up in the back to reveal her slender neck. Several tendrils had been allowed to escape and now curled delicately on her forehead and around her shell-like ears. A secret glow seemed to emanate from her, and she knew that she had never been in better looks.

Denby noticed at once, and came quickly toward her, his arms outstretched.

"You look so lovely that I hardly dare touch you in case you are a mirage and will disappear before my eyes," he murmured.

There came the sound of Aunt Matilda clearing her throat, presumably to remind them that she was there, and then the old lady said, "He's right at that, Melanie, for I'd swear you're looking better every day. Devon air must be good for you."

"It was really good for me today. I thought at first that I might freeze to death, but once it warmed up, the air felt so clean and fresh that I couldn't get enough of it." She turned to Denby. "Didn't you feel that way, Broderick?"

He grinned. "You stayed in London too long, probably, breathing all those fumes from the chimneys and the river," he told her. "I think I'd better take you with me every day until we leave, so that your body can build up a stock of clean fresh air."

"Would you?" she asked, trying not to sound as eager as she felt. "I quite obviously need the exercise, and if you're sure I'll not be in your way . . ." Her sentence trailed off, for she was certain that he had not been able to do all the things he'd planned today, because she was with him.

"You'll not be in my way, my dear, and if it will keep you from getting into mischief indoors, I'll gladly take you along with me," he said gruffly, then asked, "How did you like the mare? She seemed a bit frisky at first, but I noticed that you soon had her under control."

"She's a delight, and most responsive once she realized I meant it, but she was trying to tease me a little at first," she told him.

"She is, of course, registered with a long pedigree name," he said seriously, "but what would you like to call her?"

"Lovely Lady," Melanie said at once, "and it will, of course, be shortened most of the time to just Lady."

"That's it, then," Denby said, grinning. "I'll have the name put on her stall so that she'll know which one is hers."

"You expect me to teach her to read, then?" Melanie teased. "I'd be willing to bet you can put her name on a different stall from the one she has now, and she'll still be able to read it."

"I don't make bets with young ladies I don't trust," he said firmly. "All you'd need to do is put something with her scent on it inside the stall, and she'd go to it right away."

She shook her head. "I wouldn't even think of doing that," she told him, pretending to look shocked. "What I'd do is put something of Prince's in the stall, for she was trying to make up to him all morning."

Denby's grin widened. "I should have guessed, for she's a little flirt and I did notice her a time or two. We'll probably use him as a stud for her in a year or so, for they both have excellent bloodlines."

When he noticed Melanie's embarrassment, he just laughed. "Surely you've been around horses long enough to know how they're bred," he suggested.

"Of course I know, but Papa would never let us watch what happens, for he said it was not fitting," Melanie told him seriously.

Denby sighed. "Knowing what happens and watching it are two entirely different things. I'd not permit you to watch it either, so there I am in agreement with your papa," he said firmly.

As they went in to dinner, Aunt Matilda remarked, "I'll be leaving in the morning, for my house should be warm and cozy by now, but I must say that I will miss you both. I've not known a couple as entertaining as you two in years."

"We'll probably be gone ourselves by the end of the week, for I have things to do in London," Denby told her. "But when we come back we'll expect you to join us for dinner whenever you can."

"And I'll look forward to it, so don't let it be too long before you're back," the old lady said, smiling a little sadly.

Melanie did not really want to return to London at all, but she disliked even more the idea of him going alone, for she did not mean to let him get into the clutches of his mistress again if she could help it.

But by now she knew him so well that she was sure he would not do anything he did not wish to do, so if he went to see his mistress it would be because he felt a need for her services. And it was that which prayed on Melanie's mind to such an extent that she was unable to behave in her own natural manner, but, without meaning to, became quite self-conscious and reserved toward him.

A couple of days before they were due to leave, he asked her, "Are you sure you are feeling quite up to the journey to London? Would you perhaps prefer to stay here? If so, I'll go up alone and come back as quickly as I can."

She looked quite horrified at the very idea, and told him quite sharply, "I don't mean to be the kind of wife who stays in the country while her husband goes off to London without her. And what would people say when we're supposed to be still on our wedding trip and you were there attending balls and parties without me?"

"I wasn't aware that you cared very much about what the *ton* had to say about you," he said quietly. "And at this time of year there'll be little in the way of parties going on, for the Season will not yet be under way. But you've not seemed to be quite yourself these last few days, and I was afraid the journey might be too tiring for you. I've told you several times that I don't want to go up alone, but if you're feeling out-of-sorts, that's another matter.''

It was an effort, but Melanie managed a cheerful smile and said, ''I'm fine, really I am, and if you left me here alone I'd be so bored that I'd be forced to break my promise and redo some of the rooms here, such as your bedchamber and the study,'' she teased.

''Oh, you would, would you?'' he said, pretending to scowl. ''Well, in that case, I'll have to take you with me, won't I? Otherwise I might come back to find the house in such a state that I'd be forced to take you up to Yorkshire while the place was put back in order.''

She smiled a little sheepishly, recalling the things she had done to him at Denby Downs, and he drew her toward him, tilting up her chin and placing a tender kiss upon her waiting lips.

''We'll take it in easy stages,'' he promised, ''and if you wish, you can ride with me part of each day, or I'll join you in the carriage if you prefer.''

''I always prefer to be where you are,'' she told him, ''for though I like Bridget very much, a conversation with her for several hours is necessarily quite limited, and can become most tedious.''

''Then it's settled,'' he said, ''and I'll give the necessary instructions to the coachman. Outriders can go ahead each day to secure our accommodations, and we'll travel as comfortably as we can. I do hope, however, that we run into no more snowstorms.''

It was a risk they had to take at this time of the year, but when they set out two days later, the skies were sunny though the air was quite chilly, and apart from one day of rain, when Denby rode in the coach with both Melanie and her maid, the weather was reasonably pleasant.

Denby was a man of his word, and he made sure that his wife got as much exercise as she wanted each day, and every night he trounced her soundly at piquet. She learned quickly, however, and by the time they reached London, her game showed signs of considerable improvement.

"Are your mama and sisters still in residence at Denby House?" Melanie asked, wondering how they would all get along together if this was the case.

"Not my sisters, for they returned to their homes immediately after the wedding, thank goodness," he said, smiling with relief. "However, Mama may still be in town, but she has her own large suite of rooms and would not disturb us unless we invited her to do so."

"You mean she won't dine with us every evening?" Melanie asked, quite surprised.

He shook his head. "She has her own friends, and before you and I were married I was out almost every evening, so we lived in the same house but went our separate ways. Don't mistake me, however, for the arrangement works very well, and we're the best of friends."

"I have to take your word for it, I suppose," Melanie told him, "and if your mama likes it that way, then that is all that matters."

"Of course," he said quickly, "and on the nights when I happen to be out, which may be quite frequent, for I may often have to be with the prime minister or other cabinet members quite late, you might want to ask Mama to join you rather than eat alone."

Melanie nodded, but hoped that this would not happen too often, for her imagination was quite vivid and she might easily wonder if he was at Seymour Place instead.

As it turned out, however, the dowager Lady Denby was not in residence when they arrived, having gone to visit friends in Brighton for a few days, and so they had the house to themselves.

"What is there to do in London at this time of year, for it will be a month before the Season starts," Melanie asked.

"It's really not much different from December, when you stayed in town last year, before our wedding," Denby told her. "There are always a few friends here for some reason or another, with Parliament in session, and once the knocker is on the door, we'll start to get invitations to dinner and the occasional ball."

"Perhaps we could ride in the park when we're a little more settled," Melanie suggested, "and see if anyone we know is here yet."

"Of course," Denby said with a smile. "Don't worry about getting bored, my dear, for you'll soon find there is plenty going on. I must check in with Lord Liverpool in the morning, but I'll be back in the afternoon if at all possible, and take you for a ride, if you like."

"I would like that very much, but I'll fully understand if you cannot do so," she told him.

But the following morning Melanie had not even finished giving instructions for dinner to Cook when Fowlkes came through to tell her that a gentleman who said he was her brother had called, and he had put him in the morning room.

Melanie's face lit up at once, and she hurried through to see Michael and get the latest news of the family.

They hugged warmly; then Michael pushed her away and stepped back, scrutinizing her carefully from the top of her head to the tips of her toes.

"I must say, you look extremely well, Mellie," he told her. "Married life seems to be doing you a deal of good."

"I'm sorry that you missed Denby," Melanie said. "He had to go to the Houses of Parliament, I believe, for he's been doing a lot of work on this wretched Corn Bill, and hopes that it will go through very shortly."

"I've heard Papa talk about it, of course, and he's all for it, but I don't know enough of what's going on to decide anything for myself, and I'm quite sure you do not," he said with a little laugh.

"I most certainly do," Melanie said proudly, "for Denby's been explaining it to me, and it is extremely important that it go through at this time. It is an interim measure only, of course, but there is quite naturally a great deal of opposition from people not connected with farming, who fear that bread will become too costly for the poor to afford—and it is, after all, the main food for a great many of them."

Michael shrugged. He was now twenty-one and had a generous allowance from his father, but was constantly with pockets to let. This was one of the reasons he had come to see Mellie this morning, for he hoped to get a loan from her to see him through until next quarter. It had been a stroke of luck that she had married one of the wealthiest men in London, for he had been allowed a deal more credit on the strength of it.

"Are you staying at the house?" Melanie asked.

Michael nodded. "Mama has this thing now about leaving it in the hands of the Godfreys, particularly as Papa feels there might be riots and looting if that bill goes through." He chuckled. "I don't know what good they think I would be alone there should a mob come in that direction, but Mama feels more comfortable with me in residence."

"When are they coming to town? I know Mama will want to buy gowns for Martha again, before Madame LeBlanc gets too busy, so I would imagine they'll be here in a week or so." Melanie suddenly realized that he might be free for supper. "Would you want to have supper with us this evening? I don't know if Denby will be here or not. It depends on how much work he has to do, I suppose, but you could dine with me if you've not had any better offers."

"I have offers every evening, dear sis," he said with an exaggerated leer, "but not from people you would like to meet. What time are you dining?"

"Eight o'clock, I should imagine," she said thoughtfully, "for that will give Denby time to get home if he's going to. And we'll have sherry first in the drawing room."

"I'll look forward to dining with you in all this grandeur," he teased, then said quickly, "By the way, I was wondering if you might be in a position to make me a small loan until I get the money from Papa. I'll pay you back, of course, when they come to town, but I had to spend quite a bit of this quarter's allowance on things for the house."

"You should have put it on account, for all the stores know us. That's what I did last year," she told him, "but of course I can lend you some money. How much do you need?"

"A couple of hundred will be enough for now," he said quickly. "It should see me through until they get here."

"Wait here," Melanie told him, "and I'll go and get it." She was back in a moment with the money he wanted, and after giving her a brotherly hug, he hurried away, promising to be back at seven-thirty prompt.

Now that she was alone, Melanie knew exactly what she wanted to do with the next few hours, and she started toward the music room that she had seen on the very first visit she had made to this house.

A small chuckle escaped her as she glanced at the beautiful statues her mama had been so shocked about, and she wondered if she might, as a joke when her mama came to visit here alone, put cloaks around their shoulders.

Then she stepped into the music room and, walking over to the grand piano, ran her hand over the fine wood. She had been right, it was by Sebastian Erard, and very costly, she knew. This time she was not just going to look, but wanted to try it out for herself, so she sat down on the piano stool, raised the lid, and ran her fingers lightly over the keys.

It would have broken her heart, she thought, had this one not been in tune, like the ones at Denby Downs and Moorland House, but she knew she need not have worried as she began to play one of her favorite pieces.

As usual, she completely lost herself in the music, then went on to another piece, then another, and as she was about to begin yet a third or fourth concerto on this magnificent instrument, she glanced up and saw that Denby was in the room, propped against one of the cabinets, and he looked as if he had been there for some time.

He was gazing at her with an expression of sheer delight on his face, and he murmured, "Bravo," as he walked over to the piano.

"Why didn't someone tell me you played so very well?" he asked. "There were pianos in the houses in both Devon and Sussex, yet I never saw you touch them."

She laughed, then told him a little mischievously, "Oh, I did. I touched several keys, in fact, and found that neither piano was in tune."

He wagged a finger at her. "They would have been tuned the very same day you touched them," he told her, "had I but known that you played like this. I could listen to you all day long."

"Don't you play?" Melanie asked.

He nodded. "I was taught, but I'm afraid that my fingers suddenly all become thumbs when I attempt anything more than a few simple chords. What I don't understand is why I never heard you playing in your own house."

"Mama gets a megrim at the sound of the piano," she explained, "so I learned when I was quite young that I should practice only when everyone was out."

He shook his head. "Not anymore, I hope, for it would be most unfair to me. Promise?"

"Of course, if you enjoy it so much, Broderick. I'm so glad, for it's something I can share with you at last," she told him, her delighted face echoing her words. "I'm very pleased to see you, but I didn't think you would be home for luncheon."

"I shall be out to dinner tonight, I'm afraid," he said with a grimace, "and I wanted to tell you rather than just send a message. I hoped you had not eaten luncheon yet, so that I might join you."

She rose and took his outstretched hand to go with him into the dining room. "If you're not home for dinner, you'll miss my brother, then, for Michael came by this morning. He's staying at the house until Mama brings Martha to town in a couple of weeks, for she was worried about just the Godfreys being there when Papa said there might be riots."

"I'm glad you will have company, anyway," Denby told her, "for I feel guilty about bringing you up to town and then leaving you to eat dinner at home alone. Perhaps Mama will be back soon."

But the dowager Lady Denby did not return as soon as he had hoped, and Lord Liverpool either had to meet with Denby every evening or had work for him to perform, and Melanie became increasingly upset at having to eat dinner alone so very often. The only time they were together seemed to be in the early morning when he took her riding in the park.

Even Michael seemed to have deserted her, for she had not heard from him since the night they had dined together.

When he did finally stop by, however, he made matters rather worse than better.

"Are you and Denby still getting along all right?" he asked her, trying to sound casual but not succeeding very well.

"Yes, of course we are," she said sharply, for she had no desire to confide in her young brother. "Why do you ask?"

"I was just wondering," he told her. "You see, the other night I was with a couple of friends of mine at a house on Seymour Place, across the street from where Mrs. White-head lives, and I saw Denby come out of her house."

For a moment Melanie felt as though she could hardly get her breath. Because of the delightful warmth and affection he now showed in her bedchamber, she had begun to believe that he had broken off that particular relationship.

She did not know she had gone very pale until Michael leaned forward to look at her.

"I say, Mellie, are you all right?" he asked. "You look like a ghost. Can I get you something?"

She shook her head.

"No, I'm all right now," she assured him. "It was just a sudden faintness, and it's passed altogether now. What was it you were saying about Denby?"

"I saw him, quite late the other night. I'd forgotten all about Mrs. Whitehead until I saw him come out of the house across, and walk away toward a hackney stand," Michael said, "and I thought at first that he might have been going there just to pay her off, you know, now that he's married."

"How do you know that he wasn't?" Melanie's voice sounded strange even to her own ears.

Michael looked embarrassed. "Well, Mellie, the place we were in was a kind of gambling house, with a few ladies around, all perfectly harmless. You know the kind of thing."

"No, Michael, I'm afraid I don't," she said a little sadly. "It doesn't sound a very harmless place to me, but go on with your story."

"When I realized it was just about the time we had left the night before, I went outside for a little air, and stood waiting for my friends to join me. It took them a minute or two, and I stood there quietly waiting, and the same thing happened again. Denby came silently out of the house across, looked around a little as though he thought someone might have seen him, then went off at once in the direction of the hackney stand.''

''Are you sure it was the same house, for there must be a lot of other people besides Mrs. Whitehead living on Seymour Place.'' She desperately wanted him to be wrong, but her brother gazed at her with an expression of dismay.

''Do you think that I would make a mistake like that?'' he asked angrily. ''I know how it must make you feel, although it's a well-known fact that half the married gentlemen of the *ton* have mistresses.

''Look, I know you're upset, for it's early in the marriage for that to be going on. I tell you what, I have the very thing,'' he said, sounding very pleased with himself. ''I know where I can get tickets for a new play that's just opened. Why don't you let me take you there tomorrow night, if Denby's going to be late home again. You'll enjoy it, I know, for they say it's going to be the hit of the Season.''

''When do you need to know,'' Melanie asked. ''I'll ask him when we're out riding in the morning, and send you a note. We can dine here first, and take the carriage, for Denby doesn't usually use it when he's alone.''

When her brother had left, she went up to her bedchamber and sat there thinking about what she could do. The trouble was that she had convinced herself that he was beginning to grow as fond of her as she was of him, but it must have been all an act on his part.

She couldn't bear the idea of his coming to her tonight, so she wrote a note to Denby, asking him not to disturb her tonight, as she had not been feeling well today. She left it with his valet and was quite sure he would receive it as soon as he came in.

When Denby did get it, he immediately felt alarmed, for Melanie had always seemed to be in the best of health. His first thought was that she might be expecting a child, which was, of course, what they both wanted, and he crept silently into her chamber and looked down on her as she slept. Her cheeks looked a little flushed, but otherwise she seemed to be all right, he decided, then returned to his own bed.

The next morning, Melanie was awake before seven, for she had slept somewhat restlessly, and she rang for Bridget at once.

"My, you're up and about early this morning, milady," the maid said as she pulled back the curtains and set a tea tray on the table beside the bed. "Did you have trouble sleeping?"

"No, not really," Melanie said. "But as I was already awake, I thought I might as well be ready for an early ride if Lord Denby cares to go."

She was already dressed in a new apple-green riding habit when Denby came in, and he looked at her closely before asking, "Are you sure that you want to go? It's cold outside this morning, you know, and if you were a little under the weather yesterday, it might be best to give it a miss."

She smiled, a little more brightly than usual, and assured him that she was fine today. "I need the fresh air," she told him, "for it always seeems to do me good."

"Very well," he said, "I'll be ready in ten minutes and will meet you downstairs. Have another cup of hot tea while you're waiting."

When he had left the chamber, Bridget gave her a puzzled look. "You didn't tell me that you weren't well yesterday. What was wrong?"

"Nothing at all, Bridget, and you surely would be the first to know if there was. I just thought it might be a good idea not to always seem as robust as I do. Maybe I'll see if I can be pale and interesting for a while," she said, smiling mysteriously.

The maid just shrugged and opened the door for her mistress to pass through. "Enjoy your ride, milady," she said.

They were already in the park before Melanie broached the subject of that evening.

"Do you think you will be home tonight, Broderick?" she asked him. "Michael has tickets for a new play and he said he would take me if you are going to be busy again tonight."

"I'm afraid I am going to be busy again, my dear," he said with a sigh, "and I'm sorrier than you realize, for I do enjoy seeing a good play. Give him dinner here first, and take our carriage, and be ready to tell me about it when you get back."

He reached over and squeezed her hand for a moment. "I'm sorrier than you can imagine that I cannot take you myself," he said earnestly. "But this won't last much longer now, and then I'll take you to all the theaters you wish, and even to Almack's when they open. And, though you may not realize it, that is indeed a sacrifice for me."

11

Melanie sent the note to her brother, accepting his invitation to the theater and inviting him to have dinner with her at Denby House first; then she went to great pains to choose the dishes and wines that she knew he liked most. She could not recall when the two of them had been anywhere together since they were little children, so she wanted it to be very special.

Shortly before he arrived, however, she realized that the evening would have been altogether different if it had been Denby she had planned the dinner for, and he who had been taking her to the theater, but that was only as it should be.

She had chosen to wear a rich green silk gown with a rounded neckline that seemed a good deal lower than the ones she usually wore, and she kept looking down at it, wondering if it was perhaps a little risqué, but Bridget was adamant. A lace insert would most definitely spoil the appearance of the gown.

She had just reached the foot of the stairs when a footman opened the door to her brother.

"You know, I could have got another ticket, I'm sure, if Denby had wanted to join us," Michael told her as they went into the drawing room, "but I supposed that he had other plans for the evening."

"He had some meeting or other to attend, and it seems that the dinner hour is frequently the only time when everyone can be available," she told him.

"You know, you really shouldn't let him get away with leaving you alone every night, Melanie," Michael declared, pausing to lift his glass of sherry and take a sniff, followed by a sip, as though sampling the quality. He nodded and said, "Mm. Quite a nice bouquet. But as I was about to say, you've blossomed out in just these two months and are in far better looks now than you ever were before. I declare, I wouldn't have recognized you had I just seen you in the street. Why don't you have a shot at making him jealous? I'll warrant that if he sees you with another man he'll soon start paying you more attention."

"I'll give it some thought," Melanie told him, though the very idea of going out with some man other than her husband was most repugnant to her. "I certainly don't mean to let him overlook the fact that I'm here, of course."

"I should think not," Michael said stoutly. "If word got around that he visited Mrs. Whitehead almost every night, you would become the laughingstock of the *ton*. I must admit, though, Mellie, that he is extremely discreet. It was pure chance, that first time, that I happened to look out of the window on the other side of the street just at the time when he came out."

There was the sound of the dinner gong in the hall, and Melanie slipped her arm through his. "Don't let's talk about it in the dining room, Michael," she said, "for you know how servants gossip, and it would seem they have all been with Denby since the day he was born."

"Of course not," her brother snapped. "Do you think I don't know how to behave?"

"You know very well how to behave, Michael," she said, "but you have, at times, forgotten for a moment that others were within earshot."

Tonight, however, proved not to be one of those times, for Michael was quite impressed by the dishes Melanie had selected, and even more so by the quality of the wines that were served. As a result, he was in the most amiable of moods when they left for the theater.

The play was excellent, well-written, and even better executed, and Melanie thoroughly enjoyed it. Then, as the end of the performance drew near, Michael whispered,

"Come with me, Mellie, I've arranged a little surprise for you." He took her arm and led her quickly through a door by the side of the stage.

Melanie was a little annoyed, for she would have much preferred to see the play through to the very end, but he had taken so firm a hold of her arm that she could not refuse without causing a commotion.

She saw at once that they were at the side of the stage, and from where she stood she could see the players lining up at the very front of the stage, ready to make their bows as soon as the curtain rose again. When it did, she found it most interesting that she could not really see the audience. The glare of the footlights was so intense, even from this distance, that everything beyond it seemed to be in total darkness.

Then the actors who had only small parts came running off as the curtain fell again, and Melanie could distinctly smell the greasepaint as they hurried past her.

She recognized some of the props that had been used onstage in the earlier acts of the play, a couch on which the heroine had lain, and a small table, still set with cups and saucers, a teapot, and a sugar bowl.

Just then the heroine ran by, having made her bow, and Melanie smiled at her as she passed. She was wearing heavy makeup, but Melanie was surprised to find that the girl did not look even as old as she herself was.

"Melanie," her brother called sharply, "I want you to meet Donald O'Malley, the star of the show, whom you've just been admiring from the other side of the stage."

She put out her hand toward the young actor, but instead of taking it lightly in his, he took a firm grip on it, and when Michael nodded and said, "It's all right, Donald, go ahead." Melanie found herself being hurried up the steps and onto the stage—right up to those bright lights.

"Just put on a big smile and bow to the audience first," the actor instructed, steering her into position, "and then bow to me."

Though she could not see anyone, she knew that the house was packed and that they could all see her, so despite her shaking legs, she followed his instructions to the letter, except that she clasped her free hand to her bosom as the neckline of her gown appeared to be slipping.

It took only a minute, but it seemed ages to Melanie before she was back at her brother's side and the actor was hurrying off to his dressing room.

"Michael!" Melanie said in a shocked voice, completely horrified at what had just happened. "What on earth did you do that for? It's a good thing that I haven't been out much as yet, for if anyone in the audience recognized me, I'd be the talk of London."

"Nonsense, Mellie. I thought you'd enjoy it," her brother said, sounding a little hurt that she did not recognize what a favor he had done her. "It'll make old Denby realize that you're not just a quiet little mouse waiting for him to come home each night."

"It will make him think that I'm doing something with that actor that he knows nothing about, and he will probably be extremely annoyed with both of us," she snapped.

"Don't bring me into it," Michael said huffily, "for it was you who went out there with O'Malley. I didn't force you to get up on the stage with him, and I'll tell that to Denby or anyone who asks."

"I'm sure that young man does not do that to everyone who just happens to be standing backstage, Michael, or he'll get himself into a lot of trouble," Melanie said severely. "And you've already as good as admitted that you took me there deliberately, without telling me you had arranged the whole thing."

His boyish face seemed to crumple. "I thought you'd enjoy it, Mellie, really I did. He's no longer just a newcomer, but is making a name for himself, and before long he'll be famous."

"That's what I'm afraid of," Melanie said, "and my name will be linked with his. However, I can only assume that you really thought I'd enjoy it, so let's go home and forget all about it for now. I may just be lucky and no one will have recognized me."

The coach was waiting, and on the way to Denby House

they discussed the merits of the play and its actors. Both agreed that the show was bound to become a real hit as soon as the *ton* came to town again in large numbers and discovered the treat that was in store for them.

Before they reached the house, Melanie asked, "Would you like to come in for a drink, or are you going elsewhere?"

"I'm going to meet some of the fellows a little later, but I could certainly come in for a few minutes," he said. "As a matter of fact, I was wondering if you could spare a little of the ready, for getting such good seats at the last minute was not easy, and a palm or two had to be greased to secure them."

Melanie looked surprised, for she knew her papa had always been quite generous with her brother.

"Don't look at me like that, Mellie," he said. "I knew I was a little short when I told you I'd get the tickets, but I thought it would be a treat for you at this time. You know, take your mind off your problems for a while."

"How much were they?" she asked quietly.

"Sixty pounds would cover them," he told her, "and if you don't have it right now, I'm sure Denby would give you an advance on your allowance. At least he's in town, but Papa is not, and won't be for some time yet."

They had reached Denby House, and a footman was already at the door of the carriage, so no further conversation was possible until they had discarded their outer clothes and were sitting in the drawing room.

Melanie sipped a glass of sherry and her brother held a large glass of brandy he had poured for himself. She put down her glass on a small table and rose. "If you'll excuse me for a moment, Michael, I'll just go upstairs and get the money for you," she said as she hurried across the room, "for Denby may return at any time."

She came back a few minutes later, clutching the money in her hand, and gave it to him.

Without a word, he took it and slipped it into a pocket. Then he emptied his glass in one gulp and made a show of putting it back on the tray before turning around.

"Now, don't forget what I told you, Mellie," he said.

"You'd be surprised what a little jealousy could achieve, and it would serve him jolly well right."

"I won't forget, Michael," she said quietly. "Thank you for a lovely evening. It was, indeed, most entertaining."

On this formal note her brother departed, and Melanie stayed where she was for a moment, wondering how she would be able to face Denby if she had ruined his good name. Then she went up to her bedchamber, where she knew that Bridget was waiting to put her to bed.

"It'll be a good thing when your mama and papa come to town, milady," Bridget declared. "Michael was never very strong-willed, and you've got to remember that at twenty-one, he's still very young."

"There are times when you see too much for your own good, Bridget," Melanie said, but there was no anger in her voice, for she had been one of the family for too long.

"It's got you worrying, and wondering if the last money really was for what he said, hasn't it?" the maid asked.

Melanie nodded. "I can think of nothing he could need it for except gambling debts, and, yes, it will be good to have Mama and Papa in town soon."

They both heard the heavier tread as Denby made his way to his own chamber, and Bridget said, "Come along, and I'll get you out of that gown and your hair brushed in a jiffy."

As she spoke, she unfastened the gown and slipped it off Melanie's shoulders.

After his dinner with the prime minister, Denby had gone to his club for a game of cards, for he had a couple of hours to waste before he was due to meet with one of the people from whom he got vital information.

He had been there not more than an hour, however, and was on a winning streak, when Lord Worthington, a fellow with whom he had never been on the best of terms, came into the card room.

"So this is where you're hiding out, Denby," Worthington said jovially. "I'm glad to see you're lucky at cards, even if you are unlucky at love. But then, aren't we all, old chap? At least your little lady can't be serious about this actor fellow, for he'd never be able to give her the things you can, now, would he?''

Denby smiled slightly and shook his head. He would not for a minute let Worthington realize he didn't know what on earth he was talking about, but he'd certainly find out before the night was out.

Then young Willoughby, who was a friend of Martha Grenville's, came over, and Denby excused himself from the card game, cashing in his winnings.

"Did she do it for some kind of dare, Denby?" Willoughby asked. "I was never so surprised in my life as when I saw Melanie appear on that stage tonight with Donald O'Malley. It was a jolly good thing she hung on to her gown, though, for she was nearly falling out of it."

Denby recognized the actor's name, and recalled that Melanie had said she was going to see the play with her brother. He could not imagine her doing anything so foolish as to appear on a stage with the male lead, however.

Being most careful not to reveal that he had known nothing about it, he was gradually able to put the whole thing together, but could not for the life of him understand why she had done such a thing. To him it made no sense at all. After careful consideration, he decided that unless she told him about it herself, he would not broach the subject this evening, but would sleep on it and decide what to do in the morning.

By the time Denby walked into Melanie's chamber, her face had been washed and she was sitting at the dressing table enjoying the feel of the even strokes of the brush down the length of her hair.

Denby was not yet out of his own clothes, and he motioned for Bridget to continue what she was doing.

"How was the play, my dear?" he asked.

"Excellent," Melanie said, smiling a little stiffly. "That young actor, O'Malley, will do very well indeed when the Season is really under way."

"I rather thought Michael would still be here, for you can't have been home very long," Denby remarked.

"Time enough for him to have a glass of brandy, that's all, for he was meeting some friends later," Melanie told him. She wished that their relationship was as good as it had been when they were in Devon, for she could then have told him what had happened this evening, and of her worries in regard to her brother.

"When did you say your parents would be arriving?"

"In about two weeks, I believe, and it will be so good to see them again," she told him feelingly.

"Do you miss them so very much after only a couple of months, my dear?" he asked, sounding surprised, and also a little hurt.

Neither of them seemed to notice when Bridget slipped quietly from the chamber.

"I'd miss anyone right now," Melanie snapped, "for I ride with you in the morning, and occasionally we have luncheon together, but after that I don't see you again until past midnight."

He moved over to her and delicately stroked behind her ear and down the side of her neck. To her dismay, Melanie started to get that familiar warm, wanting feeling inside.

"I'm sorry, my love," he said softly. "It was selfish of me to have brought you here, I know, but I didn't want to be in London and have you so far away from me. In a couple of weeks this wretched bill will surely go before both houses, and once it is presented we'll go out of town immediately, either back to Sussex or up to Yorkshire, if you like. Do you think you can be patient just a little longer?"

When he asked her like that, Melanie could do nothing except agree to do whatever he wished, although deep inside she resented the hold he seemed to have over her.

She consented wordlessly, and he drew her into his arms, his lips claiming what he knew to be his.

When they made love that night, it was with a passion much deeper than they had yet known. But with daylight the next morning, alone in her bed, sounder reasoning came, and Melanie bitterly resented the ease with which Denby had been able to make her forget everything that had happened the evening before. She had meant to tell him about it, but dared not before they made love, and had not even thought of it afterward.

When Denby awoke that morning, his first instinct had been to go and see this actor and rearrange his probably effeminate face. But later, he reconsidered though he still wanted to see the young man, so he found out his address and paid him a call.

The lodging was in an unfashionable but quite respectable part of London, not far from the theater, and when Denby asked for the young man, he appeared at once and seemed almost to have been expecting him. Denby was surprised to find that he rather liked the look of the fellow, for he appeared to be more masculine-looking than most of the actors he had met.

"My curricle is outside," Denby said after introducing himself. "Would you care to go for a drive somewhere where we can talk?"

"By all means, my lord," Donald O'Malley agreed. "I'll get my coat from the peg in the hall as we go out."

"I understand that you know my wife," Denby said bluntly when they were some distance away.

"Not in the biblical sense, my lord," O'Malley said smoothly. "I actually met her for the first time last evening when her brother introduced her to me backstage."

"What is there between you, then?" Denby asked abruptly, believing that there must be more to it.

"Nothing, and I'm sure she'd not say there was," O'Malley said in the deep voice that was captivating his audiences.

Denby raised his eyebrows, and O'Malley continued.

"It was her brother who came to me a day or two ago and told me that though she was a little shy of the stage, she was simply longing to just take a bow with me out front. It sounded a little silly to me, but he crossed my palm with silver, so I saw no reason to refuse.

"Last night, however, I did wonder if what he said was true, for she seemed most surprised, and though she smiled when I told her to, she was trembling when I put her back into her brother's hands.''

"I see," Denby said. "You've not been in London before, have you?''

"No, sir, I haven't," O'Malley told him. "This is my first appearance here.''

"And I suppose that you were not aware, then, that for a lady to do what my wife did last night is frowned upon by society?" Denby suggested.

O'Malley looked worried. "No, sir, I was not. It seemed harmless enough to me, but surely her brother should have known?''

"I've no doubt that he did," Denby said, "but he's still very young and foolish, I'm afraid. I'd like you to do me a favor, and in return I'll be happy to do one for you.''

"What is it?" For a moment the young actor looked a little like the truculent young Irishman he had once been.

"I'd like you to come back with me to my home and have lunch with me and my wife. And then I'd like you to take a ride with us in the park this afternoon, for I do not believe you have a matinee performance.''

O'Mally grinned. "I'd be glad to, my lord, if you wouldn't mind me going back to my lodging first and changing into something a little bit more showy, if I'm to be on display.''

"By all means," Denby said, and turned the curricle around.

It was no more than an hour later that Denby returned to his home with O'Malley beside him. On the way back, he had driven through the park and waved to quite a number of his friends and acquaintances, and now the two men stepped down and entered Denby House.

"Mr. O'Malley will be joining us for luncheon," he told Fowlkes, and asked, "Is Lady Denby at home?''

"I believe she is in her chamber, my lord," the butler replied.

"I'll go up and see her," Denby said, frowning. "Show Mr. O'Malley into the drawing room, Fowlkes, and pour him a drink. I'll be only a moment.''

He found Melanie sitting at her escritoire, and she looked up when he came in, her eyes giving clear evidence that she feared he had found out about last night.

"Although I have not seen your brother, I believe I know what happened last night," he said gently. "Do you think that you could put on something very striking and come down in half an hour for luncheon? We have a guest who will join us for a drive in the park afterward—a very nice young man by the name of Donald O'Malley."

She looked frightened for a moment, but when he said, "It's all right, my love. We've had a talk and he's quite willing to help stop any scandal."

"You're not angry?" she asked, unable to believe the way he was taking it.

"Not with you," he said, placing a gentle kiss on her inviting lips.

She rang for her maid, and he left then and returned to join Mr. O'Malley in a preluncheon drink.

"My wife will be with us in about twenty minutes," he told the actor.

"Now, what can I do that would help further your career?" Denby asked bluntly. "Not because I have to, but because I want to. Before this was brought to my attention, I had already heard that you're a promising new talent, and I have the funds to back you if you have another show in mind after this one."

There followed a strictly business discussion for their mutual benefit, and when Melanie came downstairs, looking lovely once more in a pale lemon muslin gown, both gentlemen rose, and she went into the dining room between them with a hand on each man's arm.

It was a pleasant, lighthearted meal, and O'Malley kept them most amused with his tales of things that had gone wrong both onstage and with a group of actors on tour.

Denby explained to his wife the business arrangements he and O'Malley had made for his next play, adding, "I have no doubt whatsoever that we shall all make money on this new show, for you and I, my dear Melanie, are now partners with Mr. O'Malley.''

"Do you really mean that, my lord?" Melanie asked. "I was not aware that a woman could be a partner in her own right.''

"I mean it," he said, smiling softly at her surprise. "The papers will go to the solicitor today, and your signature will be required, you'll see.''

It was a lovely sunny day, though the air was quite crisp, and Denby had sent word that they would use the open landau for their ride in the park.

"Run upstairs and put something warm over your gown, my love," Denby told Melanie, "for I don't want you to catch a cold. But don't cover it completely.''

It was the first time that Melanie had ridden in this particular carriage, with a liveried coachman in front and a liveried groom on the box.

"I don't believe I ever saw a landau like this before," O'Malley, remarked. "It's most interesting.''

"You'll probably never see another," Denby said, "for I bought a landau and was most unhappy with it, so I had a fellow I knew redesign it almost completely.''

"It must have cost a fortune," the actor murmured as he examined it in detail.

"It did," Denby cheerfully admitted, "but I now own what I believe is the most comfortable landau in London, and if I ever wished to sell it, I could do so many times over, for it is the envy of most of my friends.''

They drove slowly through the park and back again, stopping time after time to speak to their friends. Many of the women looked as though they would have liked to snub Melanie, but not one of them dared do so with Denby there. When a few of them had been introduced to the handsome young actor, word went round that it had all been a mistake, an ugly rumor spread in an attempt to discredit the young lady who had stolen the most eligible bachelor in London from under their noses.

When Denby felt they had done enough, they took Mr.

O'Malley back to his lodging before returning to Denby House. Once she and Denby were alone together in the carriage, however, Melanie suddenly felt embarrassed, and her eyes filled with tears.

He moved over to take the seat next to her. "Don't be upset, my love," he said softly. "It's over and done with now, and no one will dare say another word about it."

"Thank you for everything," she said, "and I give you my word that I'll not let anyone get me into that kind of a situation again."

To Denby's relief, the Somerfields arrived in London a week later, somewhat earlier than they had planned. Lady Somerfield was most anxious to get the modiste started on new gowns for Martha and, as she said to Melanie when she came to call, she had been eager to see how her older daughter was getting along when she heard they were in town again.

"Your marriage to Denby will most definitely improve Martha's chances of making an excellent match," she told her, adding, "and with Denby's niece coming out also, I was wondering if perhaps a combined come-out ball here at Denby House might be just the thing to set the *ton* back on its ears. The ballroom here is so much larger, and if it were planned with tasteful extravagance, no one would talk of anything else all Season."

It was, of course, a gross exaggeration which Melanie chose to ignore, saying, "I very much doubt that Denby and I will be here much longer than a couple of weeks now, Mama, for we're still on our wedding trip and only returned to London because of this wretched Corn Bill."

"But you'll have to come back to town for your sister's come-out ball," Lady Somerfield insisted. "How could we have it here without you and Denby in attendance?"

"Quite easily, I should think," Melanie said sharply. "And in any case, wouldn't it be best to discuss the matter with Lady Settle when she comes to town? I know that Denby would prefer you to do so, for he intensely dislikes getting involved in such things."

"Perhaps you're right, but I'll expect you to give me a hand, young lady, in persuading them, for it's now your duty to help Martha make as good a marriage as you did," Lady Somerfield declared.

Melanie saw her mama again a couple of times during the following week, which relieved one kind of boredom but brought on another, for she still intensely disliked all the planning that went into a come-out.

She told Denby about it when they rode out early one morning.

"Let me tell you now, my love," he said, grinning quite wickedly, "that you have already done your duty to your mama. It is now your duty to protect me from all these planning ladies. Once we are away from here, I really don't care what kind of parties they give at Denby House, just as long as you and I do not have to attend them."

"We won't," Melanie promised. She would have said more, but Denby had a breakfast appointment and they had to hurry back.

12

O ne of the troubles with Denby, Melanie decided, was that it was almost impossible to make him angry, or even more than a little annoyed.

Perhaps, she thought, it might be easier if he spent more time at home, but when she saw him for only a few hours each day—other than late at night, of course, which was quite another matter entirely—there was hardly time enough to discuss with him all the things of importance that had come up in his absence.

Shortly after they were married, he had put a sum of money into a special account for her that she could draw upon whenever the need arose. This was to be replenished by him every quarter, and it had, at the time, seemed far larger than was necessary.

Her brother, however, had not repaid the money he had borrowed from her, even though her parents were now in town, and with a month of the quarter still to go, she was feeling the pinch a little.

As she saw it, she had one of two alternatives—to ask her brother to repay the money he had borrowed or to ask Denby for an advance on her next quarter's allowance.

After some consideration she decided that the former might be the more proper and the easier thing to do. Accordingly, in the middle of the morning she asked Fowlkes to have the carriage brought around, and she paid her first formal visit to Somerfield House.

"What a surprise, my dear," Lady Somerfield said after embracing her most affectionately. "I only wish that you had let us know you were coming, though, for Martha and I are just going out."

"That's quite all right, Mama," Melanie told her agreeably, "for it is really Michael I am looking for. Is he home this morning?"

Lady Somerfield looked extremely worried for a moment, but she quickly recovered and said lightly, "I've not seen him this morning as yet, Melanie, though I understand he did have breakfast sent up some time ago. He rarely leaves his chamber these days before noon."

Melanie looked puzzled. "When I was still at home, we all had to be downstairs for breakfast unless we were ill. Is there something wrong with him?"

"Your papa feels that I have been mothering Michael too much, and says that I should treat him like a grown man instead of a little boy," Lady Somerfield declared. "He was extremely impressed with the way in which Michael managed the house and everything until we came to town, and though he spent a great deal more of the money advanced to him than your papa felt he should have, young men are always inclined to do this, so I am told."

"You mean, I suppose, that in addition to his regular allowance, when Papa sent him to town ahead of you, he gave Michael an advance for any extra expenses that might come up here," Melanie suggested.

"Yes, that's right," Lady Somerfield agreed. "It was meant to pay for anything needed in the house that couldn't just be put on our account somewhere."

There was the sound of footsteps hurrying down the stairs, and Martha appeared at the foot of them, looking lovely as ever in a gown and pelisse of light blue and white bombazine.

"We really must run now, my dear. Do remember to send a note next time, to make sure we are going to be home, won't you," Lady Somerfield suggested, and then looked surprised when Melanie did not go with them to the door.

"Actually, Mama, I really do wish to see Michael," Melanie said again, "so if you don't mind, I'll send word to him that I am here, and will wait for him in the drawing room."

"By all means do so, my dear, if you have the time, but it may be quite a while yet before he comes down," Lady Somerfield warned. "You see, it's extremely important to him that his cravat is tied in a very special way, and it sometimes takes him an extraordinarily long time to achieve this perfection.

"Come along, Martha," she called, and the two of them hurried out of the front door.

As soon as they left, Masters, the butler, appeared in the hall.

"It's good to see you looking so well, milady," he said quietly. "Is there anything I can do for you?"

"Yes, there is, Masters," she said, moving toward the drawing room. "I'd like to send a note up to my brother in just a moment, and I was wondering also if perhaps Papa is home."

"He's in his study, milady," the butler informed her, "and if you'll give me the note to your brother when it's ready, I'll make sure he gets it right away."

She sat down at the familiar little desk in the drawing room and penned a note stating the fact that she wished to see him on urgent business and would be either visiting with Papa or in the drawing room when he came down.

After handing the note to Masters, Melanie then went toward the study and knocked lightly on the door, waiting for her papa's response before walking in.

"Oh, my dear Melanie, how good it is to see you looking so very well. I do believe you're in better looks than you've ever been," he told her. "You're not increasing, by any chance, are you?"

She looked surprised. "I don't think so, Papa, but I must admit I haven't given a thought to it. I may quite easily be, for all I know."

He looked at her a little strangely. "I doubt it," he said, "for you may be rather vague about such things, but that Bridget of yours would not be. How's Denby?"

"Fine, as far as I know," she said ruefully. "But I really

see so little of him that it's difficult to tell. Anyone might think he was married to Lord Liverpool instead of to me.''

He chuckled, then shook his head, smiling. "You always were outspoken, my girl, and I see you've not changed much. It was a good day, though, when Denby came and asked for you, for I knew that the two of you would rub along pretty well, once you got used to each other.''

"You're looking very well, Papa, but then, you've only just come up to town," Melanie said. "Do you mean to stay the whole Season?''

"Certainly not," he said, frowning at such a ridiculous suggestion. "I just wanted to be sure that Michael had done all he should about the house. Then I'm going back to the country for a week or two.''

There was a knock on the door, and Michael strolled in.

"My goodness! What happened to you?'' Melanie asked in a sisterly fashion. "You look as if you haven't slept for a month.''

"And good morning to you too, Melanie,'' Michael said with a slight sneer. "I'd like to be able to say that you look bad also, but I don't think I ever saw you looking so well. Is Denby finally paying you a bit of attention?''

"He's attentive enough when I see him, but unfortunately I don't see much more of him these days than I ever did,'' she said with a shrug.

"No, I don't suppose you do,'' he said, smiling meaningfully, "for I still see him quite often. Actually, almost every night, but of course he does not see me. I believe, however, that you wished to see me.''

He took her arm and began to steer her into the hall, but in his haste he forgot to close the study door behind him.

"Yes, I do. You remember the money you borrowed from me before the family arrived in London?'' Melanie asked.

Michael scowled, and started to bluster, saying, "What money? I don't know what you mean, Melanie, unless it's the theater tickets you insisted on paying for.''

Melanie's eyes narrowed, for she had never expected this kind of response.

"I'm talking about the two hundred pounds you said you

had spent on the house here from your allowance. You told me you would pay me back when the family came to town and Papa repaid you," she reminded him. "It was the morning when you stopped by Denby House and I invited you to come back for dinner that evening, which you did. Now do you recall?"

"I have not the slightest idea what you are talking about, Mellie," Michael said sharply. "Do you have an IOU?"

"Of course I do not," Melanie said, shocked. "I would not think of asking my own brother for an IOU, and just to set the record straight, I did not offer to pay for the theater tickets when you took me there. It was you who invited me, then asked me to pay you for them afterward, and I must say that sixty pounds for two theater tickets sounded quite exorbitant to me. What are you doing with the money, Michael? Are you losing it at that gaming house on Seymour Place that you seem to go to so often?"

There was a loud cough behind them, and they both swung around to see Lord Somerfield standing in the doorway of his study.

He said quietly, "I think you two had better come back in here. You should have made sure to close the door behind you, Michael, if you did not want me to overhear you."

"Now look what you've done," Michael snarled in Melanie's ear.

"I'm sure it wasn't deliberate," Lord Somerfield said mildly, "but I would say myself that Melanie has done you one of the biggest favors she has ever done in her life by coming here today. I believe I know now what has been happening. How much money do you owe, my boy, and to whom?"

Michael sank into an armchair and his cheeks turned a deep red. Then, as he looked at his father, his still-boyish face just seemed to crumple and he dropped his head into his hands. His shoulders shook with silent sobs.

Melanie looked questioningly at her father, and pointed to herself and then to the door. He nodded gravely, and she quietly rose and left the room. Her presence could only cause more embarrassment to her brother, and she knew that her father could handle it from here. She had no doubt that the money would be sent around to her before the day was out.

Masters appeared from out of nowhere and sent for her carriage, and then, with much relief, Melanie returned to Denby House.

She stayed in for the rest of the day, half-expecting that her mama might come to call and give her a dreadful scold for her part in her brother's downfall. She need not have worried, however, and when a message came from her papa, she knew that the envelope would contain the exact amount of money her brother had borrowed from her.

It gave her no satisfaction, though, for she could still hear Michael saying that he saw Denby often, almost every night—and he meant at Seymour Place.

She went upstairs and was much relieved that Bridget was elsewhere, for when she lay down on the bed, she suddenly found herself crying her heart out on the pillow.

It all seemed so terribly unfair. She hadn't asked to fall in love, but it had happened, and what had once been simply annoyance that he showed so little regard for his wife had now turned into real pain at the thought of him being there with another woman, giving himself to Mrs. Whitehead, and then returning to her bed.

"Milady, whatever is the matter?" It was Bridget's gentle, soothing voice, and her strong arms that clasped her mistress to her generous bosom and held her close until the tears ceased. Then Melanie found herself being undressed, put into a night rail, and given a draft to sip that soothed the heartache and put her to sleep.

She did not awake until after the dinner hour, but Bridget had already told Cook that her mistress was a little under the weather and would have a light supper in her bedchamber a little later.

When the meal arrived, she ate as much as she could, but she was not very hungry. She then asked Bridget to give her another draft so that she would sleep through the night.

Denby looked in on her a little later, and found that she

was deep in slumber. Smiling gently, he pulled up the covers that had fallen away from her shoulder, then slipped quietly back to his own chamber.

Ever since her come-out, Melanie could clearly recall her mama's remarks about riding in the park. Lady Somerfield had not really liked Melanie doing so at all, and had tried to prevent it for as long as she could, but of course she had no control over the morning rides which Melanie and Denby now took. They both galloped, but only very early in the morning, when no one was about, and at other times Melanie complied strictly with the unwritten rule and walked her horse daintily along the grass.

Lovely Lady still let her know, on such occasions, that she would enjoy a gallop, but Melanie always kept her under the most rigid control.

Today Melanie was restless, for it was a beautiful day, when everyone who was anyone was bound to be in the park in the early afternoon. For once, Denby was home for luncheon, and it was he who suggested they go out for a while.

"Why don't we take a ride in the park this afternoon?" he asked. "I was going to do some work, of course, and I'll have to make up for it afterward, but it's a shame not to take advantage of a day such as this. It's a little early for such nice weather, and we'll probably pay for it later, but it would be pleasant to drive along and greet all our friends and acquaintances."

Melanie shook her head. "I'd love to go there, but I'll guarantee that it will be so congested that carriages will be virtually at a standstill," she said feelingly. Then she had an idea. "Why don't we go on horseback? If we're mounted, we can get much more easily around the carriages, and we missed this morning's ride because of your breakfast appointment. I know that Lady, for one, would thoroughly enjoy it."

Denby looked at her vibrant expression, which had been sadly missing these last few days. Though he knew that it could be equally difficult to get a mount out if some carriages caught a rider in their midst, he decided they would be all right if they stayed on the grassy side.

"Very well," he said, smiling warmly. "If you like, you can go up and start getting changed, and I'll come up as soon as I've sent a note around to the stables."

As Bridget helped her into a new light gold habit, Melanie could not help but think of how very charming Denby was to her—on the occasions when he was at home. She supposed, however, that he was equally charming to Mrs. Whitehead, since he spent so much time with her.

Once outdoors, they found that it was indeed congested. Even the streets seemed to be busier than usual as they carefully guided the horses through the traffic. Lady lived up to her name until they reached the park, and then the sight of what must have looked like a field to her seemed to make the mare a little impatient. Denby's mount, Prince, was, of course, behaving like a perfect gentleman.

"You'd best keep a tight rein on Lady, for she appears rather too eager to be off, for my liking," Denby said as he passed in front of Melanie to lead the way. "You were right, though. I don't recall ever having seen so many carriages out at this time of year."

Melanie waited until Denby's head was turned, talking to Lady Jersey; then she guided the mare around a clump of trees and looked longingly at the stretch of green grass they frequently galloped across of a morning. She did not notice the bees that were buzzing around the purple and yellow crocuses that bloomed beneath the trees, but she did feel the sting on the side of her neck, and her sudden jump was all that Lady needed. She took off like the wind, and though Melanie thought she heard a shout behind her, she couldn't have stopped now if she had tried, for the mare had got what she always wanted when she caught sight of the open land, and she was thoroughly enjoying herself.

Melanie heard the thunder of hooves behind her, and knew it must be Denby. She was about to veer away so that he could not grab her reins, for she still felt she could bring the mare under control eventually. But to her surprise, Denby made no attempt to do so. Instead, he passed her, and she thought at first that something clipped the mare as he passed, for she was now going even faster. She realized then that it was the sight of the stallion ahead that had encouraged Lady all the more. The mare was running away with Melanie now, and it took all her skill just to remain in the sidesaddle, let alone try to bring her horse under control.

Her hair was streaming behind her, for it had come loose when her shako was knocked off by a low branch, and for the first time since she was a very little girl, Melanie realized that she was in grave danger of falling off her mount. If only she had been riding astride, she could have had the mare under control in minutes, she told herself, silently berating that stupid sidesaddle.

She had caught up with Denby now, and he was racing beside her, shouting to her to free her foot from the stirrup, but she shook her head, for she was afraid of what might happen if he did not succeed. She motioned for him to ride in front and try to cut the mare off, but before he could do so, another rider swung in front of her. Denby then came up on the other side, and between them they slowed the half-crazed horse, and Melanie gradually brought her to a canter and then to a walk.

"I say, George," Denby said to the other rescuer, "would you mind going to tell Lady Jersey that everything's all right now, but my wife is quite badly shaken by the whole thing, and I'm taking her directly home."

"Of course, Denby. But do you think the mare will be all right on the road?" his friend asked.

Denby nodded. "Something must have frightened her, for she's normally placid enough, but she's on a tight rein now, and will soon be very tired, I imagine."

Once his friend had galloped off, Denby did not say another word, to Melanie's surprise, until they reached the house. She didn't mind, however, for now that the excitement was over, her neck had begun to hurt quite badly, and she hardly felt like talking.

But after a groom had led the two horses away, Denby took Melanie's upper arm in a painful grasp, as if helping her along, and muttered threateningly, "Don't you dare say a word until we're upstairs."

She was already close to tears because of the fright, and she had to bite her lip to stop crying out with the pain of his grip, but she was determined not to let him know.

As they reached Melanie's chamber, Bridget opened the door for them to come in, but as soon as they were inside, Denby said to the maid, "Get out," with such forcefulness that she nearly ran from the room.

He almost flung Melanie into a soft chair, then stood over her, glaring so fiercely that her body threatened to tremble, but she managed to control it as she realized that he thought she had planned the whole episode.

"Now, I don't know what you are trying to do, young lady," he growled, "but you have gone just as far as I mean to let you. It would seem to me that, for some reason I cannot clearly discern, you have decided to disgrace yourself and me also, for I realize now that you must have been in league with your brother all the time. I had not thought you to be the kind of person who would deliberately try to harm my good name and yours, but I do not intend to let you succeed.

"Just remember this. There had better not be a third attempt. The very next time you try anything of this sort, I will do what the *ton* will expect me to do. And that is to give you a sound thrashing and send you back to the country in disgrace.

"You will stay in this chamber for the rest of the day and the whole of tomorrow, and visitors will be told that you cannot see anyone, as you are badly shaken after such a narrow escape."

He turned to leave, then, as he reached the door, added, "I don't know what condition Lovely Lady is in, but she will be on her way back to the country before the day is out."

If he had but turned around, he would have seen the tears suddenly pour down Melanie's face at his last words, but he left the chamber at once, and sent for Bridget, giving her instructions as to the care of her mistress, and what she was to say to visitors.

"He said I was to give you a sedative, milady," Bridget

told Melanie, "for you almost had a very bad accident. Is that true?"

Melanie nodded. "It was not my fault, though," she told her. "However, Denby seems to think that I meant to shock the *ton* by galloping in the park."

"What happened, then?" Bridget asked, completely puzzled by the whole incident.

"We were under a tree, and I suppose I did not notice the bumblebees buzzing around the crocuses beneath until something stung my neck," Melanie told the maid. "I jumped, of course, and that was about all Lady needed to take off at a gallop, for she had been eyeing that stretch of grass for several minutes."

"Let me take a look, milady," Bridget said, and Melanie put her head on one side so that the maid could see more easily.

"That's a nasty bee sting, milady. It's all swollen, and I'm going to have to get something to take the sting out with, for it's still in your neck. Let me get you out of this jacket, and I'll go and look for a pair of tweezers and something to ease the pain. What I can't understand is why you didn't tell his lordship what had happened when he was shouting at you and accusing you of heaven knows what," the maid said.

"Because I hoped he was so angry that he might just send me home—back to Devon, I mean, for I wish I'd never come with him to London. Papa asked me if I was increasing, when I saw him. Do you think I might be?" she asked hopefully.

"You could be, I suppose," Bridget told her, "but then, you've never been 'regular' so it's difficult to tell. Did you want to be in a family way so soon?"

"Yes," Melanie said with the first glimmer of a smile. "I'd like nothing better right now."

"Then you're going to have to look after yourself better than you do. No more galloping anywhere, never mind in the park, and no more getting upset like this, for you've not been happy for quite a while, have you?"

"No, I haven't," Melanie admitted.

"What's the matter with you, anyway? Can't you take to his lordship? If that's your problem, it's rather strange, for everyone here thinks the world of him, and he's always been most courteous to me before today," the maid asserted as she turned to get a robe for her mistress to put on.

"I can't just *take* to him, Bridget," Melanie said softly. "You see, I'm in love with him, and I don't want to be."

Bridget gave her a strange look and shook her head. "I'll just go and find some tweezers to get that sting out for you," she said. "And I'll bring you a sedative, for you'll feel a lot better after you've had a good sleep."

She was right, of course, for once she had removed the sting and put a blue bag on Melanie's swollen neck, she gave her the sedative and waited until her mistress fell asleep.

By suppertime Melanie was feeling less teary, for the sleep had done her good. But the maid didn't at all like the look of her mistress's neck, which had swollen a lot more and was warm to the touch.

"The best thing was his lordship saying that you were not to have any visitors," the maid said. "Your mama came this afternoon, absolutely demanding to see you, for she had heard about what happened in the park. She really had her nose put out of joint when she was told that orders were for absolutely no visitors."

"I'm glad that they didn't let her come up," Melanie told her, "for I don't really think I could face scolds from both Mama and Denby in the same day."

"Now, don't you start worrying again, milady. Everything is going to come out grand in the end, just you wait and see," Bridget assured her. "I understand from Mr. Fowlkes that his lordship isn't expected back until late. And I'd think that he wouldn't disturb you tonight after all the upset, for it was him as ordered the sedative for you."

Remembering the fury in which Denby had left her chamber, Melanie did not think that he would disturb her for many nights to come. It seemed ironic, she decided, that just a couple of days ago she had thought it impossible to get him angry—or even annoyed. Now she knew better.

Denby did go to her chamber that night, however, when he came home, and was surprised to see Bridget doing some mending while her mistress slept fitfully.

He went over to the bed, and when he saw Melanie's flushed face and the bandage around her neck, he turned to the maid and beckoned her to follow him out of the chamber.

"She looks feverish to me," he told her, frowning. "And what is wrong with her neck?"

"She was stung by a bee, milord," Bridget said to him accusingly. "It startled her and made her horse gallop. She never did it deliberately, like you thought."

"Dammit, why didn't she tell me?" he asked angrily.

"It didn't sound to me as if you gave her a chance to," the maid said boldly.

"Has she been stung before?" Denby asked. "It looks as if she might be having a bad reaction to it. Some people do, you know, and it can be dangerous."

"I think she has been stung before, milord, but I don't recall that it did more than swell up and hurt for a day or so. But she doesn't look very well. That's why I stayed with her, for I thought you might stop in to see her," Bridget said, "and I'd have knocked on your door if you hadn't."

Denby nodded. "Are you sure that you got all of the sting out?" he asked, frowning.

"I'd not swear to it, milord, but I thought I did," the maid said, looking to him for suggestions. "I did save it, though, for I felt she might need to prove it to you."

He swore under his breath.

"Go get it," he said, "and let me take a look at it."

When she brought it, he took one look and said, "I don't think it's all out. Go downstairs and boil a pan of water. I'll stoke up this fire, and it can keep simmering on there."

When she had gone to do his bidding, he went to a desk drawer and took out a dangerous-looking knife, which he placed on top of the desk.

Then he heard Melanie's voice and hurried into her chamber.

"What is it, my love?" he asked softly.

"I hurt," she told him, frowning, "and I'm hot."

She started to put her hand up to the bandage, but he took hold of it in his own and said, "Try not to touch your neck, my dear."

This time Melanie awakened at the sound of his voice, and Denby was glad to note that she sounded quite lucid as she asked, "What is wrong with my neck? Why does it hurt so?"

"It's where you were stung. I don't think Bridget got it all out, and it's causing some swelling. Why didn't you tell me about the bee?" he asked gently.

"You didn't give me a chance. You just decided that I had deliberately galloped to bring shame on myself," she said quietly.

"I suppose I did at that," he admitted. "And now on top of everything else I'm going to have to hurt you to try to get at the rest of that sting. Thank God it's on the side of the neck and not on the front, or I'd not dare touch it."

She tried to smile, but it was not her best effort.

"It probably hurts you to talk also," Denby said, "so let me do it instead. I'm very sorry I shouted at you without finding out what had actually happened, and somehow I'll try to make it up to you, I promise," he said.

Melanie nodded, and reached out a hand to touch his face, as though understanding how dreadful he felt. Then Bridget came in with the pan of boiling water.

After that, Denby took complete command, giving Bridget orders as though she was on a battlefield with him.

From his point of view, it was one of the worst things he had ever had to do, for he could hardly bear the idea of hurting Melanie, but it was all over in minutes, the rest of the sting was out, and the small incision disinfected thoroughly before being bandaged once more.

All he could do now was wait and see if the fever went away, and if it did not, he meant to get the finest doctor in London out of his bed early in the morning.

This proved unnecessary, however, for in just a few hours it was obvious that Melanie was much more comfortable, and by breakfasttime she was complaining that she was hungry, but Denby would only allow her to swallow a thin gruel at hourly intervals.

When he was sure she was going to be all right, he left for a meeting, but not before giving Bridget strict orders as to what she might and might not do.

She did have one visitor, however, for even Fowlkes could not deter Lord Somerfield.

"When your mama said that you were not seeing any visitors, I was not really too concerned," he told Melanie, "but I was surprised when she could not gain admittance again today, and became very worried about you."

"It was Denby who gave the instructions, Papa," Melanie said hoarsely, "for I was extremely shaken up after such a close call. You know that I've always hated sidesaddles, and I believe that when we get out of town I shall try to persuade Broderick to let me ride astride, as I used to do at home."

"That horse really did run away with you, didn't she?" her father said. "I don't know where your mama got the idea that you were just wanting a gallop and Denby covered for you."

"Papa, I've never been as frightened in all my life as I was when I realized that I simply couldn't bring Lady under control," Melanie told him. "We usually gallop in the morning when we go riding, with the park empty, but we hadn't been out that morning, and I suppose Lady still wanted her gallop, and thought I was permitting her when the bee stung me. Then, when Denby came racing up on Prince, she became excited and was determined to beat him. I soon found that a woman is quite helpless on a sidesaddle atop a horse that is out of control."

"Well, no one would doubt what happened if they could see you now," he told her, "but you sound quite jaunty, if a little husky, and I'm sure you'll be as right as rain in a day or two."

"Thank you for sending me the money, Papa. Is everything all right with Michael now?"

"It will be," he said firmly. "As I said at the time, I'm

glad you came around that morning, for though I knew he wasn't looking good, and was coming in very late each night, I thought it was just young men sowing a few wild oats. It was a gambling ring, though, that had got its hooks in him—or at least was beginning to.'' He patted his daughter's hand and then got to his feet. "I'll let your mama know that you're all right and will be out and about again in a day or so. Just take care of yourself in the future.''

He stooped and gave her a kiss on the cheek, then let himself out of the room.

Fifteen minutes later, Denby entered the chamber.

"I met your father as I was coming in,'' he told her.

"I'm sorry, Broderick, but I had to countermand your order for Papa, or I believe he would have broken the door down,'' Melanie said apologetically.

"I don't blame him. I would have too, if it was my daughter,'' he said. "It was your mother I was trying to keep out—along with Lady Jersey and a few other ladies who came around, but have never called before.''

He crossed the room toward her, checked the bandage around her neck, then bent down and moved the shawl from her shoulder, revealing the bruises on her arm, which he had noticed last night. He swore softly to himself.

"Forgive me, my dear,'' he begged, "for I didn't know I had done that to you. I certainly didn't mean to.''

Something seemed to melt inside of her. "Of course,'' she said. "I know you didn't, and it really doesn't hurt anymore.''

He bent down and touched his lips to hers. "Do you feel better now?'' he asked.

She nodded. "Much better now,'' she told him.

He sat down on the edge of her bed. "Your father tells me that you ride astride at home, or at least you did when you were younger,'' he remarked. "I'll agree to it if you can have some sort of a divided skirt made, for I don't really want to see you walking around in trousers.''

"I'll come up with something that meets with your approval,'' she told him, smiling now.

"You do that, and I'll have a saddle made for your use in the country," he promised, then asked, "Do you feel like seeing your sister tomorrow? She wrote me a note asking if she might call on you."

"But of course," Melanie told him. "You're not still stopping me from seeing people, are you? I thought it was just yesterday and today."

"It was," he agreed. "I think your sister is trying to be amusing, that's all."

13

When Martha called the next day, she was anything but amusing. She said she had brought a message from Michael, who apparently blamed Melanie for the fact that he had forgotten to close the door of their father's study. It was a verbal message, however, and Martha told her that he had sworn to get even with his older sister.

"He said that I was to tell you he is still going to the gambling club, though he will, of course, deny it if you say anything to Mama or Papa," Martha said, adding, "and he wanted you to know that Denby's visits to Seymour Place are getting longer, for he now stays with his mistress at least four hours each night."

They were sitting in the music room, for Melanie had been playing the piano when Martha called, and it had, fortunately, been designed so that little sound escaped its closed door.

"Do you get some kind of pleasure out of bringing this type of information to me?" Melanie asked her sister curiously.

"Of course I do," the younger girl told her. "You stole him away from me, and I am glad that you are not enjoying a happy marriage."

"Did you love him so very much?" Melanie asked the girl. "I didn't think you cared for him at all, but merely wanted his title."

"Love him?" Martha looked incredulous at Melanie's naiveté. "Of course I didn't. People like us should never marry for love, you idiot. I know that Mama and Papa did, but it's simply not the thing to do anymore. All my friends mean to marry for money and title, and then have a series of discreet affairs once they've given birth to an heir.''

All Melanie wanted now was for her sister to go away and make her mischief somewhere else. She wondered how much of this was true, and how much Martha had invented, but it was impossible to tell. Even the story about Denby did not sound quite natural, for she couldn't imagine him spending four hours with his mistress. What could they possibly do all that time?

To her relief, Martha suddenly stood up. ''I've got to go now,'' she declared, ''for I promised Mama that I'd be back in time to go with her on afternoon calls. They're really the most boring visits imaginable, but one has to keep on the good side of the patronesses of Almack's. At least I have. You quite obviously don't care what anyone thinks about you.''

When she had left, Melanie felt quite drained, and hoped that her sister would not condescend to pay her any more calls of such a nature, for she simply did not know how much she could believe and how much was a figment of Martha's most active imagination.

She turned back to the piano and started to play the second of Dr. William Boyce's Eight Symphonies in Eight Parts, and was so deeply immersed in it that she did not hear Denby enter the room until he bent down and placed a kiss on her cheek.

He startled her, and she turned around quickly, a flush of pleasure staining her cheeks.

''I wondered if you might care to go for a drive with me in the park,'' he suggested. ''It would give us a chance to find out what, if anything, people are saying about us.''

''I'm really not sure that I want to know,'' Melanie said, but she was smiling, for at this moment her wounded pride needed the kind of bolstering a drive with Denby could very well accomplish.

''I promise to hold your hand,'' he told her, ''and not let anyone start to cross-examine you.''

''They're far more likely to just make nasty little insinuations,'' she told him somewhat wearily.

''Then I'll stop them doing that too. I understand that your sister called and you did not even offer her any form of refreshment," Denby said. "Was it so bad?"

Melanie looked startled. "It never occurred to me to offer her anything, and I'm sure she did not think of it either."

"You didn't answer my question," he said, a puzzled frown on his face. "Was it such an unpleasant visit?"

"Martha is, I believe, a rather unhappy young lady," she told him thoughtfully. "She thinks that Mama and Papa are quite old-fashioned because theirs was a love match."

"Oh, I wouldn't worry about that," Denby said, smiling to himself. "Most girls of her age think their parents a trifle old-fashioned. She'll grow out of it as soon as she develops a romantic attachment to some gentleman. You mustn't think that she was ever in love with me, my dear, for I know quite well that she was not."

"Oh, I knew that also," Melanie told him, "for had it been the case, I would not have married you."

He shook his head, and his eyes twinkled merrily.

"That is not true. Do you think that I would have had no say in the matter? Run upstairs and put on something warm, and I will meantime see if I can play this piece at least half as well as you were doing," he said a little ruefully, and took his seat on the bench she had just vacated.

Once she was away from Denby's self-assured manner, however, Melanie started to feel scared just thinking about how the members of the *ton* might behave toward her. Then she scolded herself sharply. If they tried to be unpleasant, Denby would make sure they knew what had actually happened, and she would, after all, have to face them sometime.

Bridget was not in her bedchamber, so she quickly slipped into her light beige pelisse, which had a ruffle around the neck that almost hid the bee sting from sight. Then she put on a new pale blue bonnet trimmed in beige, and tied the bow so that it covered the rest of her neck on that side. Picking up her kid gloves and reticule, she hurried down the stairs, for she wanted to steal into the music room and listen to Denby's performance on the piano.

She knew he had not heard her enter, and was completely

concentrating on the work before him, so she closed the door quietly and stood there listening. As she had been sure would be the case, he played extremely well, and she decided there and then to try to obtain some music, before they left London, that they could play together. It would, she felt, be one way in which she might be able to get a little closer to him.

Then she heard the faint sound of a commotion in the hall, and opened the door just a crack.

"Now, Fowlkes, just make sure that these boxes go up to my chamber, and these others go . . ." There was a pause, and then, "You didn't tell me that my son was home. Leave everything until I come back."

Melanie stepped away from the door as the dowager Lady Denby came hurrying in, her arms outstretched.

"Broderick, I thought you'd be down at Whitehall or somewhere at this hour, dear boy," she said, stepping into his arms as he jumped up from the piano stool. "It's so good to see you. But where is Melanie?"

"Right here, my lady," Melanie said, stepping forward. "I'm so pleased that you've arrived at last."

"But you look as though you were just going out," the dowager said, giving her daughter-in-law a warm hug also. "Please don't let me keep you, for I want you to completely forget that I'm here and do just what you would normally do. It's the only way we'll all be comfortable together in one house."

"We were just going to take a carriage ride in the park, Mama. You see, Melanie had an unfortunate incident in the park a couple of days ago, when a bee stung her and her horse ran off with her. She almost had a very bad accident, and I want to make quite sure that none of the gossips turn it into something it wasn't."

"In that case, take me with you, for I'm not at all tired, and I do so hate all this confusion with the baggage. Now I won't need to feel at all guilty about leaving it to my abigail to attend to," she said with obvious delight.

While Denby went off to make sure the right carriage had been sent for, his mama steered Melanie through to the drawing room.

"I must say that you are looking very well, my dear Melanie. Married life must really agree with you. Do sit here and then we won't need to shout," she said, taking a seat on the large sofa and patting the cushion by her side. "Do I detect a little more about this accident than meets the eye?"

Melanie had always enjoyed the dowager's company, and was delighted that she had arrived at last, but she had had no idea that she was so intuitive.

She nodded. "Denby hadn't realized that a bee had stung my neck," she said as she removed her bonnet for the dowager to see the small wound and the red and puffy place around it. "And if he thought I was deliberately galloping, then some of the *ton* may have thought so also. It very nearly turned into a bad accident, however, for my mare was out of control, and I was rather frightened."

The dowager patted Melanie's hand. "I'm sure you'll have no problem once people realize what happened, my dear, so you need not worry about it. Now, you mustn't think I mean to interfere in all you do, for I am not going to become one of those dreadful mothers-in-law who won't leave their sons alone. But in this situation I know that my presence can lend you almost as much countenance as can Denby's."

Melanie nodded. "I realize that, and I am indeed very grateful," she said softly.

The dowager shrugged. "You don't need to be, for I was forever in hot water when I was young, and I must admit that I sometimes deserved it. Fortunately, I was never caught," she said with a twinkle.

"Are you lovely ladies ready?" Denby inquired from the door. "Your carriage awaits you."

Melanie allowed the dowager to go first, and as she reached Denby he murmured, "I meant that, for you do look very lovely, my dear."

Denby sat in the middle of the carriage, with the ladies on either side of him, and once they entered the park, the poor coachman had a terrible time of it, for it seemed that they could not go more than a yard or two at a time before a carriage would stop them, either to greet the dowager or to ask how Melanie felt. This was, however, the very reason they had come out this afternoon.

Lady Jersey was the one Melanie had been dreading meeting, and when she hailed them and had her carriage draw over to them, she cringed inside.

After greeting the dowager effusively, Lady Jersey turned to Melanie.

"And how are you feeling after such a close call, my dear?" she asked, eyeing her carefully. "I hear that a bee was the apparent cause of it."

"I feel very well now, my lady, but I don't believe I ever felt so frightened in all my life. I was sure that I was going to fall off, with my foot caught in the stirrup, and be dragged," she said quite truthfully.

"How dreadful," Lady Jersey said with obvious surprise. "Was that really a possibility, Denby?"

"A very definite one," he said, looking almost as worried as he had felt at the time, "for the mare seemed to be almost flying. Melanie is feeling much better now, though, aren't you, my dear?"

He took his wife's hand in his and held it while he looked warmly into her eyes, and Lady Jersey exchanged a knowing look with the dowager.

"And you, too, are looking extremely well, my lady," Lady Jersey went on. "Have you been in town long?"

"About an hour at the most," the dowager said, smiling, "and I'm afraid Melanie may always bear that scar on her neck, but it's a small price to pay for what could have been such a terrible accident."

"A scar from a bee sting?" Lady Jersey sounded a little dubious.

"I'm afraid so, Sally," Denby said. "The sting had broken off, and we dared not leave part of it inside, for she had started to run a fever."

"My goodness," Lady Jersey said, looking quite contrite, "and I thought it was just an excuse for rather naughty behavior on her part. I am so sorry, my dear."

She leaned over and patted Melanie's hand, then ordered her coachman to drive on.

After a while Melanie was feeling emotionally exhausted, and thought that they must have stopped to speak to almost every single member of the *ton* by now. Then she saw the Somerfields' carriage approaching, with her mama and Martha inside.

Lady Somerfield greeted the dowager first. "How long have you been back in town, my lady?" she asked, a little curious.

"I arrived just today," the dowager told her.

"Then you were not in time to hear of the exhibition my older daughter made of herself the other day?" Lady Somerfield asked her.

"I have heard from my son and Melanie about the dreadful accident that was narrowly averted, my lady," the dowager replied, "and I am grateful that it did not turn into the tragedy it might so easily have been."

"I cannot believe that it was anything so serious," Lady Somerfield insisted, "for Martha said she saw what happened, didn't you, my dear?"

"Well, I didn't actually see it, Mama," her younger daughter stammered, "for I was in a different area of the park at the time, but I was told that it was not at all serious."

"Do you mean to tell me that you heard your sister had an accident, and you didn't go to see how she was, my girl? You took someone else's word for it, when you were actually in the park at the time?" the dowager asked, a shocked expression on her face.

Martha looked decidedly embarrassed, and when her mama turned to her in anger, she burst into tears.

Denby quietly told his coachman to move along.

The dowager heaved a sigh of relief. "I shall be glad to get home now and have a nice cup of tea, and I am sure you will also, my dear Melanie."

"Take the Oxford Street exit from the park, Tom," Denby called to his coachman, "and we'll go home along Park Lane." Then he turned to the two ladies. "I, too, have had enough for one day. I thought it went awfully well, for the most part, but I never realized just how much of a shrew your sister is becoming, Melanie."

Feeling that some explanation was necessary, Melanie said, "Both she and my brother seem to have become involved with the wrong kind of friends, but when the Season gets under way, they're bound to meet a much nicer group of people who have some sound common sense. At least, I hope so."

"I'm not sure I understand what you mean," Denby told her.

Melanie sighed. "It's difficult to explain, Broderick. Apparently Michael has been going with friends to a gambling house and losing a lot of money, and Martha seems to have met young ladies in search of rich, titled husbands whom they care nothing for, and mean to give them heirs, then go their own way."

"It's probably just part of growing up," the dowager said kindly, "and those young ladies will change their ideas when they realize how foolish they are being."

"Have you any idea where Michael has been doing his gambling?" Denby asked, frowning, "for I've never noticed him in any of the usual places."

There was a silence; then Melanie finally said softly, "I believe it's somewhere on Seymour Place."

"I didn't know there was a gambling house there." Denby frowned as if trying to recall where it might be. "Unless he means the one on the corner of Curzon Street and Seymour Place. If that's the one, then he really is in trouble."

"Do some of the windows overlook Seymour?" Melanie asked, and when he nodded, she said, "Then that must be the one."

Denby looked away, a puzzled expression on his face.

Turning to the dowager, Melanie asked, "You will be in for supper tonight, won't you, my lady, for I'd like to ask Cook to serve some of your favorite dishes, if it's not too late."

"That's very sweet of you, my child, but it's not really necessary to disturb the meal you planned for this evening. I would love to have dinner with you, but I'm quite content to have whatever has been ordered," she told her. "I hope it won't be for an hour or two yet, however, for I believe I would like to rest for a while in my room first.''

"Of course, you must be dreadfully tired after all that traveling, Mama," Denby put in. "We rarely eat until eight o'clock, though, so I think you'll probably be more than a little rested by then. If not, however, don't hesitate to say so, and Melanie will have a meal sent up to your chamber.'' He sighed heavily. "I'm afraid that I have appointments this evening, for both dinner and afterward, that simply cannot be canceled, but I know that my wife will be glad of your company, won't you, my dear?''

Melanie's smile did not quite reach her eyes, for she had thought that surely he would have changed his plans for once, and stayed home this evening. "There are times when I'd be glad of almost anyone's company of an evening," she said with a decided tartness in her voice, "but having dinner with your mama is a pleasure I have been looking forward to for some time.''

She did not see him again that evening, but did enjoy dinner with the dowager, whom she had known only slightly during the preparations for the wedding, but whose kindness on the actual wedding day she had not forgotten.

"Has my son been going out every evening since you came back from Devon?'' the dowager asked when they were sipping their tea afterward.

"Very nearly every evening, my lady,'' Melanie told her, the expression in her eyes revealing her feelings in the matter.

The dowager frowned. "I don't at all like my son's wife calling me 'my lady,' and I would not, of course, try to usurp your own mama's title, but I wonder if perhaps you might like to call me 'Maman,' for I am part French, you know.''

"I'd love to do so,'' Melanie said. "But I think I should add, Maman, that Broderick did tell me before we left Devon, that he would be out a great deal on government work. I simply did not realize that he meant almost every evening.''

"But what does he do each night?'' the dowager asked, quite obviously puzzled.

"He tells me that he dines with the prime minister and

meets with people about that wretched Corn Bill, and he says that it will soon be passed by both houses and we can then return to Sussex. Those are the things he says, Maman, but I am afraid that he . . .'' She shook her head, too close to tears to continue.

The dowager smiled sympathetically. ''Are you perhaps allowing your loneliness to interfere with your own good sense, my dear? I am quite sure that my son would never do anything to hurt you. The men in our family are always very gentle and *galant* where their ladies are concerned,'' she assured her daughter-in-law, then, to her own dismay, was forced to stifle a yawn.

Melanie, having recovered her composure, said calmly, ''Of course they are, Maman, but I can see that I am keeping you up when you should have been in your bed long ago, getting some well-earned rest after your journey.''

She rose and offered her arm to the older lady. ''Shall we assist each other up the stairs, for I, too, am quite tired after the events of the day.''

She insisted on taking the dowager to the door of her suite and putting her into the hands of an elderly abigail; then she went back to her own bedchamber and allowed Bridget to get her ready for bed.

''Shall I put out the candle, or are you going to read for a while?'' the maid asked.

''Leave it as it is, Bridget,'' Melanie said. ''I may read for just a little while, I believe.''

Sometime later she awoke and saw in the light of the still-burning candle that it was three o'clock in the morning. She could hear movements in Denby's chamber, and assumed that he had just come home, but she felt sure that he would not come to her at this hour.

Her book was lying on the counterpane, and she picked it up again, but the words blurred as tears filled her eyes, and when no further sound came from her husband's chamber, she leaned over and snuffed the candle, but it was a long time before she went back to sleep.

When Bridget brought in a morning tea tray several hours later, she asked, ''Will you be riding this morning, milady?''

Melanie shook her head. "I doubt that I shall need my riding habits now until we return to the country," she said, remembering that Denby had told her that he was sending Lady back to Devon. "Just get out my lemon gown and the things to go with it, and I'll ring for you when I need assistance."

She was just finishing her second cup of tea, however, when there was a tap on the adjoining door and Denby came in wearing his riding habit. He raised his eyebrows when he saw that she was still abed.

"Do you not feel well, my dear?" he asked, smiling. "Did my mama perhaps tire you out last night?"

"Not at all, but you told me that you would be sending Lady back to the country that day," she reminded him. "Did you not do so?"

He sat down on the edge of the bed and placed a hand on either side of her face, then bent his head to kiss her mouth most tenderly.

"Don't you know by now that my bark is far worse than my bite?" he asked, and when she shook her head, he added, "I spend little enough time with you at the moment, without having to forgo our morning ride. In any case, after that fright you need to get back on a horse again. Get up, lazybones, and I'll ring for Bridget, then have a cup of tea downstairs while I wait for you."

He tugged on the bell rope, then went out of the room, and Melanie leapt out of bed and hurried over to the washstand.

When she entered the breakfast room in a smart black riding habit, he pulled out his watch and looked at it. "Fifteen minutes! That must be a record, I'm sure," he said, grinning mischievously as he took her arm. "Come along, let's go around to the stables. Now that you're all ready, I do hope that Lady is no worse for her gallop around the park."

The mare was not only uninjured but also most happy to see her, nuzzling up to her jacket in search of the apple she knew now to expect, and eager for some exercise when they reached the park.

"How was Mama last night?" Denby asked when they

slowed the horses to a walk and conversation was possible once more. "Did she have dinner downstairs?"

"Yes, she did, but she was very tired when she went to bed. I think that perhaps she will sleep late this morning," she told him.

"I would seriously doubt it," he said, "but then, of course, you do not yet know my mama as I do. She was a wonderfully loving wife and mother, and when Papa died, she devoted herself to the remaining family. Unfortunately, however, she got the idea into her head that I must get married, which was the reason for all that entertaining back and forth last winter."

"Were you like me, and didn't want to get married, Broderick?" she asked him.

"It wasn't a case of not wanting to get married, my love, but simply not wanting to do so at that particular time, when I was much too busy to carefully select a wife for myself," he tried to explain.

"And so you got stuck with me," she said a little glumly.

"Stop fishing for compliments, young woman," he teased. "As I've told you before, except for a few small problems, I am delighted with the way things have worked out."

"What kind of small problems?" she asked in an equally small voice, averting her eyes.

"Oh, it seems that my bride has an extraordinary tendency to disturb my equilibrium—in fact, I cannot recall a period when my relatively peaceful existence was so frequently challenged," he said, a hint of amusement in his voice. "I have even wondered at times if she bears me some kind of deep-seated grudge that I know nothing about."

"What a strange idea. Do you perhaps have a guilty conscience?" Melanie suggested.

"None that I know of, but I believe that one of the problems is that she is left alone a great deal, particularly at night, and I can of course understand her annoyance at being neglected," he murmured. "But if that is all that is wrong, I can assure her that in less than two weeks now we will return to the country, and I will be under her feet so much that she will wish that she could get rid of me for even an hour or two."

"If your peace of mind is so disturbed when she is in town, why don't you send her to the country for the next two weeks, for she might prefer living there to living in London," Melanie suggested.

"Pure selfishness, I suppose, for I am so much happier when she is with me than I've ever been before in my life," he said, his voice deep with feeling.

Melanie turned then to look up at him, and he saw the tears that were glistening in her eyes. He reached out a hand to caress her cheek, and she leaned her face against it while a tear rolled slowly down and into his palm. But after a few minutes Lady became restless, and they had no alternative but to move apart.

"Come on, my love," Denby said, "let's get our gallop in before anyone disturbs us, and then I'll take you back home. I wish I could have you to myself for a few minutes when we get there, but I know that Mama will be already up and about, and most probably eating breakfast."

"That's all right," Melanie told him, "for I enjoy her company and she'll be a big help when you're gone in the evenings."

Nothing had been settled, but they both felt better for just being together and talking. But for Melanie this lasted only until she reached her chamber and remembered Mrs. White-head on Seymour Place.

14

Denby was quite correct, for his mama was eating breakfast when they returned to the house, and she appeared completely rested.

"I had a wonderful night's sleep in my own bed," she told them, "and now I'm going to leave you two alone while I write a few notes, for not quite everyone was out in the park yesterday. Will you be gone all day, Broderick?"

"I'm afraid so, Mama," he said apologetically as he helped himself and Melanie to some breakfast, "and I'll be out this evening also, but the following night I am keeping clear so that I may dine with you ladies here."

"In that case, I think we had better have a very special dinner tomorrow night," Melanie said a little tartly. "A double celebration, in fact, of your mama's arrival and of your finally spending an evening at home. I'll order all our favorite dishes."

Denby reached for Melanie's hand and squeezed it. "I'm sorry, my dear, but it will be over very soon now, and you'll then see so much of me that you'll be sorry you did not take better advantage of your freedom when it was there."

He ate quickly, and left shortly afterward, for he really did have an important appointment, and as the front door closed behind him, Melanie went in search of his mama.

She found her in the sun room at the back of the house, where she herself often spent time working out menus and the like.

"I have decided that it's time I had a few simpler gowns made for the country," she told the dowager, "for it would

194

seem that we will be going there very soon now, and everything I wear here seems a little too elaborate.

"Just before the Little Season began last year, before Mama and my sister came to town, I visited a young French modiste who is not at all well-known, someone my abigail had heard about, and I believe I will go back to her. The gowns she made were quite lovely and cost only a fraction of what Madame LeBlanc charges."

There was a distinct twinkle in the dowager's eyes. "I was not aware that my son's wife needed to practice such strict economy, my dear," she remarked.

"It's not that at all," Melanie asserted. "This modiste is truly French, and is not really established as yet. I believe in patronizing people who really need the money, and I'd like to see her business pick up considerably so that she can employ more seamstresses. I mean to see if I can make her name a little better known."

"I cannot but agree with you, Melanie," the dowager murmured, still smiling, "for the modiste I have used for years now charges me the most outrageous prices, and I have heard that her seamstresses work for practically nothing. If you mean to go there this morning, I would very much like to accompany you, if I may."

"Of course, for I would appreciate both your company and your opinion on the styles that suit me," Melanie told her, delighted that the dowager wanted to come with her. "She's not on Bond Street, but neither is she in an unsavory location. She is on Chapel Steet East, not far from Shepherds Market and the Mayfair Chapel."

They decided to go that morning, and Melanie ordered the coach to be brought around, but before joining her mama-in-law inside, she had a word with the coachman, asking him to go by way of Seymour Place and Curzon Street, for she wanted to see what that area looked like.

"I'll 'ave to turn around at the bottom of Seymour Place, milady," he said, "for there's no way for the carriage to go through, but it's plenty wide enough."

She did not quite know what he meant, though she was,

of course, familiar with South Audley Street, which they proceeded along, and, of course, Curzon Street at its foot. Instead of turning left when they reached the latter street, however, the coach turned right, and then swung left into Seymour Place.

Melanie saw at once the large house on the corner, which had windows on both streets, and realized that this must be the gambling house her brother frequented. It was the only house on the east side of Seymour Place, for beyond it was a long row of trees with an iron fence in front.

On the west side of Seymour Place was a row of seven houses, and as she looked at them, Melanie wondered if Mrs. Whitehead might even now be looking out of one of the windows.

She glanced at the dowager, who had a questioning smile on her face.

"I just wanted to see where the gambling house is that my brother has apparently been frequenting, Maman," Melanie explained. "It must be this one on the corner, with its windows overlooking both streets."

"At this hour it does not look at all disreputable," the dowager remarked, "but I assume from your tone that it's not a very nice place."

"I would not know such things myself, of course," Melanie assured her, "but when I told Broderick where it was, he indicated something of the sort."

The modiste's establishment was quite close by, and a moment later the carriage stopped outside Marie Dubois's small establishment, and the young proprietress, an attractive dark-haired, brown-eyed woman in an elegant black gown, came out to greet them.

She offered them tea, which was very carefully served by a diminutive girl of about ten years who was dressed in black with a snow-white apron, and looked like a tiny image of her mama.

"I do not employ child workers," Madame Debois said, smiling, "but my little Simone enjoys to serve the tea to my patrons as much as to her dolls. How can I assist you today,

Lady Denby? I read in the newspaper of your lovely wedding, and would like to wish you much happiness.''

''Thank you, Marie,'' Melanie said. ''This is my husband's mama, the dowager Lady Denby. I would like some gowns for the country, for I expect to return there very shortly, and prefer to wear something simpler than the ones I wear in London.''

Madame Dubois began to bring out bolts of fabrics and fashion books for them to look through, making suggestions where she thought it necessary.

''If you will stand for a moment, I'll just measure you again, my lady, in case there have been any changes,'' she said, giving Melanie a critical glance.

She put the tape around her a second time before asking, ''Is my lady perhaps . . . increasing, as you sometimes call it? I measure more here, and here, than before,'' she said, pointing to the bust and the waistline.

''I don't think so,'' Melanie said, somewhat confused. ''I feel very well, so I don't suppose that I am.''

The dowager frowned at her. ''But surely you would know if the menses still come regularly,'' she suggested.

''Oh, that,'' Melanie said airily. ''I've always been most irregular, so I never think about it, but Bridget did ask me the same question a couple of weeks ago—and so did Papa, as I recall.''

''Do you perhaps have the tenderness here?'' the French-woman asked, pointing to her breasts.

''Yes, I do, sometimes, but I thought that was probably because . . .'' Melanie hedged, her cheeks flushing with embarrassment. She had thought they were tender because of the frequent attention they'd been receiving.

The dowager Lady Denby was watching her daughter-in-law's expressions and chuckling softly to herself.

''Oh, my lady,'' Madame Dubois said, smiling widely, ''I design a gown when I have my little one, that is perfect for such a . . . condition—is that what you say?''

''Did you really? Whether I need it now or not, I would be most interested in seeing it,'' Melanie told her, then, recalling something else she had wanted to discuss with the modiste, she added, "and I also need you to design a riding habit that has a divided skirt so that I can ride astride in the country. My husband says that I may have one, as long as he approves the design—as being ladylike, I suppose."

"But, Melanie," the dowager said, now not even trying to conceal her laughter, "if you really are enceinte, my dear, you'll not need a riding habit for the next nine months, for my son will never permit you to get on a horse in such a condition."

"But that's completely ridiculous," Melanie said, without giving sufficient thought to it, "and in any case, it's probably nothing more than my having eaten a little too much lately, for I always eat more when I'm un . . . when I eat alone."

The modiste and Melanie discussed the design of the special gown, which consisted of gussets that were quite easily let out as the body enlarged, and slots with tape or ribbon threaded through on the inside. Madame Dubois also promised to have a complete design of a divided skirt, made up in a thin cotton fabric that would be unpicked and used for a pattern if it met with the earl's approval.

While this was going on, the dowager was looking over the fabrics and designs and making notes for when the modiste had finished with her daughter-in-law.

This was quite soon, for it became obvious that very little could be accomplished until Melanie had the time to sit down and talk with Bridget on the subject of dates.

While her mama-in-law spoke with the modiste, Melanie went outside and sent the coachman on an errand, telling him he need not hurry, for they could not possibly be finished here in less than a half-hour. She made herself comfortable in the waiting room there, and began to look through some books on the latest fashions.

When the outer door opened and someone entered, she did not as first look up, thinking it to be some messenger, for she had not heard a carriage stop outside.

But when the newcomer took a seat in the pleasant waiting room, Melanie glanced up and saw an attractive woman of about thirty years of age, fashionably gowned, and with an air of quiet dignity about her.

She smiled and wished her a good day, and the woman smiled back, murmuring a greeting.

Madame Dubois put her head around the door to see who had entered, and called, "Good morning, Mrs. Whitehead. I'll be about fifteen more minutes. Will you wait, or would you rather come back a little later?"

"I'll wait," Mrs. Whitehead said in a quiet, well-modulated voice.

Melanie knew that she should not stare, but she could not help it, for this was the woman whose bed Denby preferred to her own. What did he find so appealing about her? She tried to look away, but her eyes were drawn back to her until the woman finally asked, "Is there something I can do for you, my lady?"

Melanie wanted to tell her to stop seeing her husband, but of course she must not do so. Instead she said, "I believe you are acquainted with my husband. I am Lady Denby."

The soft brown eyes that looked at Melanie were not in the least unfriendly. Then, "I was acquainted with your husband before he became affianced," she corrected quietly, "but when that happened our relationship of quite long standing was terminated in a most satisfactory manner. I have not seen Lord Denby since."

"But he goes to a house on Seymour Place, I know," Melanie blurted out, her cheeks turning pink.

"He frequently had business with a gentleman two doors away, and this possibly continues, but it was something to do with the government, I believe, and not a personal matter," Mrs. Whitehead told her, adding, "I can assure you that your husband is an honorable man, my dear."

Melanie blinked away the tears that threatened. "Thank you," she said, "I'm awfully glad I met you like this."

"So am I, if it has helped clear up a most unfortunate misunderstanding, and I wish you both a long and happy marriage," Mrs. Whitehead murmured.

As she finished speaking, the dowager Lady Denby and Madame Dubois came in.

"I'll expect you back for a fitting in two days, then, my lady," the modiste was saying to the dowager as they approached, "and perhaps you, Lady Denby, will have solved your little problem by then?"

"Perhaps," Melanie said, smiling brightly, "but if not, you will have my measurements and I have the samples, so I will send word to you from the country."

The carriage was waiting outside once more, and as it proceeded the short distance back to Denby House, Melanie felt as if she was in a world of her own—an extremely happy one.

"Will you be pleased to start a family so soon, if that should be the case, my dear?" the dowager asked, smiling.

"Of course, I'd love to have children of my own, and I'm sure Broderick would be happy about it also. I'll have to find out if Bridget wrote down my dates, I suppose, but it seems very early to talk about it."

"It is a little early, my dear Melanie," the older lady said, smiling as she tried to recall the events preceding the births of her own children. "But it's never too soon for you to begin taking care of yourself, once you start to have other signs, and I'm not at all sure that riding, particularly galloping, is a good idea at the moment."

"Perhaps not, but I would like to tell Broderick myself, when I am quite sure, of course, Maman," Melanie said softly, hoping the dowager would agree.

"But of course you must, my dear. I would not dream of spoiling your pleasure, and in any case, it is your prerogative. You will tell me what Bridget says, however, won't you?" the dowager begged.

"I most certainly will, Maman, for I wouldn't think of keeping it from you," Melanie assured her.

When they arrived home, Melanie excused herself and went directly to her chamber, where, as it happened, Bridget was going carefully through her wardrobe to make sure that she had not overlooked any garment that needed some attention.

"Ah, I'm so glad you're here, Bridget," Melanie said, "for I want to talk to you. Come over here and sit down."

There was a twinkle in the maid's eyes as she perched on the edge of the bed, facing her mistress, who had sunk down into a small armchair.

"Do you think that I could possibly be enceinte?" Melanie asked gravely.

"Of course you could," Bridget said, smiling now. "With the way you've always been, early one month and late another, it's difficult to tell exactly how far on you might or might not be. But you've only been married just over a couple of months, you know."

"I know, and though I've gained a little, it could be because of Cook's expertise, for the food here is always most delicious—she's much more proficient than Mama's cooks ever were."

"You've also got a look about you," Bridget said, "particularly today, and if I was a betting person, which the good Lord knows that I'm not, I'd be putting my money on you."

Melanie went downstairs then to join her mama-in-law for a light luncheon, but she declined the invitation to accompany her on some afternoon calls.

"I won't be in town much longer now, and with my aptitude for saying or doing the wrong thing, I believe it best to see as few people as possible before I go," she said with a mischievous grin. "Then, when I finally return to London, my supposed indiscretions will all have been forgotten and I'll be an old married lady."

"While on that particular subject," the dowager said, giving her daughter-in-law a calculating look, "do you always converse so freely with ladies of doubtful reputation? I most certainly knew who Mrs. Whitehead was, but I would never for a moment have acknowledged her. You, however, appeared to be having a lengthy discussion with her."

Melanie examined the food on her plate most carefully, pushing it around with her fork, before lifting her head and asking, "Oh, was that her name? I'm afraid I must have missed it when the modiste asked her to wait. She seemed to be a most pleasant person, and she was, in fact, very kind. However, we no longer have anything in common, Maman.''

."That's good,'' the dowager said, smiling. "I'm very pleased to hear it, and now, if you will excuse me, my dear, I must go and decide what to wear for my afternoon calls.''

As Melanie watched the dowager leave the dining room, she could not help but wonder just how it was that her mama-in-law had been aware of who Mrs. Whitehead was. This was one thing, however, that she did not intend to ask her.

She rose from the table feeling suddenly full of a number of strange emotions, and a moment later found herself seated at the piano in the music room. She allowed her fingers to select the music they knew well, and began with rousing marches and unthinkingly worked her way gradually into more peaceful compositions, until she ended with a gentle lullaby.

As the last notes died away, the dowager's voice asked her softly, "Do you feel better now, my dear? It was such a wonderful performance that I had to stay to the very end, but that last piece might have given you away, you know. Now I think I'd better send for my carriage.''

Melanie had swung around on the piano stool to face her. "I feel much better, Maman,'' she said softly, "but I thought that I had closed the door when I came in.''

"You did,'' the dowager said with a laugh, "but those marches were so loud that even this room could not contain them. I'm sure my son has heard you play.''

Melanie nodded. "I've bought the music for a number of duets so that we can play together when we get to Sussex.''

The dowager was about to leave as the doorbell sounded, and Melanie almost groaned when she heard her exchanging greetings with Martha, who must not have forgotten the way that the older lady had scolded her in the park, for her voice sounded a little cool.

Then Melanie realized that this was probably an excellent time for Martha to call, and she walked into the hall and joined them for a few minutes, then took her sister into the drawing room and closed the door behind them.

"I should think that it is a little early yet for tea, Martha, but I will send for some if you wish," she told her.

Her sister smiled and shook her head. "You needn't bother, for I can stay only a few minutes. I wanted to make sure that you were now feeling better after your bee sting, Melanie. Mama did not believe it, of course, but there was little she could say when that unpleasant old woman came so quickly to your defense."

Melanie looked at her sister and slowly shook her head. "I don't know what kind of people you are associating with these days, my love, but they're turning *you* into a most unpleasant person to be around. You don't even look as lovely as you used to, and that's a shame, for you were once a joy to behold."

"What a nasty thing to say," Martha exclaimed. "You're jealous, that's all, and you always have been."

"You're wrong, for I always enjoyed just looking at you, ever since you were a tiny little girl. As I said, I don't know who your friends are at the moment, but what they're telling you is not true," Melanie said softly. "Forget about marrying just for title and money, and look for someone you can love and who will love you also."

"Just like you did, I suppose." Martha sneered.

"You know very well that I didn't," Melanie told her quietly, "but I've been lucky, for I believe that we're learning to love each other more as time goes along."

Martha opened her mouth as though to say something, but Melanie held up a hand.

"Don't try telling me any more stories about Mrs. White-head, for I know that they're not true. Denby has not seen her since before we married, and I know it to be a fact," Melanie said firmly. "I'm sure I don't have to ask you to tell Michael, for you will in any case."

As her sister sat staring at her in disbelief, Melanie rose. "We'll be leaving for Sussex soon, so I won't be here to see your come-out, my dear, but please think about what I've said, for I love you and I want you to be happy."

Martha reached for her reticule, then got up also.

"You'll believe what you want to, I'm sure," she said, "but if I were you I'd keep him down in Sussex, out of her way."

Melanie made no further comment, but went with her sister to the door and kissed her cheek, then made her way upstairs, for suddenly she felt in need of a rest. More than anything, however, she wanted to see Denby, and hoped that he would not be too late home that night.

But once she had retired for the evening, after dining with the dowager, Melanie simply could not keep her eyes open, and she was asleep long before Denby came home.

He was, in fact, quite late, but he still went into her chamber and looked down at her peaceful, sleeping face, though he could not bring himself to disturb her.

Instead, he wrote a note asking her to ride with him at seven in the morning, and placed it on her nightstand where she would see it when she awoke.

15

They started out toward the park, and suddenly Denby said, "I have good news for you, my dear. In two days' time the Corn Bill is to be presented in its final form to the House of Commons, and my own work will be at an end unless and until they ask for revisions."

"Do you mean that we'll be able to leave for the country quite soon, then?" Melanie asked cautiously, for she had no wish to jump to conclusions and then be disappointed.

"In three days at the most," he told her, then watched as her whole face seemed to light from within, and he realized just how much she wanted to leave town. "I'm not saying that I will not need to return to help with the revisions, but that won't be immediately, if it even becomes necessary at all."

She heaved a sigh of relief. "I can't tell you how wonderful it will be just to get away from London," she said thankfully.

"There is one thing, however," he told her, looking a little grim.

"What's that?" she asked, frowning, for he sounded so very serious.

"I must have your solemn promise that you'll not disturb my study, my bedchamber, or, for that matter, any room that I make use of in Denby Downs, without my consent," he told her, and though she could see a distinct twinkle in his eyes, and the telltale twitch at the corners of his mouth, she knew he meant it.

"In writing and signed before witnesses, I suppose?" she asked solemnly.

"Not necessarily," he said a little suspiciously, "for when

I give my word, I do not break it, and I expect no less from you.''

''What if I do not wish to make so deep a commitment?'' she asked, half-seriously.

He shrugged. ''Perhaps, in that case, I'll keep you in London until you change your mind,'' he said.

''I'll consider it most seriously over the next two days,'' she promised solemnly, ''and now I think I'll race you to the crooked oak tree.''

Almost before she stopped speaking, she was off, for it was Lady's only hope of beating the big stallion, and soon she could hear the hoofbeats as Prince drew nearer and nearer. The little mare was valiant, however, and he beat her by only a head. They started back with some reluctance, for Denby had to leave immediately after breakfast, and would not be home until a little before the supper hour.

When they reached the house, the dowager was already risen and about to begin her breakfast, but, seeing them, she waited until they had washed off some of the dirt and joined her.

''Well, I must say that I feel very well rested,'' she told them. ''I am, fortunately, a comparatively good traveler, but there is still nothing quite like sleeping in a bed of one's own, is there?''

Melanie suddenly recalled the attic room in that small inn on her and Denby's wedding night, and as she looked across at his twinkling eyes, she was absolutely certain that he was thinking of it also.

''Will you tell her about it, or shall I?'' he asked, and when Melanie said, ''You,'' he recounted the story, which caused his mama a great deal of mirth and Melanie a warm feeling of sharing, for she could not recall anytime when she had known so clearly that another person had the exact same thoughts she had.

Denby ate quickly, for he did not wish to be late for his appointment, and Melanie took the dowager with her to the kitchens to speak with Mrs. Horsfall and Cook. She wanted dinner that evening to consist of the mother's and son's favorite dishes, for Denby had given his word that he would be home in time to dine with them that night.

When everything had been taken care of in the kitchen to her satisfaction, she went up to her bedchamber to have a word with Bridget about what she meant to wear for the occasion.

"I have not yet worn the new gown in deep gold silk," she told the maid. "Would you mind making sure that it has not become creased while in the armoire? With it I believe I will wear the amber necklace and earrings that Denby gave me."

"Is it a special occasion, then, milady?" Bridget asked.

"A very special one, Bridget," Melanie told her, "for my husband is going to be home for supper, for once, and in two or three days we'll be leaving for the country."

There was a knock on the door, and Bridget went to see who it was.

Melanie looked over and saw a footman standing there with an note in his hand.

"A man from Somerfield House who says he's the young master's valet has just brought this for milady," he said to Bridget, then gave the note to Melanie, who had walked over to see what it was about.

"He says as he's supposed to wait and take the mistress back with 'im," the footman added.

While Melanie opened the letter and sat down at her escritoire to read it, Bridget went to the top of the stairs and took a look at the man waiting in the hall below.

When she returned, Melanie gave her a questioning look.

"It's that new valet of your brother's, milady," Bridget told her.

Melanie nodded. "The note is from Michael," she said quietly, "and I must say that his writing gets worse every day. He must have done something foolish, I suppose, for he says he must see me at once because he is in deep trouble, and asks that I go back with his man. Let me have my gray pelisse and bonnet, would you, Bridget? And I'd best change into some heavier shoes."

Turning to the footman, she said, "You may tell the man to wait, and I'll be down in just a moment."

"Don't you think that I should go with you, milady?" Bridget suggested, but Melanie shook her head.

"I'm only going to my parents' home, and I should be safe enough with one of their servants. He must have a carriage waiting outside," she said, "but I cannot imagine what could be so urgent. I don't suppose, however, that I shall be gone long."

A moment later she was ready, having put some money in her reticule in case she should need it, and she hurried down the stairs, nodded to the servant who had brought the note, then allowed him to precede her out of the house.

She was a little surprised to find that it was a hackney cab that was waiting outside, and not one of her parents' carriages, but as her brother quite often did things without thinking, she allowed the man to help her into the vehicle and then take the seat across from her.

The windows of the hackney were not exactly clean, nor was the smell inside as pleasant as it might have been, but she had ridden in cabs on other occasions, and these things did not seem of importance when the journey would take just a few minutes.

She suddenly realized that she had been in deep thought and that they should surely have reached Somerfield House long ago, so she leaned over toward the window to take a look and see where they were.

When she realized that they were no longer in Mayfair, but were traveling through one of the poorer parts of London, she turned, and then saw a club of some sort in the valet's raised hand, and before she could even move, she felt a sharp pain in her head, and, mercifully, nothing more.

She came around some considerable time later, and did not at first know what had happened, for she was lying upon some foul-smelling sacks on the stone floor of a cold, dismal room that appeared to be used for storage, for there were several packing crates and barrels on the floor.

One dirty cracked window let in a little light, but it was

quite impossible for her to tell how long she had been unconscious, or what time of day it was.

Her head was throbbing so that she could not think clearly, and she put up a hand and found a painful swelling on her right temple. She remembered the club that Michael's valet had had in his hand, and felt angry, and then, suddenly, very frightened.

She had decided that robbery must be the motive, when she noticed her reticule on the floor beside her, as if, when she had been thrown into this place, it had been tossed in after her. And she soon realized that "thrown" was the right word, for her left arm and hip felt bruised, and her left cheek seemed to be grazed.

Opening the purse, she found that the money she had put inside when she thought Michael was in trouble was still there. This meant, of course, that robbery was not the reason she had been brought here—kidnapped, she supposed, but why? And what had her brother to do with it? Probably nothing at all, she now realized, for the writing had not really looked like his.

She got slowly and painfully to her feet, then leaned on one of the crates, for her head was swimming, but after a moment she was able to move over to the door, which she found, not at all to her surprise, to be bolted on the outside.

The crates were wooden, and not as cold as the floor, so she picked up some of the sacking and placed it on top of them, then sat down to rest, for she knew that she was going to need all of her strength if she was to get out of this place alive. A tear trickled down her cheek, and she brushed it away angrily. This was no time to feel sorry for herself!

After a while, feeling somewhat stronger, she got up and looked at the window, which was big enough for her to climb out of, but she would need something to stand on. A barrel would do very well, if only she could move it into position.

At first it seemed impossible, for the barrels were filled with something and were very heavy. She tried to move the nearest one, but found that she could push it only a few inches at a time.

However, it would be foolish to try to escape until dark anyway, and she had nothing else to do, so over the next few hours she patiently tugged and pushed the barrel two or three inches, then rested fifteen minutes or so in between. Her fingers were sore and her nails torn by the time she had it in place, but she was so proud of herself that she did not even give them more than a casual glance. She was much more interested in climbing on top of the barrel and seeing what was outside.

It took not more than one look out of the dirty window, however, to realize that the area she was in was very poor indeed. There were a number of dirty, rough-looking men moving around, and old crones in rags sat against a wall, occasionally cackling to each other. It was not difficult to imagine what would likely happen to her if she suddenly fell from the window into their midst.

The only thing to do now was to wait, and hope that when it got dark she could break the window, for she had tried and found it impossible to open. She would then drop to the ground and find someone, a woman perhaps, who would help her make her way out of the area.

Denby's day had been long and tiring, and he was glad to be returning to his home in the early evening for a quiet supper with his wife and his mama, who, it seemed, got along together amazingly well.

To his surprise, Melanie did not appear to be anywhere around, and when he went up to change, he knocked on the door of her bedchamber and went in, only to find a very worried abigail.

"I cannot understand it, milord," Bridget told him earnestly. "The note is here where she left it, and she said she'd probably not be very long. And that was at ten o'clock this morning."

"You've not heard from her all day?" Denby asked, looking worried for he knew it was unlike Melanie to go out and stay so long. "Why didn't you go with her?"

"Because she said she didn't want me to, milord. She said she'd be all right going to her parents' home in their coach and with one of their servants as escort." Bridget shook her head, wishing that she had insisted on accompanying her. "But when I spoke to the footman who let that valet in, he told me that there was no carriage outside, only a hackney."

"That is more than strange," Denby said, frowning. "Did anyone see her get into it?"

"Yes, sir. The footman said that she got in first, and that man of her brother's followed her."

He went into his bedchamber and started to dress for dinner, but could not get Melanie out of his mind. When he was only halfway through, he called his man over.

"I think you'd best go to the Somerfields', Godfrey, and see what is detaining my lady. Take the small carriage with you to bring her back, if she's still there."

Denby then continued to get himself ready, and was impatiently making his fifth attempt to tie his cravat in the style for which he was famous, something he could normally achieve on the first try, when Godfrey knocked, then came into the chamber once more.

"The family is all out to dinner, milord," he said, looking very worried indeed, "but I spoke to Masters, their butler, and he informed me that no note had been sent here today, and that Lady Denby had not been near the house. He also said that the new valet of Mr. Michael's was dismissed by that young man two days ago."

Denby suddenly felt ice cold, for he had the most awful feeling that the thing he had dreaded most had happened— Melanie had been kidnapped.

Godfrey, who had been with him for many years, said quietly, "There's still a chance that it could be something quite innocent, milord. Her ladyship's brother may have been at some other address, or was perhaps playing a practical joke upon her."

Denby shook his head. "I don't like this at all. I think I'd best get over to the Somerfield house myself and find out just how much they know about that valet," he said; then he heard a loud knock at the front door and hurried to the top of the stairs.

Fowlkes himself had opened the door, and had then stepped

outside. He came in a moment later with a stone and a piece
of paper in his hand.

"Bring that to me," Denby called hoarsely, and they met
halfway down the staircase.

He left the stone in the butler's hand, and took the note
back to his bedchamber, going over to his desk to read it.
Printed in block letters were the words:

"WE HAVE YOUR WIFE. DO NOTHING UNTIL YOU HEAR
FURTHER."

For a moment there was complete silence in the chamber;
then Denby said, "Godfrey, I have another errand for you."
He reached for a sheet of notepaper and started to write.
"You remember Bert Billings, from the Peninsula days? He's
now a Bow Street Runner and this is his address. I want you
to go there at once and bring him back here with you, for
if anyone knows where to start looking for her, it will be
him."

When he left, Denby remembered that his mother would
be going down soon for dinner, and though he was no longer
hungry, he also recalled from his years on the Peninsula that
fighting on a full stomach was always much better than
fighting on an empty one.

He met the dowager on the stairs, and there was a very
worried expression on her face.

"I've just heard that something has happened to Melanie,"
she said quietly, noticing the lines that had already formed
on his grim face. "Please tell me what I can do to help."

He took her arm and steered her into the dining room. Then
he poured a glass of wine for each of them, and told her as
much as he knew at this time.

"It's my fault, of course. I should have sent her down to
Sussex, where she'd be safe, but I wanted her near me,"
he said bleakly. "Do you remember Bert Billings, my old
sergeant, Mama?"

"Why, of course I do, Broderick. He's a Bow Street
Runner now, if I recall. Is he going to help you find
Melanie?" she asked.

"I know he will if he's not out somewhere on a case,"
he told her. "Godfrey's gone to see if he can get him now."

They had finished as much as they could eat of the main courses, and Fowlkes was just about to serve dessert when they heard the sound of breaking glass coming from the drawing room.

Denby was on his feet in a moment, and the first to reach the note that had been thrown through the window, wrapped around a stone. He quickly unwrapped it and read:

"IF YOU WANT HER TO LIVE, STOP THE BILL GOING THROUGH."

Dessert was forgotten, and Denby helped his mother to a glass of brandy, then poured one for himself. They sipped it in silence, each deep in thought, for there was nothing to say. Through the open door they listened to Fowlkes as he instructed one of his staff on the proper way to put a temporary covering over the broken windowpane.

It was a relief to both of them when Godfrey came back with Billings. Denby excused himself at once, and took the little man into his study.

After giving him as much information as he could about what had happened, Denby showed Billings the two notes.

The little man was a true cockney, and proud of it, born within the sound of Bow bells. And he was tough, fully capable of licking men twice his size, but he was also very astute and he knew London better than anyone Denby had ever met.

"Where will they have her?" Denby asked grimly.

"In t'docks is where they'll be, and I can pin down where they are to . . ." He paused, calculating, then went on, ". . . within a quarter-mile, I should say. But I can't tell you that's where they'll 'ave 'er," Bert said. "And it'll not be exactly a cuppa tea going in there tonight, for they're mean an' they're dangerous. Y'see, you think you're right about the bill, an' wot they think is it'll mean 'alf of 'em'll starve to death."

"I know I'm right, Bert," Denby told him. "If we keep the price of imported wheat high, it *will* be a hardship for some of them who work in the new factories and such, there's no doubt about it. But if we were to let imported wheat come in from Europe at low prices, we would put our own farmers out of business altogether, for they would not be able to compete.

"And it wouldn't be just the farmers themselves who would be out of work, Bert, but all the people who work for them, as well, and right now they represent a great deal more than half of the total workers of this country. With no wages coming in, they would be the ones starving then. It's only a temporary measure, though, and room has been left for adjustment as things improve."

"I 'adn't thought about it like that," Bert said, "but don't you try to convince the fellers we'll meet up with tonight, whatever y'do. Fists an' clubs are the only ways we'll convince that lot, but I'd rather avoid it if we can."

They went into the servants' quarters, and Denby bought a worn overcoat from one of his footmen and an old hat from another. Then he had Godfrey take the shine off his shoes, but it was not done without protest. Bert already looked the part, for, once Godfrey had told him the problem, he had come prepared.

They took the carriage only as far as Bert thought it wise, and left the two coachmen with it a short distance from a hackney stand. Then Bert met alone with a couple of men he had sent ahead, once Godfrey had told him what had happened.

"They've been doing a bit of nosing around," Bert said to Denby when he rejoined him. "I think we've 'it on t'place they've taken 'er to, or very near, at any rate, for it seems that an 'ackney was seen there this morning, in a place where nobody'd think of using owt but their own two feet. And that's where we're goin' to start."

"We're not taking a hackney, surely?" Denby asked, fully prepared, however, to do whatever Bert thought best.

"That we're not. An' try not to open yer mouth, milord," Bert told him, "once we're inside, for anyone listening'd know in a minute that y'didn't belong around 'ere, an' word travels fast."

At first they just walked slowly, but at Bert's signal they began to move from shadow to shadow, pausing to listen for any sounds unusual to the area.

"We're just a street away from where the 'ackney stopped," Bert said, "so keep yer eyes open for anything unusual."

The streets were filthy, and they could not see where they were going well enough to step around anything lying there.

From somewhere there came the sound of glass breaking, but there was no way to tell if one of the hovels around them was receiving the attentions of a burglar. Then Denby thought he heard a sound he recognized, and he put out a hand to stop Bert proceeding further.

"Listen," he murmured.

"Ouch" and "darn it" came softly on the air.

Bert asked in a whisper, "Is that 'er voice?"

Denby looked at him and nodded. "But where can she be?"

It took some time to find her, for the sounds had stopped, as if she had just realized she had made them.

Denby was getting desperate as he followed Bert slowly from building to building, occasionally stepping away from the wall as he walked around a bundle of rags that might or might not have an occupant.

Finally there was a crunching sound as he trod on pieces of glass, and he stepped back and looked up at a broken window from which a slight muttering had been coming, but it had stopped as soon as he did.

There came the sound of a light thud, and then, as Denby's eyes grew accustomed to that particular darkness, he discerned a small hand holding something with which it was hammering the window frame.

"Melanie," he said so softly that even Bert could hardly hear it.

But just as a squeak started to come from above, Bert made a shushing sound, and what looked like an old man shuffled past them.

As soon as he was out of earshot, however, Denby put his mouth to Bert's ear and said softly, "It's her, but I don't know what she can be doing."

"I'm removing pieces of broken glass from the frame," came the whispered response from above.

"Can you get your leg over the sill?" Denby whispered, while Bert looked carefully about to be sure no one was watching them.

Then Denby handed a wool cloak through what had been a window, saying softly, "Cover the glass with this, but bring it out with you."

Bert stepped away now, to walk completely around the small building and be sure no one was paying them attention; then, after Bert returned and gave him the nod, Denby whispered to Melanie to put a leg through the opening.

He had not yet set eyes upon her, of course, and the first portion of her that he did see was a slim leg; then an arm and shoulder came into view, and he reached up and clasped her waist, lifting her down to the ground.

Rather unnecessarily he put a finger to his lips; then he took back the cloak he had passed to her and wrapped it quickly around her. He pulled the hood up to completely cover her hair and most of her face, then clasped her so closely to him for a moment that she could scarcely breathe.

"We're not out of the woods yet, sweetheart," he murmured with a catch in his voice. "Whatever you do, don't breathe a word, and try to crouch if you can."

To Melanie, clasped tightly to Denby's side in a powerful grip, it seemed to take forever before they got out of this grim place. The light fog that had been hanging around earlier was now getting thicker, and figures seemed to materialize out of nowhere, then fade away once more into the mist. Their progress was slow, for no one else was hurrying, and they did not want to draw unnecessary attention to themselves.

A dark, threatening form suddenly appeared in front of them, and she saw Denby's small friend quickly and quietly dispose of it, with scarcely an interruption in their own slow progress.

But at last they were able to move more swiftly, in fact Denby was almost carrying her along through the dark streets, for his strong arm was still around her, and her toes were scarcely touching the ground.

" 'Ere we are," the little man said, and there was Denby's

carriage, a much more welcome sight than any of the fairy chariots Melanie had dreamed about as a little girl.

Once inside, she was introduced to the little cockney who had played such a large part in her rescue. She would, of course, have liked anyone who had helped her escape, but there was something about Bert Billings that she responded to at once.

"I think I'd have been glad to meet you at any time," she told him, giving him a warm smile, "but tonight was very special, wasn't it?"

Bert shook his head. "To be honest, milady, I didn't think we had a cat in hell's chance of finding you, but now I've met you I know why the colonel married you. You're just the little lady he deserves, for who could have dreamed you'd be already trying to escape on yer own when we came along."

"I'd never have succeeded, though, and I hate to think what would have happened to me had I been alone in that area for long," she said, suddenly shuddering at the very idea.

"What did your captors look like, my love?" Denby asked, still holding her close to his side.

"I never saw any of them other than Michael's valet," she told him. "It was he who knocked me out, and when I came around I was in the place you found me. It was some kind of small warehouse, I suppose."

"I cannot understand why you got into a hackney with that fellow. Even Bridget knew that you should have taken her with you," Denby said, "and as it turned out, Michael fired the man two days ago, according to Masters."

"He did?" Melanie was puzzled. "Do you suppose that he did this to take revenge on my brother for dismissing him?"

"I really don't think so, my dear," Denby told her. "In fact, there is no question about it, for I received a note stating that unless I stopped the Corn Bill going through, I would not see you again. The note, by the way, was attached to a small rock and was thrown right through the drawing-room window."

"Oh, no!" Melanie exclaimed. "Was anyone hurt?"

"No. My mama and I were in the dining room at the time, and it put an end to what I believe you had meant to be a very special dinner. We neither of us had any appetite to begin with, but that incident was the last straw," he murmured dryly. "I believe tonight was the first time in her life that my mama asked for and drank a large brandy.

"Let me take a look at that bruise on your forehead," he requested. "Have you any idea what he hit you with?"

"I was looking to see where we were, then realized we were no longer in Mayfair. I remember turning and seeing a club in his hand, and then I felt the pain in my head, and nothing more until I awoke in that place."

He examined it in the dim light of the carriage. "He must have given you quite a whack," he said angrily. "It's a large swelling and it's already showing some purple hues."

"Don't touch it," she told him quickly, for it was very tender; then she added, "They must have thrown me into that place, for my cheek hurts and my hip also."

He had thought it to be dirt picked up in that filthy warehouse, and now he took a closer look.

"Yes, you do have a nasty scrape on your cheek, my love, and if I could only get a hold of the people who did this, they would be very sorry indeed," he said grimly. "I believe that the best thing to do is to send you down to Sussex first thing in the morning, and I will join you there as soon as I can."

"No, I won't go," Melanie said firmly. "I'm not going until you can go with me."

"We'll discuss it later," Denby said quietly.

Melanie was silent for a moment, realizing that if she was to persuade him to let her stay, which she was quite determined to do, the best place to achieve this would be in her bed tonight.

Three days later the Corn Bill was presented to the House of Commons, and the military had the task of putting down the riots that broke out and continued for five consecutive nights. Considerable damage was done to the homes of several members of Parliament, including that of Mr. Robinson, who had introduced the unpopular bill in the House of Commons.

Denby House was unharmed, and would remain so, for Bert Billings was keeping a close watch on it.

The family was in no danger, though, for they were no longer in residence. The dowager was paying an overdue visit to the country home of her older daughter, and the earl and countess were on their way to Denby Downs.

As before, when they had set out for Sussex, Bridget and Godfrey had been sent ahead. Denby had, however, insisted on riding inside the carriage with his wife, for it seemed that since her kidnapping and rescue, he was reluctant to let her out of his sight for a moment.

"Are you sure you're quite comfortable, my love?" he asked solicitously as he reached over to tuck the travel rug more closely around her legs.

Melanie's eyes sparkled with mischief. Despite the purple bruise on her forehead and the scrape on her cheek, she had never been in better looks, for she had finally admitted to herself that she had fallen in love with her husband.

"Of course I am, Broderick, but if you're going to fuss over me like this for the next six months or more, I'll grow not only fat but also terribly lazy," she told him.

"I've no doubt that in time I'll become a little less concerned about something happening to you again," he said softly, "but I can assure you that I'll never take it for granted. When I think of what most probably would have happened had Bert not led me to the heart of that hellhole, I shudder."

She leaned over and gently caressed his cheek. "But he did lead you there, my dear, and everything worked out very well indeed. You mustn't blame yourself for my foolishness. It was completely idiotic of me to get into a hackney with a man I had never seen before, and I can assure you that I've learned my lesson and will never do that again."

"You'd better not," Denby said gruffly, then put his arm around her shoulders and drew her closer. "And I swear that if you even try to get on Lady again until after the baby is born, I'll sell her."

"I won't," she promised him, "for your friend Dr. Radcliff gave me complete instructions as to what I may and may not do. My mama also gave me her list, which was much longer, and you'd not believe how excited she is about having her first grandchild. It's a good thing she didn't know that I had been kidnapped until afterward, or I swear she'd have gone into a decline."

She suddenly yawned, and her eyelids began to droop.

"I'm afraid I kept you awake too long last night," Denby said, sounding a little worried as he moved the squabs around so that she might nap more comfortably.

"Don't ever stop, darling," she murmured drowsily.

A moment later she closed her eyes and started dreaming of what she would do when they reached Sussex. First she would redo the bedchamber next to hers for the new baby, then turn out the old nursery on the floor above, and after that make the room next to it into a schoolroom . . . and then . . . and then . . .